THE N[...]
CHILDREN

TONI BUNNELL

To Julie
Thanks for all
your support with the
hedgehogs

www.tonibunnell.com

Toni xxx

Toni Bunnell Feb. 2018

First published in 2016 by Toni Bunnell, York, UK

www.tonibunnell.com

ISBN: 978-1-78280-734-6

© Toni Bunnell 2016

All rights reserved. No part of this publication may be reproduced, stored in or introduced into a retrieval system, or transmitted in any form, by any means (electronic, mechanical, photocopying, recording or otherwise) without prior written permission from the copyright holder Toni Bunnell.

A CIP record for this book is available from the British Library

Printed and bound in Great Britain by
Short Run Press Ltd Exeter

This book is sold subject to the condition that it shall not, by way of trade or otherwise, be lent, resold, hired out, or otherwise circulated without the author's prior consent in any form of binding or cover other than that in which it is published and without a similar condition, including this condition, being imposed on the subsequent purchaser.

Cover / text design and photographs by Toni Bunnell

www.tonibunnell.com

*'Grave the guardian of our dust
Grave the treasury of the skies
Every atom of thy trust
Rests in hope again to rise'*

Words on a gravestone
at Haworth Churchyard,
West Yorkshire, UK

Also by Toni Bunnell

Music Makes a Difference[1]

The Room Between the Floorboards[2]

A Door in Time[3]

The Fidgit[2]

Tales of Sweeper Joe the Hero[3]

A Life Well Lived[3]

The Disappearing Hedgehog[1]

Samuel and the Stolen Words[2]

Dreaming While Awake[3]

Into Oblivion[3]

Available as paperback only[1]

Paperback and ebook[2]

Ebook[3]

www.tonibunnell.com

1   In the Beginning there was Soil

Their voices clamoured to be heard. Out of the depths of the dark cloying soil came a cacophony that rose up then died away. Voices desperate to be heard and to reach beyond the grave. Their pleas cast out onto the winds. Voices that belonged to the nameless children. Children who were lost to the past, but whose voices remained as whispers. Whispers that sought out any breeze that would carry them to the ears of a passerby. Someone who could help them. Someone who might offer refuge from the never-ending darkness.

They climbed out of the ground, unseen and unheard. The first crouched low, like a leopard about to spring, the second with head cocked to the side, the third staring directly ahead, motionless. All waiting their turn, below in the fathomless depths that had been their home – until now. The nameless children had returned to claim their birthright and nothing would hold them back. But this was not their century. Their time had long gone. Finding the families that they belonged to would not be easy.

They each wore a gown, a white gown made from cotton, roughly woven. It hung in loose folds from their shoulders, lending an almost funereal look to the wearer. But appearance was not uppermost in their minds at this moment, at a time when the earth had thought it prudent and timely to release three creatures to the world above. Creatures that held only a dim recollection of life beyond the grave. A brief glimpse of a world full of light where the sun rose and sank each day and graced the landscape with tantalising promise of the day that lay ahead.

For their days had been numbered. Luck had not been on their side. Born into a world where poverty was prevalent, and disease rife, their chances of survival had been poor from the outset. Even wealthy families had not been left untouched. Where drinking water was tainted, cholera spread like wild fire. After the initial ingestion of contaminated water the disease moved between family members. Between people who inhabited hovels where space was scarce and close proximity inevitable. Cholera lit upon the vulnerable, the young, the old and the highly susceptible. Once you had come into contact with the 'humors' of this bygone age, your days were limited. Time was not on your side.

Number one had lain in the earth with no name and a millstone of guilt round his neck, denied any part of life. Until now. As the first of the nameless children, in this particular deep mass grave, he left the earth and the dank-smelling soil behind him and moved into the light, nose twitching at the unfamiliar smells that met his senses.

THE NAMELESS CHILDREN

No. 1 was born on a December morning into a family where the children already numbered eight. Thrust, protesting, into a world where his mother scarcely had the strength to raise herself from her pillow to put him to her breast, and where his father's efforts to put food on the table, in any sort of predictable manner, fell short of achieving its goal. As such the children ran free, clothes threadbare, hair tossed by the wind, feet that had not been encased in shoes for many a year. Into this family came a child, loved but ailing with his first breath. The woman who helped his mother give birth sighed as she watched the tiny rib cage rise and fall rapidly as the little scrap struggled to breathe.

'He's a fighter that's for sure,' she told his father with a face that told the truth of the matter: Being a fighter did not guarantee survival. As the hours passed the whimpering of the little mite that was No. 1 grew less and the rasping breathing sounds grew ever slower, until eventually they stopped altogether. Although he already knew the answer, the father looked hopefully and questioningly at the woman who had helped his wife with the birthing. An almost imperceptible shake of her head told him all he needed to know and he turned away in despair and left the house.

He returned a few minutes later, the ache in his heart unabated, to ask about his wife. He was too late. Seconds only after he had stepped out through the door she also gave in to the relentless call from the other side and let her spirit be pulled away from her to join the others in a world where pain did not exist and suffering was unheard of. He bent over in grief as he saw the sheet being pulled up over his wife's face.

'Do you have a name for the child?' The midwife asked. 'So he might have a proper burial?'

'I have no money for a burial. He will have to go in with the other children and have a paupers' burial.'

The words were not spoken out of animosity or a lack of compassion but by a man at the end of his tether. A man who had just lost his wife in childbirth and had eight children to feed. A man who could see no way forward. And so, through an act of not doing by his father, an impassive reluctance to conceive of any sort of future, No. 1 child was consigned to the ever-growing number of nameless children. His commitment to the earth was barely acknowledged amidst the overwhelming grief surrounding the death of his mother and, while he was not held responsible for her death, the less generous souls certainly did not exempt him whole heartedly from all responsibility.

Number two hit the ground running, knees grazed and toe nails cracked and broken in the need to be away – to be gone from this place. Gown dishevelled and muddy in the leaving of the underground pit, the hem torn on her exit from the tomb. Physical evidence that would lie there, trapped on the

THE NAMELESS CHILDREN

brambles bordering the site. Unnoticed for many months until, at some point in the future, people would come looking for any sign that would lead them to this exit point. To the nameless children that had lain below the ground for so long.

No. 2 child had her own story to tell, as sad as it was tragic. Born to a serving maid, and sired by a squire's son, she had been removed from her mother's side before ever being put to the breast. Never did she feel the loving touch of caring hands or the warmth of her mother's body. Instead rough hands, bent on harsh intent, removed her before she drew her first breath and certainly before her first cry. Swathed her in blankets to disguise any trace of the child within and to trap any cries that might issue from the mouth of this unwanted infant. Unwanted by the father but so desired by her mother.

She was bundled into the back of a cart, taken to the reed bed by the river and tossed into the water. As anyone might cast a dandelion seed to the air with a single breath, so No. 2 was cast aside, without a care in the world and without a backward glance. Weighed down by the heavy swaddling of blankets, and with her cries unheard, she quickly met her end in the icy waters of the River Eft.

It was several days before the soggy mass of blankets was accidentally hooked out of the river by a fisherman throwing his line without careful consideration. Opening the parcel of blankets to discover a drowned child caused much consternation and alarm. But then it was not altogether uncommon for unwanted children to meet their deaths by drowning. The man who found her was deeply saddened and took steps to ensure that the child received a burial of some kind. As such, No. 2 found herself lowered into a pit dug in the graveyard for the likes of her, children of no known parentage, or otherwise. The nameless children.

Number three struggled to the top and stopped to pause for breath. The climb had been steep and a long time coming. There was no planning for this. No consideration of how to escape from the dark hole that had been their resting place for many moons. The decision to release them from captivity had not been theirs to make. These three alone had been selected by someone or something unknown. In time they would learn why they had been selected, seemingly at random.

But there was nothing random about any of this. Choosing three from the many hundreds, if not thousands, of children buried without much thought, in mostly unhallowed ground, without a proper burial service. Just a few words muttered as a handful of soil was thrown over the mound that was the only sign that the earth had been disturbed. And beneath this lay a mass grave, child stacked upon child in an act of indifference and nonchalance. An act devoid of compassion and an ounce of care. A vertical grave, where space was used to the maximum, and humanity featured not at all.

It was from this now sunken mound that No. 3 child emerged, just as dusk was falling. Looking to the left and right he stooped low and crept behind a hedge, moving with stealth and cunning. On high alert he flinched at every sound. Like a hare poised to run he sat back on his haunches, resembling an animal rather than anything of human origin.

The three nameless children grouped together behind the hedge and No. 1 had the presence of mind to quickly turn back and toss soil over the hole from which they had just emerged. Only a seasoned country dweller could now see that the earth had been disturbed.

No. 3 had the most cause to feel fear at this sudden ejection into the world above. A world of light, noise and uncertainty. He had fought for life. Oh had he fought. Born to a wealthy family he had been a wanted child but had lost his struggle shortly after birth. His father had no desire to see his wife grief stricken at the loss of her baby, one that they had desired for so many years. A longed-for baby. In the middle of the night, under cover of darkness, he took the still infant from the arms of his sleeping mother and passed him quickly to a waiting servant. The baby was then taken to the Dead House and placed, unnoticed, with other children awaiting burial, nameless and discarded.

The father, having realised that the death of his only child, his first born son, was imminent, had arranged for the procurement of another boy child of similar size and features. He paid a handsome sum to the farm labourer and his wife, who would not normally have considered selling their child but had no option. With seven children already they could barely put enough food on the table as things stood. Another mouth to feed was something they could not countenance.

The child was handed over amongst spoken endearments, kisses and tears, to the same servant who had only recently discarded a child's body. And so the nameless child was replaced, some would say by a changeling, but for the fact that the imposter was not of faery origin.

2 The Awakening

In the years since their initial incarceration, numbers one to three of the nameless children had grown while resting in the grave. Slowly, but surely, they had increased in height and body size to the extent that they could now be considered young teenagers. They were not aware that they had been growing as consciousness had only recently been conferred upon them. Prior to this they had essentially been in a vegetative state. Alive, but not alive. Not even breathing as such, for what oxygen would there be to take in several feet below the ground?

Only now that they had been released from their dark chamber had they become sentient beings. Suddenly aware of the rush of the wind through their hair, bracing cold against their face, the feel of the hard ground beneath their feet, the three found their senses overwhelmed to the point where they had become almost trancelike. Captivated by bird song, a musical crescendo now dying as the birds retreated into the trees and a murmuration of starlings swooped down into their night-time resting place.

No. 1 moved with his nose twitching, testing the breeze in all directions. This heightened sense of smell would serve the three well when danger lurked and their very lives were threatened. Indeed this was the crucial change that had befallen them. From inert beings, lying still in their burial spot, they had been woken to a world of change and wonderment. Fully awake, with seeing eyes, ears that pricked to the slightest sound and skin that knew the direction of the wind, they viewed their new world as visitors from an alien world might. Thoughts buzzed through their heads, relentlessly sweeping across their consciousness, as they attempted to make some sense of what they saw and heard, creating a mental map of their surroundings.

The final rays of the sun fizzled out against the fields on the skyline, leaving stark rows of hedges dividing the land into stretches of burnished gold and dark green. Three faces looked towards the forest that bordered the fields and, as one, three bodies moved into the open then blended into the hedge. They knew, instinctively, that if they kept close together they would appear, to an onlooker, as one large creature, rather than three smaller ones. They would be much less vulnerable, less open to attack. New to a world fraught with danger, both unseen and unexpected, they would need to learn quickly.

As they left the hedge to turn into the forest their movements had not gone unnoticed. A boy's attention was drawn to their strange gait – to the object that appeared at times to be composed of three beings and at other times to adhere to produce but one. Saul was a child of the countryside. Slightly built, and small for his age, he was adept at staying hidden, at crouching in the bushes and observing life from a distance. He knew, by sight and sound, all the native wild creatures that haunted these parts and, beyond all doubt, he knew that what he was looking at was none of these. The silhouette remained fixed in his mind long after he had returned home, closed his eyes and fallen asleep that night.

The last leaves closed over the group as they moved into the forest. The only evidence that they had entered the world of the living lay behind them at the edge of the graveyard, where unhallowed ground tentatively touched the sanctified area. The area blessed by God where beautifully kept gravestones stood proudly, offering their faces to the sun. Carefully inscribed descriptions of the occupants of each grave told their own story. Some touching, some merely documenting the end of a life well-lived. Whatever the message intended to be conveyed to the outside world one thing was certain: the people who lay in these graves had been loved and cherished.

Care had been taken to prepare each resting place and ensure that all visitors to the grave would be in no doubt about who lay there and who their family was. Little matter that, with very few exceptions, usually where a child was involved, the visits to the gravestone, regular at first, would gradually peter out, until one day no-one would visit at all. Indeed it has been said that the majority of people alive in the twenty-first century do not know the Christian name of their grandparents. So soon does the memory dim. So soon do we forget the past. Enough then that we should ensure as good a burial as possible for those we knew and loved in our lifetime.

It was a different story for those buried in unhallowed ground. They had no headstone carved from the smoothest granite, no message carefully inscribed by the hands of the stone mason at great expense, and under strict and close instructions from those left behind. These were the unloved, the discarded, the dispossessed, and amongst them were the nameless children.

Sleep did not come easy to the hidden three, an unruly looking trio who clung to each other for comfort and warmth. Like a startled rabbit trembling in fear, while knowing full well that a stoat had it in its sights, they darted furtive glances at their surroundings. Shadow layered shadow as the bushes appeared to close in on them and the trees seemed ever nearer. This was not their world and they knew it. They had been thrown from a world of oblivion, where they had had no interaction with their environment, into a world that had changed beyond belief. But to those that had caught a brief glimpse of life, before they had found themselves rudely covered by damp earth and confined to a small space underground, this mattered little.

They were not totally naïve however. Their genetic memory, often of questionable existence, would stand them in good stead. It would help them become independent and find their place in the world. Meagre and unsubstantiated as their memory was, they would need every ounce of support, every thread of an idea, if they were to survive in this new world. As such, access to their genetic memory was invaluable. Delving into its coffers they would learn where they came from, how they had died, which family they were most closely related to. And more. Much more. They would learn who they really were. The nameless children would go in search of their birthright and lay claim to a life that should have been theirs.

Saul woke to the cock's crow as dawn broke over the hills. Rubbing his eyes, as if to brush away the last traces of sleep and vanquish the lingering remnants of a dream, that had the edges of a nightmare spun round it, he suddenly jolted fully awake. What was it that he had seen last night near the graveyard? Three creatures – or was it one? Or two? He couldn't decide exactly what had been walking slowly away from a low mound at the edge of the walled churchyard. Although he had been watching very intently, and had focused his eyes as hard as he could, he had been thwarted. The prevailing dusk had robbed him of the light necessary to see anything clearly. While there was movement he could detect a shape, but once all motion had ceased they became invisible. Vanished in plain sight. Blended in with the background and become instantly undetectable by the human eye.

All small mammals know instinctively that the essence of their survival lies in their ability to remain still, to stay motionless and avoid detection by a predator. Move and all is lost. It is not a lesson that can be learned for, once disobeyed, life ends. It is as sudden and unrelenting as that. Final and irreversible. We are hard-wired to survive. The laws of survival are something we are born with. Fortunately for the trio, hidden in the dark, their innate abilities were very much operational. As such, they lay low.

On the night of their emergence, from the long-forgotten isolated grave, they had their wits about them, and luckily Saul, the teenage boy out too late after dark, did not reveal their whereabouts to others. He could not, however, forget what he had seen. But he did not know where they had gone. Their secret was safe, but for how long? Saul was bored with his life and this had given him something to focus on. He intended to investigate further. He had seen something and, with the patience of a cobra waiting to strike, he would not give up until every stone had been turned, every aspect considered. Saul was nothing if not persistent.

For over a century the skin covering the bodies of the nameless children had been encased in a light, loamy soil. It had lain over them and acted as both insulation and protection from the worst avarices of the weather. The long probing fingers of frost had not graced the depths of the pits that served as vertical mass graves.

Orphans, those born out of wedlock, those born to wealth and riches but deemed lacking in one way or another, those unwanted waifs and strays; whatever their origin they had one thing in common. They had all been consigned for burial without the dignity of a name. Clad only in a simple gown, a shroud, and with no distinguishing jewellery or otherwise, they were the unvalued. Rejected by society, dismissed out of hand by the world of humans, they had lain uncomplaining and unnoticed for five generations.

With the first gleanings of thoughts starting to turn in their minds, they had begun the transformation from unfeeling, inanimate objects to sentient beings intent on leaving their grave with haste. But with their exit came the inevitable separation from the only place that had ever offered them sanctuary. Their fingers had clawed at the soft soil as they forced their way towards the surface and up above the ground. As their eyes met the light, and their hands felt the damp grass beneath them, so did energy flood through their being. As if charged by electricity they were invigorated.

Now hidden in the forest, close to the graveyard, they sat in deep fearful watchfulness. Sleep was welcome, although not altogether necessary. They had been asleep for many lifetimes. So far no sound had been uttered by any of them, no question posed, no demands made. They would have to wait until their brains configured to enable them to speak. Until then they must communicate using touch and primitive sign language that they made up as they went along.

But spoken language would come to them, and it would come soon – and with the development of speech a plan could be formulated. The nameless children would not have to wait long to stage their return to the land of the living. Not long at all.

Number one was the first to stir. Although not, strictly speaking, asleep they had all rested their bodies amongst the grass. Gowns now damp with the dew that hung everywhere, adorning the forest paradise and imbuing everything with a glistening whiteness, as if frost had visited the grove during the night and laid its spidery fingers upon all around.

Nameless from the beginning of his short life No. 1 lifted his head and sniffed the air. He could smell dampness and decaying leaves. For this was autumn, to some the most inspiring season of the year. Full of reds and golds and evenings that drew to a close with an unexpected suddenness. When the air took on a chill that contrasted strongly with the warmth and dryness of the summer months. This was the time of year that the three found themselves in.

No. 1 was filled with a deep yearning to go back where he had come from. To seek out the low mound that lay at the edge of the unhallowed ground in the graveyard. It was the only home he had ever known, if indeed you could call a hole in the ground home. He leant on his elbows and gazed around. Then he rose and walked over to a large pond that served the forest animals. As he began to kneel, and cup his hands to draw forth water, he fell backwards in alarm, for there before him sprang an image in the water. A stranger looked back at him. In the dark, glassy waters was a face, the likes of which he had never seen before. Involuntarily he raised an arm above his head, as if to ward off danger and protect himself. To his surprise the creature looking back at him did the same.

Slowly, No. 1 lowered his arm and the reflection in the water did the same. He experimented, moving quickly and in a disorganised fashion, so that his antics began to resemble those of a mad man, or someone possessed. As his movements slowed, realisation dawned; whatever lay before him in the flat, dark water meant him no harm and seemed only to be an echo of himself. He was not sufficiently in possession of his cognitive powers to realise that the creature was indeed himself. Only when other creatures, wild animals, came to the water's edge to drink did he begin to understand. Like a shadow that lay behind you when you stood framed by sunlight, so a likeness of yourself would be shone back at you when you looked into water. The nameless children had much to learn.

No. 1 bathed his face and hands in the cool wetness and drank easily until his thirst was sated. A twig cracked and he was on full alert. Crouching in the grass he looked in the direction of the sound. The leaves parted and two figures ventured to the waterside. The nameless children would keep together. This would be their salvation.

They kept low to the ground, moving in quick bursts punctuated by inactivity. As a prey animal moves across an exposed space, they repeatedly darted forwards then froze to the spot. Close scrutiny, however, would reveal that not all about them was motionless. Their ears moved slowly to detect any sound. They drew breath through their nostrils and tasted the air. Their eyes took in everything, making sharp distinction between inanimate objects and sentient beings, garnering the knowledge that would tell them what posed no potential threat and what signified imminent death or capture.

The nameless three had no wish to be caught. On some deep level they were acutely aware that they were 'foreigners abroad', that they were new to this land and that they would be viewed as strangers by anyone they met. Perceived as a threat and a danger to those who saw this region as their own territory, their own home. They could not afford to be seen and they could not afford to be caught. Their survival depended on their ability to lie low – to avoid detection.

Crisp and hollow, the leaves crunched underfoot as the nameless children made their way with stealth and cunning. No concept of where they were going, just a strong abiding memory of where they had come from. Driven by forces unknown, helped by a wind from the north, inspired by a feeling and knowing that now they were alive, in a manner of speaking. But most of all they were driven by the desire to stay alive.

If danger threatened they could withdraw to the deep trench from which they had emerged only the evening before. But this would be a last resort. The drive to survive and forge new lives for themselves lay uppermost in their minds. They would not give up easily. They would reclaim their lives and continue them from where they had been abruptly cut short. By any means available to them they would strive to reach their goal and they would not suffer fools gladly. Anyone that stood in their way and blocked their path to salvation would wish that they hadn't. To the nameless children the world was theirs for the taking. 'To have and to hold' held rather a different meaning to them than to others who inhabited the world they now found themselves in.

3 Saul

Saul had spent the entire morning trying to pick up the trail of the three wandering creatures. Finally, after much searching, he had discovered some tell-tale signs. Here and there, a broken twig, a crushed leaf and – finally – a footprint. Saul stood motionless, aghast at the imprint of splayed toes that confronted him on the muddy path. Thank goodness for the light rain that had fallen last night and washed away the dry, sandy topsoil, soaked into the underlying ground and allowed a footprint to be sealed into the wetness for all to see.

The sun crashed through the trees, scattering light as it fell. Patches of ground, hitherto unseen, now lay fresh and exposed. As the day moved on it would be more and more difficult for the nameless children to remain hidden. It was only a matter of minutes before Saul spied them. From his spot on the other side of an elderberry bush he was camouflaged. It was a perfect vantage point from which to view his prey. For that is what the three had become. To the engaged, fascinated onlooker in the twenty-first century they would undoubtedly be seen as prey.

A craggy tombstone loomed over the low mound of earth from which the nameless children had escaped by pulling themselves up from the depths and onto the grass. The headstone was nothing special but served as a kind of monument, a sign that someone had been buried here – in testament to a life lived and then lost. There was no inscription. In that, the stone was unusual. Rarely did such edifices find themselves erected in unhallowed ground. The fact that it was there at all served as a reminder that, although unnamed, those who were buried here were blameless. They were not thieves or murderers. They were the unfortunates. Those whose spell on earth had not been good to them. Through no fault of their own they had lost their life and been relegated to an inauspicious resting spot.

Saul heard the distant church bell strike noon and reluctantly turned away from the path he had been following. Before moving in the direction of home he took one last, lingering look at the footprint. A person not much older than himself he suspected, judging from the size of the impression and the weight of the body that had made it. An inadvertent footprint pressed into mud. He looked around for landmarks to help him locate the spot for when he returned after dinner. A jackdaw eyed him suspiciously from under a hedge, then followed him at a distance as he retraced his path back through the forest. Saul was intrigued by the bird's behaviour, bold yet coy. Each time Saul stopped, so did the bird, as if it was playing a game that he had played as a child, a game they had called 'Creeping Indians'. Eventually the jackdaw stopped following him, almost as if it was seeing Saul off its territory.

'I'll be back soon,' he told the bird. 'You mark my words. I'll be back.'

Within the hour Saul was back on the trail. The footprint was as clear as before, neither sharper nor diminished in outline. Unknown to Saul though, was the fact that the foot that had made it was long gone. Even as Saul had turned back for his dinner, three shapes were making their way deeper into the forest, seeking a refuge where they could lie low, bide their time and make plans. The primitive signs, that they used to communicate with each other, were soon to erupt into language. But for this to happen they needed to immerse themselves amongst others. In order to do this they would need to become part of the crowd, lose their wayward appearance and their strange loose clothing and learn to blend in unnoticed.

It would not be easy, but only when they had achieved this would it be possible to search for the families that they had once belonged to. Families that had not the slightest inkling that, buried in their history, was another ancestor, one who had not made it into the record books. In the odd instance where a birth had been recorded, but the infant had died shortly after, the register merely read:

'Infant born. Died within days of birth'.

Some unscrupulous individuals even had the word 'stillborn' written on the register of innocent children, with no accompanying details. This 'slip of the pen' was relatively easy to engineer. With the changing of hands of a small amount of money, the existence of the child was erased forever. This suited both parties involved in the transaction. The 'midwife' who would stop at nothing to get her hands on some money, and the unscrupulous man who had fathered a child in less than illustrious circumstances and had no desire that his wife should discover that he had strayed. This information must stay hidden forever. It would not help one iota if the wealthy friends of a straying man should learn that he had fathered a child out of wedlock, and betrayed his wife so utterly and completely.

Other children had been born into poverty at the poor house. Their deaths would go largely unnoticed, unchallenged and most certainly uncelebrated. In these circumstances, the lack of a name was hardly considered worthy of note.

Saul would not be beaten. He pushed ahead and picked up the trail again, moving further into the forest. Not so easy to see at first but eventually dark-adapted eyes allowed him a glimpse of another footprint in the mud, a broken branch and more... A small scrap of torn white material had caught on a bramble bush and hung lifeless like a limp rag. Saul carefully and meticulously untangled the cotton and held it up to the retreating light to examine. By entire coincidence they had just covered the type of clothing worn in the recent past, in a history lesson at school. How it was produced – whether woven or not – and whether dye was used to colour it.

At the time Saul had been paying scant attention to the lesson and was now struggling to recall what the teacher had said. He must have absorbed more than he thought because key pieces of information drifted into his consciousness. He could see that, although rough-edged and dirty, the material was loosely woven, and not in a fashion typical of the twenty-first century. He reasoned that it might not have anything whatsoever to do with the person, creature or creatures that he was tailing. But he would keep it anyway. Just in case.

The light was failing as the three nameless children settled down for the night. Away from the forest edge shrubs were still fairly visible, but once across the edge, on the other side, great shadows lay under the vast expanse of trees. This was a perfect temporary refuge for them. Tomorrow they would venture out into the unknown. Into unchartered territory. But, in a manner of speaking, they were going home.

A face peered out of a hollow tree trunk and its gaze met that of Saul's directly. The eyes did not blink, nor the mouth twitch. It looked for all the world as if it had been sculpted from stone and placed inside the trunk, at the whim of someone intent on creating an element of difference to this section of the forest. Saul stared, riveted to the spot. A crow squawked and Saul swivelled in its direction, his gaze leaving the face for but an instant only. But when he looked back, seconds later, the face had gone, leaving Saul doubting that he had ever seen it in the first place.

He cast his eyes over the trunk, inclining forwards slightly to peer inside the cavernous mouth of what had once been a solid tree. Nothing. Whatever he had seen, or thought he had seen, had vanished. He made a mental note that, once home, he would sketch the face that he had seen, commit its likeness to paper, render it insensible, show it to others asking 'have you ever seen anyone like this? Does this remind you of anyone?'

But for now he was left empty handed, yet again to return home with no concrete evidence that he was on the trail of anything of substance. Driven on by a hazy recollection of a strangely-formed creature or creatures on a dimly-lit night under a fair moon.

Dusk began to lay its hand on the edge of the forest and No. 3 child ventured to look outside the dwelling within the grove, a group of stones clad in mossy green that provided the perfect sanctuary for three refugees. Refugees from what you might ask, and you would have just cause for doing so. If all had remained unchanged and unchallenged the nameless children, currently out on the prowl, would have stayed beneath the ground, fate would not have been tempted, the order of things not rearranged.

But change did happen, triggered by events unknown to them. And now the process had begun it would evolve to its inevitable climax, and nothing and no-one would stand in its way. Like a volcano erupting, once begun there was no stopping it. Lava would flow along the path of least resistance. And so it was with the nameless children. They were hell-bent on a path of destruction, the full implications of which had not yet hit them.

4 Penny

A rare moment of sanity had touched Penny that morning. A glimpse of something whole and meaningful, outside the myriad doubts and uncertainties that rained down inside her head. She was sixteen and being tutored at home. 'A disruptive element in the classroom', she had been deemed: 'impossible to educate through the normal channels'. As such, any possible social benefits that could have been gained through mixing with her peers were damned to smithereens, broken like glass, shattered before she had even started to dream about new horizons and new possibilities.

As the years had passed she had become more and more withdrawn and less willing to communicate with others. Apart from her immediate family, that consisted of her parents and elder brother, David, and of course the dog, Norman, a Border Terrier with a less than sunny disposition, she engaged with virtually no-one in the outside world – except for the postman. There was always the postman. He was eager to chat with anyone and used to make space on his rounds to pass some time with Penny.

'How's my little charmer today?' he would ask.

The reply was always the same.

'I'm sixteen for heaven's sake Brian,' she would tell him indignantly. 'I'm not five.' And with that she would stomp away, to the amused grin of the postman as he watched her go.

She might be labelled as educationally problematic but she had a brain and she intended to use it. As soon as she had taken her exams, and overcome the bouts of depression which unbalanced her, she would be off. The world would be her oyster. She had heard the expression often but had always taken it literally and, as such, had never actually grasped its meaning. The time when all this would happen was nearer than she suspected. A new drug, intended to eliminate the symptoms of clinical depression for all time, was nearing the end of the second set of clinical trials. It was expected to be available for doctors to prescribe by the end of the year.

Life was about to change irrevocably for Penny and, when it did, she would discover a passion for history and become embedded in a quest for the truth. A quest to discover where she came from. This thirst for knowledge would, after many twists and turns, take her to a place she would wish she had never visited – and to No. 1 of the nameless children.

Saul was gazing into a pond. A shiver ran down his spine. Looking back at him from the cool, dark water was a reflection other than his own. Beside his clear features sat those of another, wholly unfamiliar to him but steadfast and unflinching in the mill pond. The pond that lay as still as glass and appeared as black as soot once you averted your gaze. The features held within the reflection reminded him of someone – or something. Slowly the memory crawled to the surface and let itself be examined. The face in the hollow trunk. Not the same, but somehow similar. How many were there? Could these be the creatures that made up the weird object that he had witnessed leaving the edge of the graveyard, under cover of darkness, less than twenty four hours ago?

He spun round to confront the body that belonged to the face in the water but it was too quick for him. As soon as he turned about, it turned on its heels and ran for cover. Saul acted like one possessed and took off after it, his backpack falling to the ground with a thud at the sudden leap forward. He turned back to grab it. The compass held within could not become lost to him. But precious moments had been lost and the captivating face was gone.

'Did you see anyone come this way a minute ago?' he asked of people he passed as he hurried away from the pond.

Slow headshakes dismissed his question and, at the same time, the boy who had asked it. With a sullen expression on his face he trudged round to the other side of the mill pond and gazed into its depths. There was the face again! It was playing a game with him.

Maybe it wanted contact, to speak to him? He spun round, but this time the owner of the face remained rooted to the spot. It was a young girl, mouth upturned, quizzical look on her face.

'I am Saul.' He offered his hand and she took it.

A smooth coldness met Saul's fingertips, as if the owner was devoid of heat, had no blood supply, was (he dared to think the words) actually dead?

No response. Saul tried again.

'I am Saul. Who are you?'

Again the quizzical look but this time dominated by one of sadness and regret and something more – frustration.

Could she be deaf? Saul thought. *Unable to hear and possibly unable to speak too?* He had learned some sign language. They had been taught basics at school. 'In case you need to communicate with someone who might have hearing or speech difficulties,' the teacher had told them.

'I mean you no harm,' he managed to signal.

This was met with a sigh, or rather a murmur expelled with the breath, and a visible relaxation of the girl's features. He saw that she was dressed in a long white tunic and wore no shoes. Could this be the person who had made the footprint in the mud? Why was she out looking like this? Was she running away from someone? Had she been kidnapped by the ones she was with? Impossible to ask her all this in one go, particularly using sign language. Too much too soon. Keep it simple.

Before he had chance to assemble the next signs in his mind she turned as if to leave then, in a move that both surprised and pleased him, kissed him on the cheek. Then she was gone. So fleet of limb, so swift in flight. Saul could only stand and watch helplessly as she shot into the hedge and vanished. He might have imagined it, he couldn't be sure, but he thought he saw a hand reach out of the hedge, as she neared it, and grab her arm, pulling her into the swathes of green foliage and out of sight.

5   The Smithy

The turn of the wheel against iron, the rasping note as the blunt edge ground to a sharp, honed blade, sounded through the air. It reached the ears of No. 1 child. A dim, recessed memory jostled to be heard, pushed itself forward for attention. It is said that genetic memory holds the most fundamental essence of our being, the primitive link to our ancestors who came before us.

And so it was with No. 1 child. His father had been a blacksmith who made the links for bridles and tapped into position the metal rims on cart wheels. Before he had fallen on hard times, life had been good for him and his wife who took in laundry from the village. But with a child being born at regular intervals and, unusually for the time period, most surviving infanthood, finding enough food to feed them all proved almost beyond his means.

By the time No. 1 had been born the children still alive numbered eight, with three deaths along the way, and already the writing was on the wall. With the birth of No. 1, and the subsequent early death of the child and his wife, the blacksmith struggled to survive. But survive he did. In time he found another wife who bore him two more children and luckily, in view of the extra mouths to feed, the business thrived.

In the twenty-first century the smithy, founded by this diligent man so many years ago, had stood the test of time. Each generation had seen one of the sons take up the baton and run with it. And so it was that the clang of steel that rang out across the fields came from the same buildings that No. 1 had been carried from, still and lifeless, a century and a half earlier. Removed by the midwife who had tried, but failed, to save his life and that of his mother.

It was no lack of kindness that had seen No. 1 buried, nameless and without ceremony in unhallowed ground, but an unfortunate set of circumstances beyond anyone's control. No.1 did not know this. No. 1 did not care. All that lay in his mind and blanketed his memory, obscuring all that was kind and good, was a deep feeling that he was owed something – that he was owed a life.

Penny wandered into the smithy. Despite the constant ringing noise, or perhaps because of it, she revelled in the dark corners where she could hide away and think her own thoughts. The men that her uncle employed mostly ignored her, some following orders, others because they sensed that here was a troubled soul that wanted to be left alone. Being sensitive to her needs, they did precisely that.

THE NAMELESS CHILDREN

Penny fingered the wrought iron gate that had been commissioned for a particularly grand house in the town. Yet to be painted, the metal glinted with a pristine and sterile look about it. She longed to paint it but lacked the courage to ask if she could be involved in the project. As she drew her hand away from the spidery, ornamental top of the gate her eyes rested on a symbol that had been pressed into a central circle, a circle that served to bring together six traditional points that, in turn, met the edge of the circle. The symbol was not familiar to her so she took a quick photo with her phone, to check online later. Underneath the symbol was a simple inscription:

'You were never forgotten'.

Who was never forgotten and where did this inscription come from? What time period did this relate to? Penny's curiosity piqued, her blanket of invisibility and desire to be unseen was shrugged off as easily as an unfastened cloak falls to the floor when a person rises from their chair.

'Sorry to bother you,' she whispered.

'You'll have to speak up,' came the reply. 'Can't hear a word over all this noise.'

Unperturbed she persisted.

'I wondered who this gate was made for.'

'Look in the book over there,' her uncle, the blacksmith, instructed. 'Under 'iron gate for Grange Manor'.'

In untidy scribble she could just about make out the words, all but hidden, on the grimy page in the order book. Next to the order was the full name and address of the person who had commissioned it. 'Matheson, Grange Manor, Pendlebury'. Not a name or village that she recognised but then ironworkers were hard to find these days and this order might have come from far afield.

'Where's Pendlebury?' she asked her uncle.

'I'm not quite sure but it's not far from here. Why don't you check online?' he replied, anxious to get her out of his smithy so he could work uninterrupted. Penny was not the only one who liked working on her own. *Must be a family trait*, he thought to himself.

'I'll be off then.' Penny vanished into the yard and took off running. She wouldn't stop until she reached home and was logged on, sitting cross-legged on the floor, laptop carefully balanced in front of her.

The keywords: 'Pendlebury Grange Manor' revealed it to be an ancient building that had stood since the late 1700s. It had originally housed a member of the aristocracy but later a squire and his family had come to live there. Between 1830 and 1875 according to the records listed on the website she had found. The name of the family was not Matheson then though, but Andover. Another quick search revealed Pendlebury to be about 15 miles to the east of the village where the smithy stood. She checked the timetable. Buses were every two hours.

If she left immediately she could just make the next one. As the bus set off along the country lanes she sent her mother a quick text:

'Gone for bus ride to Pendlebury. Back for tea.'

If her mother was surprised to read the short message, from her unpredictable daughter, she didn't show it. *Showing some interest in something for a change*, was all that crossed her mind, as a pleased smile played round her mouth.

When Penny arrived in Pendlebury, Grange Manor was easy to find. She tapped lightly on the imposing front door then, realising she was unlikely to be heard, tapped again with more feeling and purpose. A tall figure, dressed in paint-splattered overalls, and not yet out of his teens, answered the door. He looked friendly but a bit irritated. From the look of him Penny assumed he had been up a ladder until the knock on the door had interrupted him.

'Yes?' he asked.

'I'm sorry to bother you but I wondered if you had ordered a new gate from the smithy at Clitheroe?'

'Well, not me exactly, but my parents have. Why do you ask?'

'My uncle has nearly finished making the gate and I was curious to know what the strange symbol and inscription mean. 'You were not forgotten'. I wondered where it came from.'

'To be honest I've no idea. My parents just wanted an exact replica making of the existing gate.

It was in a bad state, corroded and rusty. Apparently, something was written that came with the deeds of the house, stipulating that any replacement for the gate must look as identical as possible to the one already there, including the inscription. I don't think they gave the matter much thought and just decided to go along with the instruction as it's a listed building and they didn't have much choice. Why are you so interested?'

'No reason in particular. It just sort of drew me in and made me curious,' Penny petered off, thinking that she had had a wasted journey and was feeling rather silly into the bargain. But Dom, the wearer of the overalls, was not remotely fazed.

'Why don't you come in? My parents will be back soon. They can fill you in with some family history. They'll be glad to help if they can.'

Penny tentatively crossed the threshold, scraping her boots on the welcome mat as she did so. Like a vampire who has been invited into someone's house against all expectations, she could not quite believe that she was entering this house. The house that might give her answers to the enigmatic inscription on the gate. She was also mystified as to why she had become so captivated by a few words sealed into the fabric of a gate. She felt drawn to the words and the symbol in an obsessive sort of way, which some would say was linked to her particular mind set and psychological state. Possibly so, Penny would be the first to admit it, but this was something more. She felt compelled to solve the mystery and, even more so, she felt drawn to the past, as if something – or someone – was calling her.

Silence had settled on the parlour room where she had been invited to sit. Penny, unused to small talk was balancing a mug of tea on her knee and staring into space, hoping against hope for the door to open and for Dom's parents to burst in. Dom was equally tongue-tied and shy, shyness not being a word that could normally be associated with him. He glanced sideways at the rather strange girl that he had invited in despite knowing nothing whatsoever about her. Dark lashes that framed oval hazel eyes. Eyes largely hidden by a curtain of long, dark hair that hung down and served its main purpose, that of covering her face.

She was undoubtedly attractive but her allure lay in more than just her obvious good looks. She seemed to radiate an air of mystery that drew Dom in and intrigued him to his very soul. This was a girl he would not forget in a hurry. When he heard his parents talking in the hall he swung round to look at the door and missed the look that Penny gave him. Had he seen it he would have been startled, for the look held the essence of longing, as if twin souls had met without warning, and crashed headlong into each other on a cool day in autumn in a small village.

'Mum, Dad, meet Penny. She's come to ask about the origin of the inscription on our gate.' The words catapulted out of his mouth without him drawing breath and were met with a look of surprise by his father.

'And her uncle has made the new gate – the replacement,' Dom added by way of explanation.

'Let me take my coat off and we can chat properly,' said Dom's father, smiling a welcome at Penny. 'Actually, your mother might be more help Dom. She's been looking into the family tree and has come across the odd thing or two. What did you find out about the gate Sue? Anything?'

Dom's mother turned to look at Penny and was shocked to see a likeness of herself at the same age. A time when she was at her most vulnerable and feeling her way in life, finding most things frightening and challenging.

'Well, strangely enough, it turns out that I was related to the family that owned this house in the early to mid-nineteenth century. A family who went by the name of Andover. When I married I took the name of Matheson, Dom's father's name. Jim and I bought this house when it came up for auction in the 1990s. 1993 I think it was. Do you remember Jim?'

'Something like that,' he replied. 'Dom was born three years after we arrived so that just about fits.'

'Most of what I read about that period contained nothing of great interest or, at least, nothing unusual for the times. But there was something...' She paused, then continued as she recalled the details.

'Something about a child being born out of wedlock. Not unusual in those days – not by any means – but the child was recorded as disappearing shortly after birth. No-one knew the exact circumstances but a rumour was circulating the village at the time that the child had been taken away and drowned by a servant following the orders of the squire. It was thought that a serving maid at the house had given birth to the child and shortly after was dismissed from her job. The maid's father was a blacksmith. When he was asked by the squire, at some later date, to make a new gate for Grange Manor, he managed to insert a central panel with the inscription that you have seen. No-one at the Manor said anything. Perhaps they didn't notice it – who knows? Either way, each time a replacement gate was made, over the years, it has carried the same symbol and inscription. When the building was listed by National Heritage, it was stipulated that any replacement for the gate should remain true to the original.'

'And what of the symbol?' Penny blurted out. 'Did you find anything out about that?'

'Not really, but then I didn't search very hard. I have been working on a thesis and have limited time to carry out extra online searches. Are you going to try and find out what it means?' Sue looked inquisitively at Penny.

'I think I might,' Penny replied in a rather non-committal manner. She turned to Dom with a look that said: *I would like to leave now.*

Dom understood totally. This was someone who could only cope with small amounts of time engaging with other people. Now she needed to be alone. He had no idea how he knew this about her. He just did. Having promised Sue to pass on anything else she learned about the gate, Penny left the house, but not before she had swapped phone numbers with Dom and agreed to accept a friend request from him on Facebook.

Dom watched her walk away, her head bent slightly so that her face was totally hidden by her long dark hair. She resembled a raven attempting to move unnoticed along the pathway, oblivious to the actions and intentions of others. Dom was captivated. Before Penny reached home he had already sent her a friend request on Facebook and, before the hour was up, Penny had accepted it. The die was cast. The road to discovering the story behind the gate would not be travelled alone. There would be two of them travelling side by side, united in spirit, intent on achieving the same goal, of solving a mystery long held encapsulated in a few pieces of wrought iron.

Had Penny had the faintest insight into the origin of the gate she might have decided to dwell on her own family tree, though, as she would shortly discover, the gate was inexorably linked to her in ways that were both incredulous and sinister. While she delved deep into the intricate, long-lost twists and turns of the family history linked to the gate, she would draw closer and closer to the nameless children – and all the while one, in particular, would be drawing nearer to her, seeking her out.

No. 1 was hell-bound on finding his roots – getting to the source of where he came from. Every instinct would draw him closer and closer to Penny. At some point in the future, not as distant as any of them could have known, there would be a meeting of the minds and the outcome would not all be good.

The connections between the nameless children of the mid-nineteenth century and their counterparts in the twenty-first would gradually reveal themselves in a sinister unravelling of lies, deceit and hidden stories.

6   Lies and Deceit

No. 3 felt lost in the wilderness, both in the real and literal sense. He had remained closely bound to his fellow nameless children for the two days since they had left the grave. The grave that had originally held ten bodies, piled one on top of the other in flimsy makeshift coffins, now held only seven. It had already been dangerously close to collapse before the recent emergence, under cover of darkness, of the top three residents.

It was not uncommon for ten or more bodies to be buried in such a vertical grave, and for the grave to be susceptible to collapse as the coffins disintegrated. For reasons beyond explanation, the top three bodies had not succumbed to crumbling into the soil and had emerged both healthy, whole, and grown. Resembling young teens they had emerged to tread the earth and follow their hearts. To achieve their mission. To find where they belonged and to continue again with life, from the point where theirs had been cruelly ended. They would not accept an existence of eternity, laid in mind-numbing boredom beneath the soil. They wanted what was theirs. They wanted a life.

As No. 3 would discover, his ending – his final committal to the ground – was shrouded in a cloak of lies and deceit. He had effectively been wiped out of existence. It was as if he had never been born. The records would show that a boy child had been born to Lucy Elver and that the Elvers were a well-placed wealthy family who had occupied Dilston Hall for centuries. The records were indeed correct but what they would not show is that the child born to Squire Elver and his wife had died very shortly after birth. Scurried away, nameless and uncherished, to a pauper's grave for nameless children, he had been replaced immediately.

No. 3 had been denied recognition of any kind. A changeling, of sorts, had taken his place. No. 3 had every reason to feel short-changed and more than a little disgruntled. What he actually felt was a deep-seated hatred of the entire Elver family and all who ensued in the forthcoming generations. He would seek out anyone who had links to the family. Through them he would get close to his relatives, those connected to him through blood, his kith and kin. He would, through cunning and stealth, worm his way into their affections. Should they accept him as one of their own, all would turn out well. Should they, however, reject him out of hand, then it would be the worse for them. The wrath of the gods would fall upon them. The outcome would not be good.

No. 2 had survived the chiding and admonishment that she had received from No. 1. To avoid future chastisements she had agreed to stay close to the others, not to wander freely, and above all not to engage with humans without a specific purpose in mind. Casual interactions were not allowed. While promising faithfully to keep out of sight she had crossed her fingers, knowing that she would be unable to resist the temptation to talk to Saul, should she ever see him again...

The three continued to grow. Having emerged from the grave with the bodies and mental age of teenagers, they were now growing apace. Their hair lay well over their collars and, while it enhanced the appearance of No. 2, it made No. 1 and 3 look rather unkempt. The fair hair of No. 2 had a copper sheen to it, echoed in that of No. 1, the reason for which would soon become evident. No.1 had unusual blue-grey eyes which would have been an attractive feature if he had not looked so shifty, something that resulted from his tendency to avoid eye contact. And Bede – well Bede was an open book.

The basic sign language that served as communication between the three was developing rapidly and being accompanied by indecipherable grunts and squeaks, as the vocal cords prepared for action. Speech would not be long coming.

Although only brief excursions had been made into the town near the forest, to learn more about the ways of humans, they were nearer to making headway with their quest than they realised. No. 1

had already discovered the smithy, the very seat of his origin – of his birth. They were relying on primitive instincts to guide them, deep intuition to show them the path they should take. With no instructions to help them, and no sympathetic character to encourage them and support their efforts, they were alone. Cast into the wilderness, seeking a salvation that they presumed existed, they were true pioneers.

Dusk was falling and Jack, the blacksmith, reached over to turn on the table lamp. He was looking forward to an evening of uninterrupted reading. Book in hand he drew the curtains and sat in the comfy armchair, relaxing with a sigh and kicking off his boots as he did so. He was alone in the house and was not expecting visitors. Just as he liked it. Several hours of solitude in which to engage with the characters in his book. He folded back the cover and turned the page to where the bookmark had held his place from the previous evening.

There was a gentle hum of a bee that had found its way in earlier. He made a mental note to put it outside before he went to bed. Into this calm atmosphere of peace, harmony and the imagined lives of the book characters, came a sudden strident sound that pierced the silence and caused him to sit bolt upright. Someone had knocked on the door. He listened intently but, no, he was not mistaken. There it was again. A deep thud sounded on the heavy oak door. And on the other side stood child No. 1.

The blacksmith froze in his seat. Although this was the twenty-first century, or maybe because it was, he felt immediately anxious and fearful. Who was calling on him this late in the evening? The smithy and attached house were not exactly isolated, but neither were they at the centre of the town. 'Out on a limb' would be a most apt description. It flashed across his mind that he might be too isolated for comfort. No-one called after nightfall, unless by agreement. Not until now.

The knock came again, this time three short taps in quick succession. *The visitor grows impatient*, the blacksmith thought. *I should answer the door and put my mind at rest.* As the heavy wood shifted in position and swung inwards Jack stood his ground and determined to look the intruder in the face. He stared directly ahead but his eyes met only the hedge bordering the garden. Surprised he looked down and took a step backwards. There, standing only five feet five inches tall, was a young boy. *No older than fourteen or fifteen,* thought Jack.

'Can I help you?' he asked of the strangely clad child.

Answer came there none, the boy staring straight into Jack's eyes with a look of calm benevolence and purposeful intent. The combined features were not unpleasant but conveyed to Jack that, while there seemed to be no immediate cause for concern, the figure that stood before him was not entirely to be trusted.

He repeated the question but was again met with stony silence and a reluctance by the boy to look away from Jack's face. This rather unnerved Jack who was not used to being looked at so intently. As a child he had always been told not to stare and yet this was exactly what this boy was doing. Staring at him continuously – and something else was strange. The boy didn't blink. Throughout the whole time he didn't blink once. Then, with no warning, the strange boy, wearing a long, white night shirt, turned on his heel and walked away. Jack shouted after him.

'Hey, come back here. Tell me who you are and where you're from.'

But his pleas fell on unreceptive ears, and the steady footfall of the boy did not once break rhythm as he retraced his path back to the forest beyond the village. In a matter of minutes he had gone, swallowed up by the leafy foliage that delineated the edge of the forest. Jack shot a last look at the clock on the wall. The whole episode had taken less than four minutes but it had left him feeling shaken and not a little agitated. He closed and bolted the door and poured a whisky. It would take more than a hot chocolate to calm his thoughts before he went to bed.

Sleep, when it finally came, was broken and disturbed, shallow and unfulfilling. He woke feeling more tired than before he went to bed. It was only when he went into the living room, where he had been about to read the previous evening before being so rudely interrupted, that he spotted the note pad. He picked it up and examined it closely. He couldn't remember writing anything on it but there, clear as day, was his own untidy hand writing with the words: *I will be back. I belong here.*

Jack dropped the pad in astonishment. The writing was his but the message was not anything that had originated in his mind. He was quite sure of that. If he had written it then where did the words come from? The only possible explanation was the strange boy at the door. The boy who had appeared out of nowhere, under cover of darkness, and had held his gaze so steadfastly.

Jack decided to go into town and make enquiries. He would ask questions. He would not take 'no' for an answer. He would find out who this boy was. Then it dawned on him. CCTV. He had set it up to cover the area round his front door following a few acts of wanton vandalism in the town two years ago. He would look at the footage and identify the unearthly visitor that came by moonlight wearing strange apparel and with no shoes on his feet. He would track him down. No stone would be left unturned. Come what may Jack would discover the identity of the boy. Little did he know that, within a matter of days, the very same boy would be back.

THE NAMELESS CHILDREN

Jack was an early riser. He threw back the bedclothes as the first light of day forced its way through the curtains. Halfway between the Winter Solstice and the Spring Equinox the days were growing ever longer. By 5.00 am the land was lit by a flood of sunlight, scouring the countryside, challenging everything it fell upon to resist its beam. In a matter of minutes, while the kettle boiled, Jack had checked out the CCTV images from the night before. Yes, there he was. A teenage boy, his body draped in what could only be described as a night shirt, stood in the porch before Jack's door with an expectant look on his face.

Jack scrutinised the face carefully. Had he seen it before? Was there any degree of familiarity here? The boy seemed to be almost mechanical in his movements. He stood rigidly, staring fixedly at the door, waiting for a response to his initial knock. A couple of things registered unease in Jack's mind. At one point the boy tilted his head, first to one side then the other, as if listening.

He's listening to hear if anyone's inside the house, Jack thought. *He can hear from outside the door.* As the door was very thick, it was normally impossible to hear anything going on inside the house, once you had closed the door behind you. But yes, the boy was definitely able to pick up sounds from inside the house.

Jack continued to watch the footage, riveted to the images on the screen. Shortly before Jack had answered the door, the night before, the boy could be seen to drop his shoulders and assume a more relaxed position. *He knows I'm coming to the door. He can hear me,* Jack thought in wonderment. *Across four inches of solid oak he can hear me coming.*

The knowledge that the boy had superhuman hearing stunned Jack, but what he saw later shocked him to the core. As he watched the retreating figure running towards the forest he noticed something else, barely visible on the camera footage. Waiting at the edge of the forest was another figure, wearing a similar white robe to the boy.

'My God, there's more of them!' he exclaimed. But there was still the question of the words on the note pad. Had he really written them before he went to bed last night? He couldn't remember a thing about it. For some reason that he couldn't lay his finger on, he decided to slow down the playback on the CCTV to analyse the images frame by frame. All seemed as before until, during the one-sided conversation between himself and the boy at the door, he noticed that the boy had suddenly vanished but that he, Jack, appeared not to have noticed. The screen showed Jack still engaged in attempting to have a conversation.

He scrolled the images forwards slightly and there was the boy back in position outside the door. He had been inside the house. In the blink of an eye he had entered the house and returned to the door step once more. The emerging truth, hard to believe, was that the boy was capable of moving at great speed. Could it be he, not Jack himself, who had written the words on the note pad in his living room? Jack had thought that the writing was his own but could it be the boy's writing?

He rushed to get the note pad and held it to the light. On re-examination the writing no longer looked exactly like his own. The long swaying 'l' and 't', that he was so fond of doing, slanted a little too much to the right. Then there was the 'b'. Jack typically wrote the consonant with a little curl at the top. But in the note this curl was missing, the vertical line standing upright, bold as brass, straight as a die. This was not his writing. The note must have been written by someone else. It had to be the boy. The boy must have entered his house at great speed and written the note. But what for? Did the note act as a straightforward communication to inform Jack to expect another, more illuminating, visit? The boy might have a speech impediment of some kind or was too shy to explain the reason for his visit at the first meeting. Or was the message more sinister – a threat even?

'I'll be back.'

Jack was unnerved in the extreme and felt the rising clammy fingers of fear touch his spine. He clutched at the table top to steady himself and lowered himself into his armchair. This would require some thought.

Back in the forest grove No. 1 reflected on the events of the day. He was jubilant that he had managed to track down the smithy, but completely unaware that he had put the fear of God into Jack, who was now on high alert, dreading another visit.

7   The Graveyard

'Crikey. I nearly fell through that!' exclaimed Gareth, one of the gardeners tasked with keeping the churchyard tidy and relatively weed-free. With the exception of some areas that had been left untamed on purpose, to provide a habitat for wildlife, the graveyard was kept in immaculate condition. Last year's innovation of introducing a few goats to keep down the grass between the graves had gone well and was set to be repeated this summer. Totally unexpected then was this hole in the ground. A hole that seemed to resemble a well in that it was not possible, in the pervading light, to see where the bottom lay.

'I could swear that this hole was not here yesterday when I checked the area,' Gareth remarked to his workmate and friend Ian.

'Yes, I saw it too. The ground looked firm, if a little disturbed.'

'Disturbed? How?' asked Gareth. 'And who by? Do you think foxes or badgers have been at it? Do you remember me telling you about something I'd read recently? About how they used to place gravestones flat over the graves, almost touching each other? The assumption drawn was that in days gone by, when wolves were still roaming free in the wilds of the UK, they used to dig up bodies from the graves. Positioning the stones close together stopped the wolves gaining access to the ground and hence the bodies.'

'Yes, I remember that,' replied Ian. 'But, to my knowledge, there haven't been any wolves in these parts for hundreds of years. Relentless persecution by humans saw to that.'

'True, but it could have been a fox or badger that started digging and caused the whole lot to collapse in on itself.'

'Well, whatever the reason, let's get it filled in. Quickly. Before anyone vanishes down it, never to be seen again!'

'Or it could be something else,' continued Ian.

'Such as?'

'Creatures of darkness?' suggested Ian.

'Oh, very funny,' said Gareth. 'I don't think so!'

Of course he was right. This was not the work of a vampire. It was, though, the work of something equally sinister. Three children who had been buried more than a century earlier had emerged from the ground fully intact and aged by more than ten years.

The dawning realisation that they were conspicuous in their present apparel had led the nameless children to discard their night shirts and replace them with more appropriate clothes. Odd, assorted garments had presented themselves, free of charge.

Large plastic bin liners, containing second hand clothes, were to be found periodically deposited outside charity shops in the evening, despite signs advising strongly against the practice. Having found the time to clear out their cupboards, and having made the effort to transport large bags of clothing all the way to the shop, people were clearly reluctant to take the bags back home, on seeing that the shop was closed. Bounty for the harmless and the destitute – and for the nameless children.

Looking slightly strange, as not all the clothing fitted properly, they made their way slowly along the pavement into the town centre, trying not to attract too much attention on the way. They needed to be able to blend in amongst the masses if they were to make any headway in discovering the homes and families to which they belonged.

People edged to the side to make way for the trio as they moved along the street. The children might as well have been wearing placards round their necks saying 'unclean', 'beware the plague' or even simply 'homeless', judging by the wide berth they were afforded.

The casual manner with which people averted their eyes, with an air of nonchalance, showed well-practised behaviour when it came to avoiding those they wished to have no contact with. Their peripheral vision told them all they needed to know – the quick up and down scan of a person told them many things.

Clothes that don't fit properly – no money to buy new ones, or even second hand ones. Probably destitute or homeless or both. Socially inept. The conclusion drawn was always the same. Don't have anything to do with this person. They are not of your social class. They are misfits.

Propelled into the twenty-first century the three were programmed to behave as teenagers. The unknown event that had precipitated their resurrection had determined this state of affairs – had sealed it in stone. And they were effectively all but invisible.

In terms of achieving their goal of avoiding arousing suspicion they were mostly successful. The greater majority of people avoided them. Turned away. Went about their own business. All but one.

Standing directly opposite the three, on the other side of the street, was Saul, his attention caught by the peculiar movement made by the trio as they walked along. A sort of loping motion, not normally seen in humans. It did not resemble someone walking with a limp, or recovering from a stroke, but rather was an animal-like movement. Typical of...?

Saul searched his memory trying to recall a natural history TV programme he had seen recently... A hyena. A carnivore that works as a pack to bring down prey. Yes, that's what they resembled – a pack of hyenas working closely together with a common goal. In the case of the nameless children the common goal was to keep safe, find food, discover their ancestry and, of course, to survive.

With perfunctory nods of the head the three reached an agreement of sorts. Smoothing down their clothes, and adjusting their backpacks, they parted and went in different directions. If their short time in the world of the living had taught them anything, it had taught them that they needed money. This seemed to be easy to obtain if you had no objection to sitting on a cold, hard pavement busking, hour after hour in all weathers. Come rain or shine. In the snow. If you were prepared to do this you would be rewarded.

People would take pity on the plight of those worse off than themselves and would part with small amounts of change. If the three only had the patience to stay the course they would earn enough to enable them to survive. One sticking point might be their inability to converse, but then many people who were destitute on the streets of the UK did not have English as their native tongue, so maybe this would not be a problem. They would just have to try it and see. Like children learning to speak for the first time, the world of words came to them, lay itself at their feet and beckoned them to use it. And, as with their other well-developed talents, the ability to speak came quickly, with an inordinate haste that spoke of magic.

8   Number Four

A dark-cast sky hung over the small mill town overshadowed by the West Pennines. Soft earth crumbled in the deep pit that had held ten bodies for over a century. Bodies of children buried without a name, for whatever reason. Unremembered, their final resting place not commemorated or sanctified. Just a number.

A few weeks earlier three of these ten children had risen from this same spot. Children who had made their way into the local town to earn their living from begging in the streets. They were oblivious to the fact that another of their kind would soon move amongst humans in the world above. That another nameless child would soon walk the earth. That No. 4 was about to join their numbers. The emergence of three bodies from their collapsed coffins had caused a deep pit to form and with it a trembling of the earth and an awakening of the next body down.

No. 4 raised his head above ground, just as twilight bathed the graveyard with an eerie glow. He was different from the others. At birth he had been given a name, Jonas, but it had been forgotten and the headstone delivered no record of it to the observer. No thread to help them trace the history of this child, or indeed any of the ten children buried there in the 1850s.

Jonas was also unusual in that he had lived until the age of four. He had been much loved by his family and siblings. After Jonas no more children had been born to his family. He had been the last.

But a long life was not to be his. Cholera had descended on the small town and swept through it like a wild fire through a timber-dry forest, claiming all vulnerable souls and leaving a path of devastation in its wake. One of those souls was Jonas. Lost to his family, taken too soon from this life.

But he was not the only one from his family to lose his life. Cholera had also claimed his parents and four sisters, leaving two orphaned children to be reared by their aunt. And so it was that the absence of his parents led to his burial without a ceremony and without a name. Jonas became consigned to those known as the nameless children.

Now he was risen, bedraggled as he was, clothed in a woven cotton shirt that trailed across his knees. He presented a plaintive sight to anyone who might see him. But no-one did and Jonas made his way carefully out of the graveyard into the adjoining town. Another nameless child had risen from the cold clay and was now free to wreak havoc as he wished.

He moved cautiously along ginnels and alleyways, still clothed in his white burial shirt, which was now looking much the worse for wear, torn at the hem and covered in mud. He didn't get far. Falling blood pressure and blood sugar levels saw to that. As he moved past the gate that sealed in the yard of number 56 Watkins Street he stumbled. Reaching out to the wall to steady his fall, his hand met with the shoulder of a small woman who was just leaving through the gate. She bent slightly under the weight of Jonas. Slight as he was for a fifteen-year-old boy, she was slighter. Aged 52, and tiny by modern-day standards, Emily stood firm and held her arms out to support the ailing boy.

'Hang on to me. I've got you!'

Words of reassurance spilled out over Jonas and on to the pavement.

'Do you want to come inside and sit down for a while?'

Words of gentleness, kindly offered.

Jonas nodded and tried to manage a smile. Holding Emily's arm for support he let himself be led into a small, clean kitchen. Even in his weakened state he was able to appreciate the cool, cream painted walls and the comfort of the chair positioned by the stove. The chair that he lowered himself into. He even noticed the massive grandfather clock that stood in a small alcove near the bottom of the stairs. Emily noticed him appraising the clock.

'That clock's been in my family for going on two hundred years,' she told Jonas.

Having ensured his safe delivery into the chair Emily stood back, partly in order to get a better view of him and partly to give him some space. There was nothing worse than to feel crowded by the close proximity of another person, in particular a stranger, especially when you were feeling ill.

Just in time Emily stopped herself from saying: 'Cat got your tongue?' when yet another of her questions was met with the same stony silence. *Maybe he couldn't talk?*

'Do you have a name?' Emily persevered.

A quizzical look fleeted across the face of Jonas. She tried again:

'Can you speak?'

No response.

Emily had learned Makaton, a type of sign language, at some point in her life. Many years ago when she had worked with people who had learning disabilities. Without giving it a second thought she started to sign to Jonas.

'Are you hungry?'

Amazingly this generated an enthusiastic response.

Cracked it! thought Emily. *We have lift off. He understands sign language. We can communicate.*

In front of the little stove, Jonas begin to visibly thaw. His frown, that seemed to be etched deep into his forehead, was smoothing out. By the time Emily had brought him a bowl of hot soup he was almost asleep. She gently touched his arm.

'Here. I've brought you soup. Why don't you try some?'

The instrument that served as an implement for eating the soup was somehow familiar to Jonas. It jogged his memory. Damp mornings sitting in a kitchen with condensation running down the windows. The noise of others sitting alongside him. The chastisement of children by a figure who looked a lot like Emily. He clicked back to the present and slowly and gratefully swallowed the soup. As his strength recovered he tackled the hunk of malted grain bread and in no time had demolished all in front of him.

'You look as if you have been poorly. Would you like to rest here for a while before going back outside?'

Jonas nodded and fell into a deep sleep, head resting on the back of the arm chair.

Emily smiled and retreated to another room to leave her unexpected visitor in peace. Her trip could wait. Only a few things to get from the shop. No hurry. She only worked part time these days, her full-time position falling prey to the recession. She didn't mind. Emily had plans for her life and they didn't involve working behind a counter in the library, even though being surrounded by books all day had been a childhood dream of hers. Emily was a poet and once she had enough funds was going to publish her first book of poems.

She also drew. Little sketches. Nothing more. Maybe she could sketch Jonas while he was sleeping. He wouldn't know she was there if she was quiet and she could show him her attempt at his likeness later, when he woke up. Emily felt a warm glow of contentment, not just because she had done something good for another person in need, but because it filled an inner need in her.

Many, many years ago, longer than she cared to think, she had given birth to a child who had not made it to his fifth birthday. A child that she had named David. A 'treasured beyond all else' child. Loved beyond measure. A longed-for child. A child that had been born with a health problem.

The writing had been on the wall, the diagnosis made, the die cast. The doctors were accurate in their prediction, to the month. They could not have known the day though. Only God could have known the day. God... Emily's faith, once so strong and unbending, had taken a pounding all those years ago and had never fully returned.

So Jonas slept on, while Emily drew.

Emily was a woman driven. A persistent streak, coupled with an ability to focus with immaculate attention to detail, proved to be immensely beneficial as tools to guide her through life and help her to achieve her goals. Being relaxed, and open to inspiration, was one thing. Being able to structure your day, in order to get everything done, was another. Emily liked a degree of structure to be built into her day. Without it she tended to wander off mentally, becoming a little lost in the process.

A lack of structure had only one outcome – failure to achieve one's goals and the insidious, sinister creeping of depression. The long fingers that tested the air as if seeking a vulnerable subject, someone unable to resist the inviting request to:

'Come to me. Let yourself relax. No need to worry about anything. No need to go anywhere. Forget any arrangements or appointments you had. Let them all slip away. Forget it all.'

And with almost no effort the cloak of depression, the black dog, had enveloped the vulnerable person, taken them for its own, had drawn them in. The smug darkness that would, from now on, seem to hang over everything the person thought about, all the things they had considered they might do. All their plans would fall apart. Their innermost thoughts, the inner sanctum so crucial to a feeling of well-being and sanity, would disintegrate, often never to be reassembled in any useful form.

Emily knew that deep within her lay the tendency to become depressed. She had felt its fingers before, lain within its grasp for many months. The months following the gradual decline, and eventual death, of David, her beloved child. But Emily had one thing on her side, an inner strength that she could draw on. A little voice within her that fought away the lurking spectre of depression. The voice that said:

'Get up Emily. Get up now. Make a plan for the day.'

It was a fine line. Trying to maintain a balance and stop depression from taking over. Mostly she was successful. Today, drawing Jonas sleeping, drawing the face, as she saw it, of an innocent, needy child, lifted her spirits beyond all measure. She had just laid down her piece of charcoal when Jonas stirred and, opening his eyes, looked straight at her. For a split second she thought she detected an element of malice, a degree of evil intent, in the eyes. Then Jonas broke into a smile and the thought vanished.

Emily rose and went to make a cup of tea while Jonas looked round the room at his leisure. Taking in his surroundings, and registering that here was a place he could stay, he began to configure how he would trace his family, get back to those who had gone before, or rather their descendants. For now though he could relax and let Emily do the worrying.

9   Life on the Streets

It had been a slow day. Many pitying glances but little money thrown into their hats. The hats they had placed so carefully in front of them, with optimism and anticipation. But as the hours passed and the hats remained largely empty, optimism waned, to be replaced by lethargy and an overwhelming sense of defeat.

Life on the streets, as No. 1, 2 and 3 children were discovering, was not easy. Earlier in the week they had seen others gathering money in their pots or guitar cases and had been led to believe, by observation alone, that this was the way to easy pickings, a way to survive with minimal effort. They now felt cheated – deceived even.

What they could not have known though, was that there were many contributory factors that determined whether you earned a substantial sum in a day or whether you earned barely enough to survive. The day they had witnessed crowds standing round someone who was busking for money was unusual in that it was bright and sunny. Unusual as well in that this was autumn and such days were far and few between. Far more common for mist to lie like a blanket over the land and for people to resume their huddled posture in anticipation of winter.

But when the sun shone it raised the spirits. People were more prepared to part with their money. *To help others worse off than ourselves* was the general ethos behind the money throwing. In addition, the street performers with small crowds round them were not just sitting on the pavement, staring at the floor, but were often playing a musical instrument, singing, juggling or engaged in some such activity that was generally recognised as entertainment.

It is one of the paradoxes of life that those who exhibit a sunny disposition, and are able to demonstrate skills of one sort or another, are often the ones who have far less need of money than those who stare at the ground, their face lined with worry, the epitome of the social misfit, the outcast whose demeanour sums up the word 'dejection'.

The sunny, happy ones who played music on the streets were often, if questioned, found to be on a gap year before going to university and were accruing funds to support their trip to some far-flung part of the world. These people often had parental backing to boot, both emotional and financial. The street people whose demeanour signalled 'dejection' often had no-one. The lucky ones, far and few between, might have formed loose connections with others on the streets, operating under the rule 'safety in numbers'.

Some sought the companionship that a dog offered. Not just a companion in their everyday struggle but also a guardian, something to protect them should they find themselves under attack. But with the acquirement of a dog, with which to share their days, came another problem. Their chances of finding somewhere to live, to be off the streets and able to sleep in a bed at night, were dashed on the arrival of the dog.

Finding rental accommodation where dogs are welcome was nothing short of impossible but, having acquired a new friend, it would take more than the prospect of shelter under a roof to persuade the homeless, dispossessed person to part with their dog.

So the division lay between the two sets of street people, the 'haves' and the 'have-nots'. Both groups attempted to strike the right posture, the right appeal to the passerby, while all along the difference between them was as stark as it could be. The group that the three nameless children found themselves in was the group that was the most pitied, the least befriended and the least helped. And so it was that, on this their first day of attempting a life on the streets, they had not been lucky. The sun had not shone on them.

However, the three were not stupid. Temporarily lacking in any language skills they may be, but without ingenuity and an innate intelligence they were not. No. 2 was particularly adept at judging situations and garnering information. She saw that facial expression was all important, demeanour paramount and a positive attitude crucial. Back in their make-shift dwelling in the forest that night, No. 2 communicated her thoughts to the others. They would not give up or back down. Tomorrow would be another day. They would try again. They would learn. They would succeed.

Saul had been scouring the streets. His last sighting of the strange trio, he secretly referred to as 'the hyena', was as they moved with stealth along the high street, but as quickly as they had appeared, so did they vanish.

After two hours he found them again. To say that he was surprised to see the three sitting in such a public place, faces averted from the passing crowd, hope dimming by the minute, would have been an understatement. He could scarcely believe his luck. Then he began to wonder. *Why on earth were they exposing themselves to this – to possible ridicule, personal attack, verbal abuse? Why would they do this?* Unless of course they had nowhere to live.

Saul cast his mind back to when he had first seen them leaving the graveyard two weeks ago, moving furtively, anxious to avoid detection. He decided to go back to the graveyard, to retrace his steps, to discover where these three might have come from. *Maybe they had been sleeping rough amongst the gravestones. Maybe they still were?* Tearing himself away from the drooping heads, that signified dejection, he made his way back to the graveyard.

No. 1 had been mulling things over. In the deep recesses of his mind, where memories were gradually beginning to stir, he reached in and grabbed a thread of remembrance. Like following a string that would return him to his starting point in a dark wood, he clawed at the nuggets of wisdom that sparkled dimly amongst the mire that was his previous life. A life after he was born, but before he died.

Like glow worms, whose light ebbs and flows in the darkness, so the memories tempted him, drew him towards them, held him in their thrall. And when he had clutched them to him, held them aloft, gazed closely at them, more – much more – flooded back into his consciousness.

Memories of being held with love and tenderness, wrapped gently in soft material. Then – struggling to breathe. Words of kindness, sympathy, offered over him as he lay. Then, finally, utterances that held the unmistakable note of desperation, followed by grief. With his parting breath he saw his soul leave his body.

Even after death No. 1 was still aware. He could see the room where people stood and waited. He hovered above a bed, close to the ceiling, and gazed down on a figure that lay on the bed. A woman, her features pure and unworried, her life spent, her son newly born. Only minutes after the soul of No. 1 had loosened itself from his body, it was followed by that of his mother. She searched for him, took his hand and led him to the world of all souls where peace would be with them and they would find life everlasting.

No. 1 snapped back to the present and the matter he was anxious to pursue. He was desperate to connect with his past, to discover the mysteries behind his burial without a name, and needed to make contact with the blacksmith once more.

Tapping the other two, to indicate that he was leaving, he made ready to travel across town towards the smithy. In a matter of but a few days the three nameless children had closely observed the ways of others. They had seen how they moved, how they walked – mostly with an upright posture.

No. 1 straightened himself, pushed his shoulders back to heighten the image he portrayed and, with renewed intent, trod purposefully on the road to the smithy.

Jack, the blacksmith, lay down his tools. It was hot, thirsty work and sweat streaked down his forehead into his eyes. Absentmindedly he wiped it away, cursing at the grime and dirt that inescapably accompanied his profession. But he wouldn't have it any other way. It was all he had ever known and deep down he loved the life. Being his own master, being able to call the tune, to dictate the hours that he worked. There was nothing to beat it. He looked up and staggered backwards. The window, filthy as it was, held a face. Staring back at Jack with unflinching eyes. Eyes that didn't blink.

I know this face, he thought. *That's the strange boy that came to my door the other day and left a note.*

'I belong here. I will be back.'

And true to his word, he has come back, thought Jack.

Then – an attempt at a smile.

The boy was trying to be friendly. Perhaps the enigmatic note was not meant as a threat – more as a message to indicate his return at some future date. Jack recovered his composure, wiped his hands on an old rag, and moved towards the door. With some apprehension he opened it slightly. Not enough to allow the visitor in, just enough to exchange words and to allow him to bang the door shut should it prove necessary.

'Yes?' Jack was a man of few words and he wanted to see what this boy had to say.

The smile again. No words. Then a sign. A hand lifted in the air that seemed to denote a peaceful stance. As if he was saying: 'I come in peace. I mean you no harm.'

Jack was suspicious and spoke again.

'What do you want? This is a smithy.'

No. 1 had come prepared. While he had only the beginnings of speech, he could nevertheless write in a reasonably intelligible fashion. He handed Jack a torn piece of paper on which were strewn a few, seemingly random, words. Words that, after some perusal, assembled to form sentences:

'I belong here. I was born here a long time ago. I have come back.'

Jack could see that he had come back. Of that there was no doubt. What was obviously in doubt though was the fact that he had been born there a long time ago. Not possible. He couldn't be much more than sixteen years old – and what an odd assortment of clothes. They looked like they had come from a rag bag, or were left-overs from a jumble sale. Clothes that had been obtained without first trying on. Very odd indeed.

'Right,' said Jack. 'How can I help you?'

No. 1 looked past Jack into the house behind him, then back at Jack with a questioning look on his face that was not open to interpretation. Its meaning was evident.

He wants to come in, thought Jack. For some reason a scene from a vampire movie flooded into his mind. A few words in particular: 'A vampire can only come into your house if you invite them in' the vampire slayer had told the townspeople. Jack was looking into the far distance as he thought this and he swung his gaze back to face the visitor directly.

Cool, grey eyes that met his.

Eyes that did not blink.

That's creepy, Jack thought. *No way is he coming in my house. Not a chance.*

'I'm sorry. I'm sure you have your reasons for being here but I don't know you at all and I'm not about to invite you in.'

The boy's face fell and he looked disconsolate, almost as if he was about to cry but then, in a split second, his expression changed to one of total self-composure and purposefulness. He held his hand out for the scrap of paper, took a pencil from his pocket and began to write.

'I was born here. My family lived here in the 1850s. They died during the cholera epidemic.' No. 1 had learned enough to have assessed the situation and realised that the major sticking point was the century and the time that had elapsed since he had been born. Jack read the scrawled words and thought for a minute.

'Right then. Here's what I'll do. My niece, Penny, is looking into the history of our family and it appears that you are doing the same. You can't speak – is that correct?'

No. 1 nodded.

'But you can communicate using pen and paper so that's a start. I think Penny would like to meet you. I will tell her about you and see what she thinks. How can I reach you?'

No. 1 thought quickly. He gestured for more paper.

'I play music on the street in front of Gerhart's Café. Every day between 11.00 am and 3 pm. She can find me there.' He was actually incapable of playing a musical instrument but planned to learn quickly – very quickly.

Jack marvelled at how much more eloquent the writing had become and how much more coherent the words. No. 1 was also taken aback. What he did not yet know was that his skills were maturing by the minute. Like a bright child learning to read and write, and like a person learning a new language in a foreign land, being immersed in an environment that swam in all of these would allow him to develop them with great speed.

10   The Enticement

By the time Saul reached the graveyard the light was beginning to fade. And with the loss of light came the retraction of colour. The hues of amber and dark green imparted to the headstones, and the moss covering them, were turning to shades of beige. The upright stones were losing their 3-D definition and beginning to look horizontal.

    Saul became more cautious. This was not a place to fall and injure yourself. You could lie there the entire night, helpless and exposed. No-one would find you until morning. He thrust the negative thoughts away and began to focus intently on the gravestones. Nothing appeared to be out of the ordinary, but then... in his peripheral vision he caught sight of a blue light hovering over an area towards the edge of the official graveyard. 'Official' in that the area was delineated by where the grass cutting ended and the foliage was allowed to grow largely as it wished, free and untamed.

    The obsession with grass cutting in every part of suburbia, to the detriment of all hidden wildlife that kept its distance from humans and tried to exist within the confines of the remaining habitat, was part and parcel of the twenty-first century. So many hedgehogs had met their ends when confronted with the unrelenting bite of the strimmer's lashes. The cutting extended even to the graveyards. But the area permeated by the dull blue light had not yet fallen prey to the grass cutter. It had been left to follow its own way, bar a perfunctory attempt with the shears in between the gravestones where the nettles had begun to tower too high, the brambles to grow too thickly.

As Saul approached tentatively, the light seemed to dim, then extinguish completely, as if someone had thrown soil over a small fire in the forest, quickly, to avoid detection. What had caused this light? Was there someone else in the graveyard? Was someone watching him?

Murmurings within the deep pit that held the collapsed coffins and the remaining six bodies were barely audible. Saul could just about detect a low hum, almost like the sound that emits from a bee hive as one approaches it. But, while the sound emitted by bees continues unabated, the 'hum' from the grave ceased. As suddenly as the blue light was extinguished, the murmurings stopped. So quiet had they been that Saul begin to think that he had imagined them. But, like the rumblings of a volcano that has lain dormant for decades, the noise began again. This time Saul could pick up distinct words.

'Where have the others gone?'
'Are there only six of us left?'

The thought skipped across Saul's mind: *these are words from the grave*. How often had he heard the expression 'words beyond the grave'? Well now he was hearing 'words from the grave'!

'Who's there?' he called out, not honestly expecting a response.

'Who are you?' flew back the response.

Having a question answered with a question had always made Saul very exasperated and today was no exception. He felt like saying 'I asked first. You tell me!' but instead:

'I am Saul. I mean you no harm. I am searching for three people I saw come from this graveyard a few weeks ago.'

Silence.

'Do you know anything about this?' Saul persisted.

Still silence. Then:

'If you want to know more you must climb down to us.'

The deep pit looked uninviting in the extreme but Saul reasoned that he could make footholds in the soft earth of the sides as he climbed down, and use them to climb back out.

When he reached the first coffin, that contained body No. 6 of the nameless children, arms reached out to take him, followed by more arms that drew him down. Down into the depths. Saul had shown trust when he should have shown none. He had let curiosity take priority over common sense and survival. He took his last breath of earthly air from the world that he had known and let the grave claim him for its own.

One headstone, standing not far from the unhallowed area, had an inscription at the bottom. It read:

In the midst of life we are in death but God will redeem my soul from the power of the grave.

Saul had succumbed to the power of the grave, fallen prey to the nameless children that continued to occupy the vertical pit in the ground. The only saving grace, should there be one, was that, unlike the nameless children, he still had his soul. He would also discover that, like the nameless children, he would be graced with the ability to survive beneath the ground.

The shovelling had begun. Spade upon spade of loose earth was poured down the hole in an attempt to fill the deep pit.

'We don't want any casualties,' the council worker informed Stephen, the young teenager on work experience. 'We need to get the hole filled to the top and flattened down. Then we can sow grass seeds on top and it will be as good as new. No sign that the grave ever collapsed. A hazard-free graveyard.'

Stephen looked across to the main graveyard, sanctified by blessings from above. He saw the scattered, fallen headstones lying at all angles upon the ground, and doubted this very much. Tidy it might look. Hazard free it most certainly was not.

The first indication Saul had, that he was about to be buried alive, came as the first spade-full of earth hit him on the head. The incarceration of Saul had begun. He tried to shout to indicate his predicament but his calls fell on deaf ears. Too much earth now lay between him and those above and his words were lost.

Then a hand reached from below and clamped firmly over his mouth to stifle any further pleas. It was then that he knew that all was lost and that he would die alone in this deep pit. No-one would ever know what had happened to him. He was lost to the world.

A weak sun seeped between the trees in the graveyard. All seemed unchanged. The autumn red-gold leaves fluttered to the ground. Squirrels rushed about clutching nuts to their chest. The graveyard that had quietly existed since the beginning of the nineteenth century had seen much coming and going. So many people laid to rest in its grounds. So many people left to grieve. So many inscriptions on headstones.

'Your final resting place' was a common one. A nice sentiment that intimated that, once laid in your allocated space, you would lie here and dream untroubled dreams for all eternity. Except that the statement was not true. It lied. The emergence of four nameless children from their 'final resting place' had, by definition, rendered these words null and void. It was most certainly not their final resting place. Three of them were currently eking out a living on the streets of the local mill town, while a fourth had taken up residence in the house of a welcoming woman. A woman desperate to rekindle her memories of motherhood. To experience what she felt was her right. To claw back the years she would have had mothering her small son David. If only he had not died.

Beneath the mound that held six nameless children, with the perfunctory headstone that failed to tell their stories, now lay another body. That of Saul. It was only a matter of time before his absence was noticed. Then all hell would be let loose.

11   Anwen

In a terraced house, in a Welsh town that had seen the last of its mining days, someone with as yet unrealised connections to the nameless children was deep in conversation.

'Have we got any records of our family tree?' Anwen asked her father.

'Not a lot!' he replied. 'You're probably better off doing an online search. See what that turns up.'

Anwen brushed the hair out of her eyes. Remarkably beautiful, with shining green eyes, she had no awareness that her looks and demeanour captivated all she met.

'A lovely girl, so kind and inspiring,' people would often remark. No-one could have known that Anwen, leading a quiet life in the Welsh valleys, was descended from a changeling. That somewhere in the past a child (No. 3) had been replaced by another, and now the replaced child was clawing its way back. The nameless child, dismissed without any form of recognition, refused to be forgotten, under any circumstances.

Anwen had made good progress. She had tracked her family tree back to the late 1800s. Hours and hours she had spent pouring over old records in the reference library. To reach the library required a long bus journey. Chasing down your origins through archives was not for the faint-hearted. But Anwen of the valleys was driven. Driven by a passion for knowledge. Not for her a retreat from the path of hard work. No falling at the first hurdle. She had discovered much. Stories of intrigue and deception, unintentional incest. Wayward lives indeed.

Some children born out of wedlock were farmed out to distant relatives as new-born infants, never to learn the true nature of their beginnings. This led to some unfortunate alliances between siblings who, in total ignorance of their genetic background, embarked on liaisons which were best left alone. Only harsh, timely intervention prevented the unfortunate victims of the charade, perpetuated by their relatives, from marrying and bearing children.

Anwen also unearthed records that showed many of her ancestors to be the wandering kind. Listed as 'journeyman', several distant male family members had travelled far and wide plying their trade. Judging from the frequency of the surname 'Elver', in one particular town, it seemed likely that this was somewhere her family had lived, well over a century ago. This was the place where she decided she would concentrate her search.

But Anwen was following a false trail. While on paper it might appear that she had descended from the family 'Elver', in reality she was descended from another line entirely. One that belonged to the changeling. The changeling so abruptly uprooted from his home. So uncaringly taken to a strange place. Laid in the arms of another woman, not his mother, the changeling might have appeared, at first glance, to have landed on his feet. But appearances can be deceptive. The changeling had been denied his birthright and been severed from his real family. He had served to replace No. 3 child.

The changeling had just cause to be angry. But this paled into insignificance compared with the wrath felt by No. 3. Discarded and buried post-haste, denied a ceremony, denied a name. It was not his fault that he had failed to survive. Never to have felt a loving touch or to have been grieved for by his parents. No. 3 was intent on revenge and once he discovered a family member, a descendent of those who had wronged him, he would exact this revenge, vent his fury. No. 3 would not accept dismissal from this world, with no name and no recognition. The time had come to right a wrong.

Anwen tracked down the birthplace of what she thought were her ancestors in a matter of seconds. An online search revealed Dilston Hall to be the home of a family, one with the name of Elver, back in the 1850s. She felt tempted to finger the screen of her laptop, so inviting was the image of the linocut showing the Hall set in stark splendour against a brooding sky.

'Dilston Hall,' she murmured out loud. She had a vague recollection of a song she'd heard sung at the local folk club. How did it go?

'Farewell to pleasant Dilston Hall, my father's ancient seat ...' the tune was coming back to her now, in waves. Short bursts of notes that were forming a song of sorts. It couldn't be the same surely? The Hall in the song was not in a Pennine mill town for a start. It was in Northumbria. The last lines of the song ran:

'If it is in London town, I am condemned to die, carry me to Northumberland, in my father's grave to lie.'

No, it couldn't be the same place. Interesting though. Synchronicity? Anwen didn't believe in coincidence, however compelling the evidence, but she would recall the song at a later date.

'Carry me to Northumberland...' would come the whispered thoughts from inside her head.

She scrolled down the screen searching for more details but nothing of any note caught her eye, until: a small section from a newspaper cutting:

"On September 18, 1853, to the Squire of Dilston Hall and his wife, a son was born. The child has been named James, after his grandfather. He is the first born child."

Anwen was not well up on history and the traditional manner in which births and deaths were reported in the newspapers in those days. She did, however, wonder how frequent it was for such an advert to be placed in a newspaper in that day and age, considering the amount it would have cost. Further searches revealed that it was a far from common occurrence. Maybe this was a particularly longed-for child.

Anwen was now able to trace her family name back to the 1850s. The facts were there in front of her. Several generations ago her family had lived in relative splendour in a Hall in the north of England, in the shadow of a mountain range known as the Pennines. She appeared to be related to this longed-for son, James. What had happened to James?

The records showed he had led an uneventful life, working in the local mill as a supervisor in charge of the work force. He had married and had four children, two of whom had survived infancy. *Not many lived past five,* she thought, then: *I could go to Dilston Hall, if it still stands. Have a look round the local graveyards. See if I can spot the name 'Elver' on any of the stones.*

With renewed vigour, and enthused by her findings, Anwen endeavoured to head off to the north as soon as funds and time allowed. Unbeknown to her she was on the trail of the changeling.

Time hung heavy on his hands. Dom had never given much thought or consideration to the possibility of time possessing qualities such as weight. But then he had never heard of time hanging lightly. Time always seemed to 'hang heavy'. He had been trying to get on with an assignment for his course but couldn't get Penny out of his mind. As much as he tried he couldn't shift the image that he held of her walking away from his parents' house, on her way home.

Such a strange meeting. Even stranger for her to just turn up at the house enquiring about their family. He had opened up to her, as had his parents, although they knew nothing whatsoever about her. Penny had such an engaging manner, one that suggested that only the truth would be spoken by such a person. No fabricated lies would spill from her mouth. She could be trusted. Dom felt sure of this, if nothing else. A glance at the clock proved, yet again, that time does not pass more quickly when you keep checking on it.

Penny arrived by bike, threw it to the ground as she reached the end of the path, and went to knock on the front door. As she raised her hand the door swung open before her.

'Hi. I saw you from the window,' Dom tried to sound as casual as he could. While Penny let her arm fall to her side.

'Hi, I've come on my bike.'

'So I see.'

Settled in the living room, each hugging a mug of tea, they eyed each other warily with a degree of anticipation. Dom took the plunge.

'Anything to report?'

'Actually – yes. It would appear that rumours circulating at the time are true.'

'What, there really was a child that was born here at the Manor. A child that was drowned?'

'I think the word is 'murdered',' corrected Penny. 'Yes, the squire could not afford for any of the local community to ever find out that his son had fathered a child born to a commoner, a serving maid, so he had the child dispatched – drowned I think. It all fits in with what your mother said.'

Dom was visibly shocked.

'My God, that's terrible. When did all this happen?'

'Early 1850s by all accounts. Just before the cholera epidemic swept through Clitheroe, which of course gave everyone something else to think about. Pursuing justice for a possible wrong-doing, that no-one could actually prove had happened, was set aside. Plus which the squire also sat as a judge in the local court.'

'The chances of 'justice being seen to be done' were remote then.' Dom posed the rhetorical question.

'Precisely,' agreed Penny.

'Anything else?'

'I thought that was enough to be going on with. A bit of a bombshell actually,' Penny replied. 'But, yes, there was something else. The child born was a little girl. Her mother was only fourteen and the eldest child of the local blacksmith. Once details of the child's murder and disposal surfaced, mostly through gossip amongst the servants, the mother was, understandably, grief stricken. She was inconsolable. Shortly after, with a callous display of unfeeling behaviour verging on downright cruelty, a commission came in from the Manor. Grange Manor. Here,' Penny stressed the point. 'Orders for a gate to be fashioned out of iron, to serve as an entry to the walled garden that lies to the side of the Manor. Desperate for money the blacksmith made the gate, but not before he had inserted a small plaque in the centre with the inscription that you know.'

'You were not forgotten,' Dom murmured.

'Yes, exactly.' They both sat, silent, bathed in their own thoughts. Then Penny turned to Dom:

'But I didn't find out anything about the symbol in the middle of the plaque. Do you know any more?'

'No. I'm afraid I haven't actually been looking. Too busy with assignments. I'm doing a degree in farming and agriculture at the local college. I could help you look though. We could look together?' Dom posed the question in the hope that Penny would respond favourably and he could spend more time with her.

'Yes, fine with me,' Penny responded with an air of indifference.

Dom logged onto his laptop and they chose various combinations of keywords with which to challenge the internet search engine. Not knowing what the symbol on the gate was called didn't help.

'Stop! What was that?' Penny had spotted something on the page.

Dom scrolled back up and they both peered closely at the screen.

'Looks similar don't you think? Not quite the same but very similar,' Dom pondered.

Penny didn't reply but just sat staring at the symbol in front of her.

'Can you rotate the image?'

'Yes, if I save it first, then no problem.'

'Now enlarge it,' Penny instructed once the image had been flipped through 180 degrees.

'That's it,' she breathed out. 'We've found it.'

'What is it though? What does it say?' Dom was desperate to know.

'It seems to have a few different meanings.' Penny started to list them:

- An ancient pagan symbol often used to ward off evil
- A portent for the future
- A symbol to say that an act of ill-doing was committed and will be avenged
- A threat to future generations linked to the one who perpetrated an act of ill-doing

'There are a few to choose from then,' said Dom. 'Which do you think is the most likely, knowing what we suspect about the reasons for the plaque being on the gate in the first place?'

'I would say pretty much all of them.'

They looked at each other with sombre faces.

'What next?' asked Dom.

'Not sure but let's keep it to ourselves for now,' said Penny.

'Yes, okay.' Dom looked at Penny who had hidden once more behind her hair. *Inscrutable as always*, he thought. *Probably not a good time to make a move.* Desperate though he was to put his arms round her, and hold her close to him, he resisted the temptation and waved as she took off on her bike, drifting into the night. He watched her ride away as dusk fell and pipistrelle bats flitted in and out of the silhouetted trees that broke the skyline. *Another day, another time. Next time,* he thought.

12   The Forest

The three were huddled round a fire deep in the forest, hoping the smoke would not attract the attention of local residents. A small, discreet affair it shouldn't present much of a fire hazard at this time of year. The leaves were damp underfoot and the branches hung loosely, dotted with spiders' webs that held the jewels of autumn and dusk within them. Tiny droplets of water were captured within the fine strands that were so beautifully spun and constructed by a spider programmed to do precisely that. They looked like faery chandeliers.

Communication between the three had come on in leaps and bounds by virtue of their rapid development of language. Their ability to learn, and absorb information from their environment, was improving all the time. Like No. 1, the other two had enhanced hearing and the ability to move so rapidly that it went beyond flicker fusion. It wasn't that they appeared to move rapidly, as in a fast-moving sequence of film, it was that they weren't seen to move at all. This was extremely useful should they need to remove themselves from danger in an instant, or escape unwanted, lingering scrutiny from suspicious characters.

Sitting on the streets, day in, day out, with a begging bowl in front of them, would appear, on the face of it, to be tempting fate; as if they were putting themselves in the limelight and drawing unwanted attention. Not so. Apart from the odd person who stopped to talk to them, and appeared to show genuine interest in their predicament, no-one gave them a second glance.

Even the meek 'thank you' that they uttered when someone dropped a few coins in their bowl, received no acknowledgement. It was as if, in throwing down the coins, the 'benefactor' felt that their job was done. They had earned their points for the day, were a better person for showing interest towards someone worse off than themselves. Yes, it was a strange irony that placing themselves in full view of the public on the high street of a busy town should attract so little attention.

No. 2 had been pondering for some days:

'I wonder where the boy is. I haven't seen him for a while. I quite liked him,' she brooded.

'Which boy?' No. 3 challenged, looking worried. 'You don't mean the one that you disturbed by the pond that day? The one who saw your reflection in the water and tried to talk to you?'

No. 2 nodded and looked away sadly. She remembered how angry the other two had been when she had made contact with the boy, how they had called her away, dragged her back into the forest even. Chastised her. She became even more melancholy as it dawned on her that, although she had escaped the confines of the graveyard, she was not entirely free. The others, No. 1 in particular, were keeping a tight rein on her, one that she intended to break. As soon as an opportunity arose she would look for the boy.

In the graveyard, where the point of emergence of the nameless children could once be clearly seen, there was now no sign that there had been a disturbance of any kind. The council workers had done their job well. The pit, formed from crumbling coffins and the reduction in the number of bodies, had been completely filled in. Backfilled was the term they had used. The ground was entirely flat. Other than the stone that still stood, looming over the spot, there was no sign whatsoever that anyone had been buried there. None at all.

The three nameless children were learning more about each other. Words spilled from their mouths like grain in a flour mill. And with the learning came the gradual realisation that they were connected, an understanding that their lives, their roots before they had each met their end in the 1800s, were intertwined.

Genetic memory held so much within it. Although lacking in any kind of real memory from

THE NAMELESS CHILDREN

their early days – the brief moment that they had spent on the earth before being entombed beneath it – their minds could conjure up images of times past. They retrieved their own, unique, memories and shared them, throwing them into a melting pot for discussion.

The truth, when it emerged, was stranger than any of them could have imagined. No. 2 discovered that her mother, from whom she was brutally separated shortly after her birth, was related to No. 1. During No. 1's brief spell on earth the mother of No. 2 had been his eldest sister.

To add to the cruel injustice done to her by the Squire of Grange Manor, the mother of No. 2 was soon to lose her own mother and her tiny brother, No. 1. Her mother to childbirth and her brother because he was just not robust enough to survive. He was born too early and his lungs were not developed sufficiently to draw in air: so the midwife had told his father.

So there they had it. No. 2 and No. 1 were related. While No. 2 had just cause to be angry at her premature death by drowning, No. 1 had no real axe to grind other than being buried without a name. Now he knew all the facts he had more understanding of how his nameless condition had arisen. And with understanding came compassion. Compassion for his father who had lost his wife and tiny son within minutes of each other.

What did incite No. 1, though, to a state bearing on rage, was the knowledge that No. 2, who would have been his niece, his sister's child, had been drowned. On learning this he vowed to avenge the dreadful wrong perpetrated against his family. An appalling miscarriage of justice that had never been rectified.

'As if she didn't matter,' murmured No. 1.

'Sorry?' asked No. 2.

'As if you didn't matter. You were treated as if you were worth nothing. Taken away and drowned as if you were meaningless rubbish to be thrown out with everything else. This will not be left. Will not be ignored. I will set things right. I will find out more about this family that drowned you at birth.'

As he spoke No. 1 already had plans to contact Penny, the niece of the blacksmith at the smithy. The smithy that he now knew had held the family name of not just himself but No. 2 also. He must hope that Penny sought him out on the streets when they were begging.

'We must take up our places on the streets. It is a good day. The sun shines on us. We will make much money,' he said, more as an affirmation than through any firm conviction that this would actually happen.

As the straggled line of the three, strangely clad people made their way to claim a begging spot for their own, No. 1 sent a message out into the ether.

'Let Penny visit us today.'

THE NAMELESS CHILDREN

At that very moment Penny was struggling through the crowds along the same street. Seconds before the three took up their positions on the pavement she had already passed by, wheeling her bike. The meeting between her and No. 1 of the nameless children would not take place today.

The embers of hate and revenge that had been smouldering in the mind of No. 1 were now beginning to ignite. Each day that went by only served to fan the flames more. He was on a mission.

Life on the whole had taken a turn for the better. A chance discovery, when they had had to flee for shelter to avoid a sudden torrent of rain, took the form of a large brick-built building previously used as a public toilet. They had rushed through the door without looking twice at the façade of the building, faded now and no longer in use.

Through an oversight of the local council the water had not been turned off. Water that could not only be used to wash with but also to drink; a fact they discovered after observing birds drinking from the overflow, with no adverse effects. Pure, uncontaminated water. This was a great find indeed. They could not believe their luck.

By nightfall they had retrieved all their meagre possessions from the forest and decanted them into the old building. Being hidden, overgrown and off the beaten track for the townsfolk, it was ideal for their purposes. Part of the roof had started to decay so they took care to store everything in the dry part. No. 2 had even found an old mattress that was in reasonable shape.

'This place looks like it has been used by homeless people, quite recently,' stated No. 3.

'What? Like us you mean?' countered No. 2. 'We're homeless.'

No. 3 thought about this for a moment, his head bowed.

'Yes, we surely are, but that is all about to change. This can be our new home. We will make good the roof and live here quietly on the edge of the town. No-one will ever know we are here. It is only a twenty-minute walk to our begging spot. We can make this work!'

They marvelled at how quickly all three of them had adjusted to life in another century, to a culture so far removed from what they had known. Sitting, as darkness fell, clutching mugs of hot tea, with the kettle whistling away and propped up on a little outdoor wood-fuelled heater that someone had thrown away with the rubbish, they looked, for all the world, like a group of children having a camping weekend away from their families.

No part of the scene suggested that these were interlopers from another century – not even the last century but the one before that. That these were essentially visitors to the earth. Visitors who could not really be considered to be alive, having met their deaths during infancy. An apt description might be the 'living dead' although they preferred to think of themselves as the 'reborn' or rather 'the nameless children'.

As they began to drift off to sleep No. 2 gazed at the tiled walls where water trickled down from the ceiling in fits and starts, noticing how it halted unexpectedly where a tile had been broken and cracked in two, or where grease and dirt made the rivulet divert somewhat from the vertical pathway it was destined to follow. *Even water has to twist and turn to get where it wants to go*, she thought, this being her last recollection before sleep overtook her and propelled her into dream land.

13   Little James

Since coming across the newspaper cutting, Anwen had thought of little else. When she closed her eyes at night, and before she opened them in the morning, the image she saw was that of James: 'first born son to the Squire of Dilston Hall'. She had no idea what he might look like, but the image that she had formed was of a bonny-looking child with golden curls dressed in a little white bonnet, long white dress and little shoes.

She had seen photographs of children taken in the days when the camera had first been invented. These children came from families who could afford the services of a photographer and dressed their children in finery. Velvet and lace featured strongly in such photographs and little boys could often be mistaken for girls, so long and curled was their hair, so feminine their attire.

Finally the college term ended and Anwen headed for the bus station and a bus that would take her to Swansea, followed by a train to the north of England, away from her beloved Wales. The journey would be worth it though. Give her time to think, a chance to discover more about little James and his background – *her* background.

It would be many moons before she started to have any inkling that all was not quite as it seemed. Everything on paper, all the records, would seem to be perfectly in order, all in place. But behind the scenes there would be other voices waiting to be heard, other stories waiting to be told. Nothing can ever be kept entirely secret. However much money changes hands no-one can be wholly sworn to secrecy.

Whispered words carry far. Through the walls. On the breeze. To other ears. Across the centuries. It was only a matter of time before the true nature of the cover-up reached Anwen. By fair means or foul she would discover that little James, who she already regarded as her own kith and kin, her long-lost ancestor from the mid-nineteenth century, was an imposter. For now though she was oblivious of any intrigue or wrong-doing. When the truth emerged it would hit her like a thunderbolt out of the blue.

Subterfuge was rife throughout history, but buying a child from parents who were poverty stricken and could ill afford to keep it, and then using it to replace one that had died, was nothing short of a heinous crime. Carrying it out without the knowledge of the mother just added to the injustice of the whole episode.

Had Anwen known it, both No. 3 and the changeling had cause to feel shabbily treated. No. 3, as he had never known his mother's touch and had been buried without a name. The changeling because he had been sold by his parents. Passed over to strangers when only a few days old, with the exchange of a sum of money. They were not good times.

Anwen reached Manchester by mid-afternoon and took another train, followed by a bus to Clitheroe. She had booked into a local hostel. Sharing a room for one night was quite acceptable to her, particularly considering the low cost. Tomorrow, she would rise bright and early and set out to track down Dilston Hall and the descendents of little James.

In the disused toilet block No. 3 was stirring. He had also been learning about his origins. Not much, true, but enough to set him on a track that he felt compelled to follow. A journey that would take him to the people who substituted him with a changeling. He was only at the beginning of his mission but it would not be long until he found the signs that showed him the way. The way to Dilston Hall.

A light rain was falling as Anwen trod the gravel road leading away from Clitheroe. The bus had arrived in good time, pausing every now and then to collect the odd person who stood, seemingly stranded, at wayside bus stops. A visit to Tourist Information had revealed that Dilston Hall did indeed still exist, if not in name, then certainly in structure. The hurriedly drawn spidery map that the woman in the information centre had drawn for her, showed the building to lie on the outskirts of the town.

Renamed Dilston Conference Centre it had been restored, modernised and refurbished. The inside had been transformed beyond all recognition, however the outside apparently looked much the same as it had in the mid-1800s, when it had existed purely to house one family. A family that, at one time, had included little James.

The day before, Anwen had explored the town.

'Go and have a look,' the woman at the Tourist Information Centre had urged her. 'They won't mind I'm sure.'

So Anwen, fortified by the knowledge that she would finally get to see her ancestral seat, walked on apace, without even a backward glance. Had she chosen to look behind her she might have been rather unnerved by the dishevelled person who hung back in the shadows.

No. 3 was also looking for his ancestral seat. In time he and Anwen would meet, but for now they were on separate journeys. Separate journeys but with the same goal: to find out what had happened to those people with the name Elver who had lived so many years ago. People who had trodden the same path that they themselves trod now. The same path but in a different century; a century-but-one removed from this one.

Anwen's resolve faltered a fraction as she reached the reception area at the front of Dilston Conference Centre.

'Yes? Can I help?' asked the young, well-dressed woman behind the counter, checking her nail varnish as she did so and glancing at the computer screen directly afterwards.

Whatever happened to eye-to-eye contact? thought Anwen. *Died a death like many other traditions I suppose.*

'Is it okay if I just have a quick look round the building?' Anwen was not going to be put off by this woman who seemed to have lost the art of conversation, and with it most of her social skills.

'If you like,' replied the receptionist in a dismissive tone that spoke volumes to Anwen. In only three words this young woman had managed to convey so much. Indifference, lack of interest in her job, an inbuilt desire to get through the day as quickly as possible.

'Thanks,' replied Anwen, continuing with: 'my ancestors used to live here, nearly two centuries ago,' but trailed off when she saw that the receptionist had restored headphones to her ears and was no longer open to conversation. The woman had left the land of the living and immersed herself in a world of solitude where no-one could reach her. The days when listening to music was a shared experience had largely disappeared. These days headphones served very effectively as a means of isolating yourself from your surroundings and of deterring others from approaching you and attempting to engage you in conversation.

'You're in the wrong profession,' Anwen muttered as she turned on her heel and made her way along the long corridor that led away from the reception area. After roaming several corridors, and passing door after door that possessed a disturbing similarity to one another, Anwen made for the exit and left the hall.

Across a courtyard there stood several stone outhouses that may have been used to hold animals, store chicken feed etc., so the Tourist Information leaflet stated, a four-page booklet that told the visitor: 'all that is known about the Hall and its origins'.

She picked her way along the side of a building that looked as if it may have served as a pigsty. The outer walls were crumbling in places and Anwen absent-mindedly pushed her hand into a gap between two of the stones. She met with something in the hole. Closing her fingers carefully around whatever it was she had found, she withdrew it slowly. A piece of folded yellowing paper met her eyes. Gingerly she opened it out and gazed at the writing on the page.

Dearest Will, you will not believe what happened to me today. Terrible things. The new baby, James, died and

the squire told me to take him away to the poor house to be buried without name or ceremony. He said to tell no-one and never, ever, to mention it to his mother. Will, baby James's mother doesn't know he has died. But that is not the worst of it. The squire then pressed money into my hand and said to go to a nearby farm and ask to buy their new-born child, a baby boy. He said they will part with him because they can't afford to feed themselves. They will have no choice. So there you have it. The baby that now lies in the arms of the squire's wife is not baby James. He is an imposter – like a changeling left by the faeries. And I am to tell no-one. But such a secret is hard to bear so I am telling you. Will, dearest, we must let no-one know of this or our love for each other. If they should find out we will both be dismissed and it is so hard to find work these days. I will meet you at the cross roads tonight, as usual.
Your loving Emma xxxx

The writing was tiny and written without spaces, no doubt because the paper was small and left little room to write. Anwen was shocked and perplexed at the same time. Folding the paper carefully she put it in her purse and, checking to see that no-one was watching her, made her way to the graveyard to look for headstones bearing the name Elver.

No. 3 had been tracking Anwen. Like a bloodhound with head swinging from side to side, endeavouring to catch her scent, he moved forward with speed. But the meeting between No. 3 and Anwen was not destined to take place today. Nor the next. Nor the one after that. By the time No. 3 reached the graveyard Anwen had left and was sitting on a bus, relaxing in a seat by the window, watching the Lancashire countryside flash by.

She had looked round the graveyard in Clitheroe and found a few headstones that bore the name Elver. With diligence and patience she had studiously written down every last word from these headstones. She had copied every detail exactly, even to the rather random use of capital letters. This was the mid-to-late1800s after all and Anwen surmised that grammar carried different meanings compared with the twenty-first century. These meanings might prove to be crucial when she later came to interpret what had been written.

As a firm adherer to the scientific approach she knew that it was better, far, far better, to collect too much data rather than not enough. Data excess to needs could be ignored – data that have not been collected in the first place cannot be retrieved. Hindsight is of no use in these circumstances. Better to be safe than sorry. Anwen followed the tried and tested methods fastidiously. They had not stood the test of time for nothing she decided.

One headstone, in particular, had caught her attention. A simple monument, constructed using local stone, told a story of grief and fortitude:

'In memory of Susanna, daughter of Joseph and Emma Elver, of this Parish, who died December 11, 1862.' No mention of the child's age but then it continued:

'Also, Hannah Louisa Elver, their daughter, who died February 15, 1864, aged 2 years and 8 months.'

Anwen struggled to read the rest of the inscription, tentatively scraping back the dark green moss that obscured the words. Words that had been etched into the now disintegrating sandstone:

'Also, Josiah, Benjamin, Joseph and Lilly who died in infancy.'

So much loss it was barely possible to read the inscription on the stone without becoming sad and tearful. *How did these people cope, way back then?* Anwen thought. From her extensive reading of late she knew that, contrary to most people's beliefs in 2015, the death of a child in infancy was not dismissed out of hand in the 1800s. Just because something happened on a regular basis, far too often for comfort, did not make it any less terrible.

Each tiny body that a mother and father carried from their house, to the churchyard for burial, was a treasured and wanted child that they had lost. A child whose life had been denied to them – whose life had been denied to itself.

These were mostly wanted children and Anwen would remember that. The premise would lie close to her heart and unknowingly help to formulate her ideas and developing concepts when she finally learnt of the existence of the nameless children.

For the nameless children had not all been wanted, treasured and loved. And waiting in the shadows of a local mill town were three who had just cause to seek vengeance. No. 1, No. 2 and No. 3 children were already following the path that had been laid down for them, dictated by fate and circumstances beyond their control, while No. 4 child – well he was just biding his time…

14 Emily

Emily switched on the light in the living room and was startled to see Jonas sitting on the rug in the dark. He appeared not to notice her at all, nor the sudden flooding of the room with light. Emily warily moved towards him, slightly fearful that some medical catastrophe had befallen him. Seizures were not unknown in the young.

She had heard about an absence seizure, a staring spell where a person loses awareness of their surroundings for a few seconds only, then regains full consciousness and carries on as if nothing had happened. This piece of random information was something she had learnt from a discussion about seizures on the radio. Amazing how such seemingly unimportant trivia could lie dormant in the recesses of your mind and spring to life unbidden at exactly the right moment. The power of recall is truly phenomenal she thought.

Emily remembered once seeing a ferret that used to lapse into such states every now and then. The ferret was named Porritt, on account of the child in the family being unable to pronounce the word 'ferret'. The ferret went on to live a long and healthy life.

Emily pulled her thoughts back to the present and away from the ferret. She looked closely at Jonas, bending down to his level as she did so. He was sitting cross-legged on the floor, staring into space. His eyes were open but he continued to give no indication that he was aware of her presence. *It's as if he is in an opium trance,* thought Emily though, on reflection, having never seen anyone in an opium trance, this could well have been a poor analogy.

She scrutinised Jonas, his appearance and his demeanour, and found nothing to be out of the ordinary or unsettling. True he had to be reminded to shower on a daily basis, but Emily put this down to an entrenched habit that had developed from many months of living on the streets, or at least living rough in some capacity. He had finally succumbed to having his hair cut but had repaid Emily's persistence with a sulky frown that seemed to last for days.

On occasion she thought that perhaps her protégé, as she liked to think of him, could be a little more grateful for the life she had provided for him. After all, she asked for so little in return. But deep down she knew exactly why she had allowed this unbalanced, one-sided relationship to exist in the first place and to continue unabated. He filled a great need in her, a hole, an ache that had lain in her heart since her precious David had left this world abruptly at the age of four. David... She still couldn't think of him without tears welling in her eyes. Such a little mite. So young. So soon. So devastating.

The truth, should it be known, was that Jonas was of pivotal importance to Emily, while to him she was merely someone to provide him with shelter. A roof over his head. A meal on the table. Clothes on his back. Grateful though he was for the ministrations, care and attention lavished on him by his substitute mother, he was largely indifferent to her. Indeed he often had to force himself to react in a manner appropriate to the situation; to thank her, when he judged that she expected thanks.

As someone who found it difficult to interpret and judge human emotions, the behaviour of Jonas was consistent with that of the other nameless children. Those he had still to meet. The common denominators appeared to be:

Think only of yourself. Adapt your behaviour to suit the occasion. Don't attract attention that might provoke an adverse reaction. Keep together. Be true to each other. Nowhere amongst this crudely constructed code of behaviour did anything remotely normal feature such as:

Be kind to others. Strive for harmony. Make friends. In fact, one thing to be added to their code of behaviour could be: *attempt to be sociable.* But this was not in order to cultivate friendship or to form social bonds. It had another function entirely. It was the manner in which the nameless children attempted to portray a semblance of ordinariness, an appearance of normality.

Only then could they wheedle their way into people's consciousness, gain their trust, feign friendship. And only then could they begin to learn more about their own origins, find the descendants of those who had committed such great crimes, those who had wronged them. They formulated a new plan and strengthened their resolve to bring it to fruition.

Then, like a child awakening from an afternoon sleep, Jonas turned to Emily and smiled.

'Oh, you're back. Shall I put the kettle on?' he asked, and Emily clutched at this little display of domesticity, much as a drowning person clutches at a drifting log that appears to be continually evading their grasp – out of desperation and out of a refusal to believe that all was not well, that all was not as it should be. She thrust these negative, invading thoughts from her mind.

'Yes,' she smiled back. 'That would be lovely.'

Sitting down in the armchair Emily vowed to forget this 'episode', as she later came to refer to it, to bury it deep in her mind. Only later would she cast her thoughts back to this night when Jonas had been 'absent without leave' sitting tranced-out, alone in the dark.

15 On the Streets

The trio were ensconced in a shaded area set back from the main street. It was actually a large doorway for a recently vacated shop and served well as a place to beg without obstructing the flow of pedestrians along the pavement. It also reduced the chances of being spotted by the man who 'policed' the streets after a fashion, moving along all the 'undesirables' as he called them.

Apparently it was entirely acceptable to play a musical instrument or sing on the streets, but not to openly beg without offering anything in return. It was as if people had to feel that they were getting value for their money and just sitting with a bowl in front of you, while staring into space, was certainly not construed as that.

A lengthy discussion the previous evening had led to their resolve to 'become musical'. Contrary to the views of much of the general public who thought that a musician just woke up one morning and found that they could suddenly play the guitar, the piano, or any other instrument that took their fancy, the nameless children were not naïve enough to think that this would be easy, that the ability to play music would come naturally to them.

Others that performed on the streets, apart from the very gifted ones who had taken the time to practice, tended to opt for the 'low maintenance' instrument, something that did not require much, if any, tuning. Fitting nicely into this category came the whistle, the harmonica, the bodhran (Irish drum) and not much else.

The whistle, unless played properly, could suffer from 'over-blowing', producing a strident and rather harsh sound that did not sit well in terms of creating a feel-good atmosphere. That left the drum.

'One of us could play the drum softly and the other two could sing. Eventually we could maybe buy a harmonica and add that to the mix?' suggested No. 1.

'Who's going to sing?' No. 2 was secretly hoping to be voted in for this.

'Are you offering?' No. 3 asked.

'I suppose I am,' she replied.

'And I can supervise the money until I've learned the harmonica,' offered No. 3.

'Or you could play the drum and I can take care of the money,' countered No. 1.

'I'm happy either way,' said No. 3. 'How hard can it be to play a drum?' He let the question float on the air, full of famous last words, spoken by someone who had never played a bodhran in his life and for whom the concept of rhythm was hitherto unknown.

And so it was that as Penny wheeled her bike through the pedestrian area in the town centre, the whispers of a song could be heard coming from a shop doorway. An old folk song created by a disembodied voice as, try as she might, she couldn't detect anyone standing in the shaded recess.

She stopped and looked again. As her eyes adapted to the dark, three figures were clearly outlined. Three teenagers, two male, one female. The female was sitting cross-legged on the ground in a position that reminded her of the lotus position in yoga, or that adopted by the Orange People.

These were a group of gentle people who descended on the towns of West Germany in the 1980s, hoping for money in return for renditions on an Indian lap organ. She had heard about the Orange People from an aunt who had spent an entire summer busking on the streets of Heidelberg during this period.

All three buskers, as they had now become, appeared to be gazing into space, avoiding eye contact with passersby. Then something made No. 1 look directly at Penny, just as she was staring at him. A memory jolted to the fore of her thoughts. Someone, a boy, had recently visited her uncle at the smithy. Apparently the boy was keen to talk to her about family history. He'd said that he busked outside Gerhart's café every day between 11.00 am and 3.00 pm. Could this be him?

'Did you visit the smithy last week?' she asked him. 'I'm Penny.'

Penny's brusque manner, so lacking in social skills and so abrasive in usual society, struck no chord of awkwardness with the nameless children. They would look on her as one of their own. Someone who cut straight to the point, didn't mince their words, said what they meant without disguising it with meaningless frivolity, social niceties, blandness or hidden agenda. No. 1 liked Penny.

'Yes, that was me. Have you got time to talk?'

'Not now but I can come back. When do you finish?'

'In an hour.'

'I'll be back,' and with that Penny vanished into the crowds, wheeling her bike. The first real contact between No. 1 and his long-lost family had been made.

Penny headed for the smithy to see her uncle.

'Did you come across the strange lad then?' Jack enquired.

'Yes, briefly. Saw him busking with two others outside Gerhart's Café.'

'That's where he said he'd be. Good that you found him. What did you make of him?'

'Hard to say really. We only exchanged a few words. I'm going back in about fifteen minutes. I'll find out more then, about what it is he wants to know.'

'Much like you, I suspect,' Jack suggested. 'Looking into his family history for general interest or a college project. Who knows?'

'I don't think it was for a project,' Penny stated firmly.

'What makes you say that?' her uncle looked at her, surprised.

'Nothing specific. Just a gut feeling. Anyway, I'd better get back. I said an hour and it's getting on for that. See you later,' and she peddled off furiously.

Jack turned back to the piece of metal he had been working on and, like a shadow darkens a field when a cloud passes overhead, a thought flashed through his mind. A thought that putting his niece in touch with the strange, awkward boy who had appeared unheralded at his door, twice now, might not have been the wisest thing to do.

No. 1 poked his head out of the shop doorway and spotted Penny as she steered her bike through the crowds, weaving it to and fro, constantly changing direction. The trio were mid-song when Penny finally stopped her bike and stood watching. As the golden rule amongst buskers is never to stop until you have finished the song or tune you are playing, they continued to the end.

A group of children were seated at their feet on the pavement and clapped furiously when the three stopped playing. Such admiration was unexpected and they could not decide whether to be pleased or not. They were glad of the money but less delighted by the overt attention they were receiving.

'Hi. Glad you came back,' No. 1 greeted Penny.

'I said I would and I always keep my promises,' Penny managed a slight smile. Not being prone to displays of emotion this was about as much as she was prepared to exhibit for one day.

'Can you stop for a while and we can talk?' she asked.

'Absolutely. No problem.'

Not only had No. 1 and the other nameless children learnt how to speak English fluently, they had also learnt much of the nuances and jargon that tell the listener so much about the speaker. How old they are, which part of the UK they are from etc. Though there was one strange thing that had happened. The amazing speed with which the three had learned to speak new languages had resulted in a few idiosyncrasies creeping in.

Many people travelling round the UK were not native to the British Isles. Many were from China, some from the Baltic States, Croatia, Germany etc. As the three nameless children sang and played on the street they were being ambushed, on a daily basis, by a sea of foreign voices. Voices that spoke not only their own language but also English, with their own, unique accent.

The knock-on effect of this was for the vocabulary of the three teenagers to expand rather rapidly for a number of languages. They had now accrued an accent which was not immediately associated with a UK resident, influenced as it was by foreign accents.

The realisation of what had happened resulted in an attempt to back-pedal, to remove all traces of the foreign lilt. But this was not easy. Having once acquired a turn of phrase it was very difficult to lose it.

As they were learning language for the first time they were effectively becoming multi-lingual. This had its benefits, particularly with the Chinese and Japanese tourists who, on discovering that these street musicians could converse with them in their own language, were overwhelmed, the amount of money being thrown into the collecting bowl bearing witness to this.

No. 1 nodded to the other two and he and Penny walked to the fountain in the square to find somewhere they could sit and talk.

'Don't go anywhere out of the way with him,' Jack had warned. 'We don't know him from Adam. Better to play safe.'

Penny had agreed and the town square seemed as good a place as any. As they walked, side by side, Penny felt a sense of peace overwhelm her, as if she had known this boy for a long time. He seemed strangely familiar. He seemed a lot like her.

THE NAMELESS CHILDREN

No. 1 allowed Penny's words to linger on his lips. Tasted them as they filtered through the air from her mouth. Clear, crisp words that were clipped but full of meaning and promise. No. 1 did not yet know it but he and the other nameless children were synesthetes – and so was Penny. When they heard a number they saw a particular colour, while some words hung on the air and had their own flavour. The children and Penny not only heard words that were spoken, they tasted them.

'Your words taste of cinnamon,' No. 1 announced after Penny had spoken.

'And yours taste of dark chocolate and pecan nuts. It explains a lot,' Penny added.

'How?' No. 1 was curious.

'When someone says that they almost choked on their words, or even other people's words...' her sentence trailed off.

'Maybe they swallowed too many words in one go?' suggested No. 1. Penny laughed. 'You still haven't answered my question,' she prompted.

'Oh, yes. What do I want to know about the family – your family and hopefully also mine? I actually want to know everything there is to know – and more!!'

'You can't know more than there is to know. It's impossible.' Penny dismissed his statement out of hand.

'What do you know about where your family came from?' No. 1 persisted.

'I've found out quite a bit. We descended from people who lived at the smithy. The family business goes back for generations. Unbroken. I do know that they haven't always had things easy, particularly in the mid-nineteenth century. Many children died in infancy, before reaching the age of five. It was worse amongst the poor but the rich didn't escape. No-one emerged totally unscathed from the cesspool of that era with its poor sanitation and hygiene. Cholera was rife, beginning in Clitheroe with the outbreak at Broadwick Street Water Pump in 1854. I'm in the process of delving back before this period. We had links at some point with Grange Manor at Pendlebury, a village near here.'

No. 1 and Penny too, truth be told, were marvelling at the remarkable eloquence of their turn of speech. The way in which words were flowing out of Penny's mouth echoed the sudden improvement in No. 1's command of the English language.

We are feeding off each other, he thought. *This is no ordinary meeting of minds. This is something special.* And he let the thought linger a little longer before he responded.

'I think we have the same goal, you and I. We have a common mission.'

Penny smiled at this comrade in arms. After much sharing of ideas she and No. 1 parted. Where the edge of the square, bright and filled with people rushing about their business, merged with the deep shadows of the narrow lanes that ran away from it in all directions. Here was where they took their leave of each other.

Not without a little sadness did they murmur words of farewell. So much learnt in so short a time. So many confidences shared. Penny had taken immediately to No. 1 and, as the conversation had progressed, had felt a closer and closer connection develop between them.

They walked away from each other then, as if to order, both turned and looked back at the same time. This meeting of eyes prompted a slight shyness and surprise on both their parts. The looks they gave each other held more than the promise of the friendship that was to develop. They held within them the tantalising glimpse of twin souls who shared not only a joint understanding of the universe, but also a mutual attraction. In the space of half an hour Penny and No. 1 had formed a bond. A bond that would survive most things that life could throw at it. Most, but not all.

True, Penny and No. 1 shared a few genes. This was inevitable as further examination of their joint history would reveal. If anything, this knowledge added to the feelings that had already begun to germinate and would be cemented by this genetic link.

Through the ages genetic sexual attraction has been a much discussed topic. Delving deep into their family tree would unearth references to other families, including literary giants such as the Wordsworths, where genetic sexual attraction ran deep and was thought to be instrumental, if not pivotal, in helping to create some of the greatest poetry and prose that nineteenth-century Britain had ever seen.

The seeds of mutual attraction had been sown. From now on Penny and No. 1 would find it impossible to go more than a day without some form of contact. They would find that they needed it to survive; to ride the hills of adversity and tackle whatever life threw at them. They would find that their bond was unshakeable and could not be challenged. They would not let it be challenged.

From the moment that Penny arrived back at the smithy, her uncle sensed a change in attitude. A shift in her mood. It had lightened. Her expression was more relaxed. He noticed the occasional break into a smile, as if she was thinking about something secret that she had no wish to share with anyone.

'All okay?' he asked.

'Yes, fine thanks. We met up. It will be good to share the work load of looking into the family history,' she replied, thinking that that was probably not all they would be sharing. It was then that she realised that she had actually no idea where No. 1 fitted into her family history, or indeed, what his name was. She couldn't believe that, at no point during the conversation, had he mentioned his name. And she hadn't thought to ask him. It was as if it didn't matter. She made a mental note to ask him the next time they met.

At Grange Manor Dom was putting the finishing touches to an essay. As soon as he was done he texted Penny.

'Fancy meeting up for a drink later to compare family history notes?'

Penny agreed and a plan was made. She would meet him in the Nag's Head on the outskirts of the town, mid-way between their living places.

Dom was buoyant. Totally uplifted at the thought that maybe he could start to get closer to Penny. He knew, or rather hoped, that she was attracted to him, and indeed she was. Until she had met No. 1 Penny would have been totally open to a relationship with Dom. Polite, caring, thoughtful Dom. But that was before she had met No. 1. The strange boy with the eyes that lit up when he talked, who saw colours in numbers, who tasted words on the air.

No. 1 encapsulated danger, the thrill of the unknown, produced a deep stirring within that captured her imagination. But overriding all these emotions was the one that told her she had found a kindred spirit – someone who would match her step for step. Someone who would show her how clouds were made, when rain would fall and how to read her dreams.

No. 1 was both darkness and light trapped in one person. Dom would have his work cut out trying to compete with someone who, strictly speaking, was not alive. A phantom from the grave. A soul from the past and, as we all know, it is not possible to compete with the non-living. To throw out a challenge to the dead. Not possible at all.

16   Avenging the Past

No. 2 woke up gasping for air.

'I can't breathe! Help me!' she cried.

No. 1 reached over and pulled the blanket away from her face.

'You had the blanket over your mouth. That's all it was. You're okay now. Look – I've moved it.'

'No, it was more than that,' whispered No. 2, trembling now. 'I was being held under water. I thrashed my arms and legs about to try to break free, but something was holding me down.'

'Or someone,' murmured No. 1. 'It's your memories, coming back in full force. From when you were taken away and drowned.' He scowled. 'The people who did this mustn't be allowed to get away with it. They must pay for their deeds.'

'But they're all dead,' No. 3 stated the obvious.

'They might be dead,' agreed No. 1, 'but their descendants aren't. Far from it. Penny has had contact with one of them. Only recently, in fact.'

'Penny from the smithy?' queried No. 2.

'Yes, she's found out loads about the family, going back to the mid-1800s. Some really strange goings-on happened and she can prove it. Penny is descended from generations of blacksmiths who have kept the family business going for over a century. She knows about the child taken away under the orders of the Squire of Grange Manor. The child that was you.'

He turned to face No. 2 as he was talking.

'We are going to work together to find out more. But there was something she let slip the other day. Not so much a slip of the tongue as an accidental diversion in the conversation. She mentioned that she had gone in search of the people who had commissioned a new wrought-iron gate from her uncle at the smithy. She is as persevering as I am and managed to track it to Grange Manor. Incredibly, the people who live there now are descendants, on the mother's side, from the original squire that arranged for you to be drowned. No, not arranged – ordered. He ordered your murder.'

'But it was not the squire that drowned her was it?' No. 3 entered the conversation. 'Not that I think that that exempts him from any responsibility for the heinous crime. Far from it,' he concurred.

'Well, you have made a good point,' No. 1 replied. 'It is not just the squire's descendants that should pay, it is those of the servant who actually drowned No. 2, my little niece.'

Though as No. 1 looked protectively at No. 2, with compassion in his eyes, it dawned on him that she was more like a sister to him than a niece. Bearing in mind the similarity in ages, when they had both died, this was not surprising.

'But first things first. The servant's family can wait. Their time will come. It has been written in stone for generations that 'I was just following orders' is not a legitimate excuse for premeditated murder. Not now. Not ever.'

'So who do we know who is related to the squire?' asked No. 3.

'We have the mother who had the name 'Andover' before she married Jim Matheson. Her son, Dom, is therefore directly related to the Squire of Grange Manor back in the 1850s. And what would you do if you wanted to cause the most pain to someone you held directly responsible for the death of someone close to you? If you could prove beyond all reasonable doubt that they were responsible. Would you hurt or kill them?' No. 1 stated his case, ending with a question to which he already had the answer.

No. 3 opened his mouth to reply but, before any words came out, No. 1 continued with:

'No, you wouldn't. You would hurt or kill someone close to them. Someone they valued more than life itself. And in this instance the person is the first and only son born to the woman Andover. Her son, Dom.' He paused, as if to savour the words.

'Somehow, by fair means or foul, we will ensure that harm befalls Dom. We will create a situation whereby he will wish he had never been born. But we won't kill him. That would be too final. Too quick.

Nowhere near lasting enough. No, we will find his weak spot, be it physical or emotional, and we will mete out our own form of justice.'

'Isn't that a bit unfair?' asked No. 2. 'Dom isn't the one who drowned me, or even arranged for it to happen. It was his distant relative.'

'True,' agreed No. 1, 'but avenging past misdemeanours has never stopped wars from happening. Indeed it has been the cause of most of them, and the reason why they continue for generation after generation. What do you think these people are doing?' No. 1 then answered his own question:

'They are avenging the past and that is what we will do. We will look for a chink in Dom's armour and we will pierce it. Little by little we will wreak vengeance. And justice will be seen to be done. Believe me, the message will get back to those who perpetrated the deed in the first place. They, like us before we emerged, might be dead, but that is more a figure of speech. Dead they might be in some ways, but in others they are only sleeping. Remember the phrase 'tread lightly for you tread on my dreams'? What do you think that refers to?'

'I'd never really thought about it to be honest,' No. 3 replied.

'Well, it is well-meaning advice intended for people who wander round graveyards reading the inscriptions on the stones. It means, in a word, don't disturb the dead lying beneath the ground for they are only sleeping – and while they sleep they dream.'

'That's true,' said No. 2. 'I used to have some lovely dreams back in the grave.'

'There you are. My point is proven.' No. 1 smiled the smug smile of someone who has set out his premise and found that it brooked no argument. In a word, he had won. But underneath his smiling exterior was a deep-seated hatred and a determination to make someone pay for what had been done to No. 2. And that person was Dom.

Anwen was unsettled. Back in the Welsh Valleys, her home since birth, it was a couple of weeks since she had returned from her 'journey to the north' as she referred to it. She was intrigued by the note she had discovered at Dilston Hall. Overwhelmed in fact.

Spending every spare moment engaged in online searches she had stumbled upon a post about 'hidden romances', love affairs that had to be conducted without the knowledge of the employers of those involved. Any hint of a romance between those working together 'below stairs' was not merely frowned upon, but completely forbidden. Anyone discovered to be having such an illicit affair would be dismissed on the spot, *and this at a time in history when the poor really were poor*, thought Anwen.

No welfare state to support you and if you couldn't support yourself you were sent to the workhouse. Sad to say that life could be so dismal, and so difficult to master, that some entered the workhouse voluntarily, with open arms, for the protection it offered from the hardships of the streets and the inclement harshness of the weather.

Anwen could see that it was imperative that all efforts be made to avoid detection by the master and mistress of the house, the house in this case being Dilston Hall. She wondered why Will had not claimed his note from the gap between the stones in the wall. Did he and Emma meet that evening as planned, in their usual spot?

Trying to discover the outcome of a clandestine love affair, that took place over 150 years ago, was a daunting task and seemingly impossible. But she would try. She was driven by a desire to discover more about the child, 'Little James' as she referred to him in her thoughts. Next time she logged on to her Twitter account she would post a request for: *information regarding...* or would she? Was it best kept to herself for the time being – for who knew what ghosts such a request might unearth?

But one ghost had already surfaced. No. 3 was waiting in the wings. On the trail of Anwen and anything she could discover about the changeling and the 'father' who had exchanged his small dead son for an imposter; while his wife accepted the replacement child lovingly, trustingly and unknowingly, for her entire life.

But did she really? Anwen asked herself. *Surely a mother would know that a child wasn't hers? That it had been swapped? If mothers in a maternity unit wake only to the sound of their own baby crying then they must be hard-wired to recognise the distress call of their needy infant? Surely she must have known...*

Her last conscious thought before she fell asleep that night, and her first thought on waking the following morning: *If the mother of little James knew about the swap, then she is equally complicit in the subterfuge.*

17   Jonas

Jonas shifted slowly down the street. His whole demeanour suggested someone with a furtive, secretive nature. Someone who could change personality on the turn of a sixpence, whose manner could switch with a change in direction of the wind. Someone who could not be trusted. A liar. Not a nice person to know, unless of course you held similar personality traits, in which case you would not be alerted to the unsavoury disposition of such a person. Not avert your eyes when people such as Jonas passed by. Feel no sense of distaste as you observed their unwholesome, anti-social ways.

In fact, you would respond in entirely the opposite way. You would welcome them with open arms. Feel a deep sense of attraction. Look on them as a kindred spirit. Recognise in them your own nature. See in them yourself. Know that you are one and the same. And so it was with Jonas.

As he mooched along the street his eyes lifted fractionally from the pavement and he caught No. 1 watching him from the busking spot set back in the shadowed doorway. For a split second they shared a look which encompassed a shared history, of words unspoken and intentions understood. In each other they recognised themselves.

'He's one of us,' No. 1 murmured.

'What was that?' asked No. 2, anxious to start singing the next song. Time was money where busking was concerned and there was always another busker hiding in the shadows, ready to move into their place should the music slow to a halt, or they leave the spot for a short break. Spots to busk, where they were guaranteed not to be moved on by the police, were far and few between in this town.

No. 2 pressed No. 1:

'Come on. We must start again. Now.'

But No. 1 would not be pushed. The over-riding emotion at that moment was to make contact with the boy who was about to walk past them. No. 1 moved forward like greased lightning taking some passersby by surprise, to the extent that one jumped out of the way then looked mystified as he couldn't understand what had made him move. He felt only a rush of wind, like a sudden breeze through the trees alerts you to a threatening storm and chills your bones, and a sensation that something had appeared and then rapidly disappeared from his peripheral vision.

Like the other nameless children No. 1 was well adapted to life above ground, where sleight of hand paled into insignificance compared with the speed at which he could move his entire body from one spot to another.

He touched Jonas lightly on his retreating back, just as the boy was about to vanish into the crowds. Jonas spun round to face him. The expression on the face of Jonas was not one of confrontation or aggression but one of alarm. Seeing the questioning look on No. 1's face, Jonas visibly relaxed and took a step towards the stranger who had stopped him in his tracks. No. 1 was temporarily stuck for words, speechless in fact.

'I am Jonas,' said the pale boy with halting, fragmented words.

'And I am One,' said No. 1.

'Wan?' asked Jonas. 'Is that Chinese? You don't look Chinese.'

'You can call me Yan if you like. Other people do. It's easier,' replied No. 1.

'Who are you?' Jonas persisted. 'What do you want from me?'

Yan was not entirely sure what to say, but continued regardless.

'It might sound strange but you look like you might be one of us,' and he pointed to the others waiting in frustration for him to return so they could start singing again. No. 2 had gathered that it must be something extremely important for Yan to risk losing their busking spot, and she waited with interest to see what happened next.

'Come and meet the others,' Yan urged Jonas and he moved towards the comforting, secure shadows of the shop doorway, looking back to make sure that

Jonas was following. As Yan moved alongside Jonas, he accidentally brushed against the hand of the secretive, reserved stranger and was taken by surprise. No warm, burning feeling met his hand, a daily occurrence when he accidentally touched humans.

He is most definitely one of us. Absolutely, for certain, he thought. Once in the comfort and safety of his little group Yan threw caution to the wind and turned to face Jonas once more.

'We are the nameless children. We dug our way out of a grave in the churchyard. We have taught ourselves to speak. We have infiltrated society and are passing ourselves off as humans.'

There was a long silence as Jonas stood there staring, mostly at the ground, occasionally at the three of them. Then he spoke:

'So am I.'

No. 2's mouth dropped open.

'One of us,' she whispered. 'Is that really true?' And as she spoke she reached out and lightly touched the back of the boy's hand. Coldness met with coldness. No difference whatsoever in body temperature. No. 3 reached over and repeated her action.

Jonas seemed not to mind and viewed them all with a look that conveyed confidence and a distinct lack of a tendency to be disturbed by external events. He appeared unruffled in the extreme.

Many people who present a cool, impassive exterior to others are often experiencing a multitude of conflicting emotions, an inner turmoil belied by their calm front. Jonas was not one of these people. He was the epitome of the English phrase: *What you see is what you get*. Anyone meeting him for the first time might be forgiven for thinking that Jonas was at peace with the world; that he had no hidden agenda, no axe to grind. They would be wrong. One hundred per cent incorrect in their surmising of the situation.

Jonas was no different from the other nameless children, other than having been given a name initially, which subsequently vanished at his burial. He was also no less driven. No less determined to avenge his past. No less selfish or uncaring towards others. No less vindictive.

In fact, truth be told, Jonas was, if anything, more selfish and uncaring than the other nameless children. He was a master at playing on the kindness and generous nature of others. A master at reading other people's emotions. It was precisely these skills, if they could be described as such, that had resulted in the 'drawing in' of the loving, gentle Emily.

Emily, who was in his thrall. Emily who had welcomed him into her home. Had actually been instrumental in ensuring that he had come to live with her. Had made life so very easy for him, in the hope that he would never want to leave, so that Jonas could not really be held responsible for the situation he found himself in. One where he was loved unconditionally, without giving much in return.

Emily was duped from the start. Her own weaknesses and vulnerability had resulted in her creating a situation from which escape would prove difficult. For now though, life ticked along fine and the two of them lived side by side in Emily's house in relative harmony.

After Jonas had finished relating his living arrangements to the other three, an audible sigh fluttered round the group. This was accompanied by looks of envy.

'You have somewhere proper to live,' murmured No. 2 sadly.

'Why? Don't you?' Jonas asked.

'Well, it is a disused toilet. So – no – we don't have anywhere decent to live, but it's better than a grove in the forest. We make do, only I am dreading the winter as we have no heat other than an open fire which we build from time to time. But please don't pity us. We are three. We stand together. Fortune is on our side.'

'But what of your past?' asked Jonas. 'Do you not search out those who condemned you to a nameless burial in unhallowed ground?'

'Indeed we do,' Yan spoke up. 'It is an over-riding passion for me. It is the first thing I think of when I wake up and the last before I go to sleep at night.'

'And me,' No. 3 and 2 echoed in unison.

So we are as one then, thought Jonas for a moment, while the others watched and waited for his next words.

'I can help you with your mission. All of you. But in return you must help me.'

Yan had known from the moment he had first set eyes on Jonas that this was someone who didn't act out of generosity of spirit, or out of consideration for others. Jonas would only do something for another in return for a favour. That was fine though. They understood each other. No words were spoken. They looked from one to the other and gave a slight nod in agreement.

'It is agreed then,' Jonas spoke again. 'We work together. We will be a force to be reckoned with. For now we are four.'

Emily heard the back door open and creak slightly. *I must oil the hinges*, she thought and immediately remembered why she had dismissed this out of hand every time she had thought of it previously.

If the door creaks when opened at least I will know when someone is coming in, she had reasoned. Had she thought about this more carefully she would have realised that the safest option by far was not to leave the door unlocked in the first place. It was simple enough to turn the key in the lock, something Emily had previously done for years. That is until Jonas had graced her doorstep.

THE NAMELESS CHILDREN

These days she left the door on the latch. *Just in case he forgets his key and can't get in*, she told herself. Today it was indeed Jonas coming in. But he was not alone. He had in tow three rather strange-looking characters. Initially, Emily was not aware that he had company. Jonas popped his head round the living room door.

'It's me. I've brought three friends round for a cup of tea.'

Jonas was not asking Emily for her permission but rather telling her what he was doing. The niceties of social behaviour had passed him by. Missed him by the skin of his teeth. Seen that he was in need of them but found him lacking in any desire to acquire them. Jonas cut to the chase as usual. Used as few words as possible in stating his position.

'That's fine Jonas.' Emily was aware that he was not asking her permission, merely informing her. No point in asking him if he was going to introduce her to his new friends. He wasn't.

All four filed into the kitchen and collapsed into the chairs round the table. Emily's curiosity got the better of her and she rose slowly from her chair and looked into the kitchen. Her first impression was of an unkempt, unwashed group of people who had total contempt for society and its guidelines for 'normal' behaviour.

They look fairly harmless though, she thought. No sooner had this drifted across her consciousness than one of the three strangers looked up. Yan looked directly at her, staring in a way that invited no confrontation, no challenge. She found it impossible to look away. No desire to avert her eyes from the stranger's gaze.

Had she been capable of free, unadulterated, conscious thought she would have acknowledged the hold that the boy had over her. The compelling desire to gaze, trance-like, into his eyes. She was held in thrall to him. Then, suddenly, Yan turned his gaze away from her and it was as if a taut line, an invisible thread from a spider's web stretched between them, had snapped. The breaking of the link caused Emily to jerk backwards slightly. The feeling of calm tranquility was immediately replaced by one of alarm. *What had just happened? Who was this boy? Who were any of them?*

She looked at Jonas, who was engaged in conversation with No. 3, and the hair on the back of her neck began to stand on end as a cold sensation swept down her body, from her head to her feet. She felt chilled and powerless at the same time. Was she imagining it?

There was something in the way the boy was looking at Jonas – with his head cocked to one side. But, more than that, it was the way in which Jonas looked back at the boy. Seated in an identical position he was almost the mirror image of the strange boy. With his head tilted in the opposite direction Jonas could be his twin. Not in looks, granted, but certainly in terms of mannerisms and the way he held his body.

'Would you like your friends to stay for tea Jonas?' Emily regained her composure and tried to instill calmness into her words.

Jonas nodded and Emily set about making spaghetti with onions and mushrooms. She was a vegetarian and the only thing she really insisted on in her house was that no meat was eaten. Jonas concurred. As that was the only concession he had to make, he could live with it. She had barely begun to chop the onions when a figure appeared at her elbow.

'Can I help?' No. 2 asked Emily.

'Yes, you can if you want to. That would be nice. What's your name?' Emily gently asked the girl.

'Two. My name is Two,' No. 2 replied.

'Two? As in Tui?' Emily was trying to make sense of the name. 'Isn't that a New Zealand bird? One whose call sounds like a gate creaking? It should really have been the native bird of New Zealand, instead of the Kiwi. At least New Zealanders have a fighting chance of seeing a Tui at some point in their lives, as opposed to the endangered and secretive Kiwi.'

No. 2 remained silent, not having any understanding of what Emily was saying.

'So shall I call you Tui, then? Is that okay with you?'

No. 2 nodded, anxious to please and desperate for a plate of cooked food. As the smells of cooking drifted through the house everyone began to show interest and the conversations slowed to a halt.

As they ate, heads down, forks tossing food into their mouths, Emily marvelled at the effect a warm meal can have on starving people. *Concentrates your mind*, she thought. *Maybe that is all they needed. A good meal inside them.*

But a little voice at the back of her head would not lie still. *Do not trust them. Ask them to leave. They are not who they seem to be.*

She knew from experience that the 'voices in her head' were not a sign of madness. They were there to help her. To protect her from evil. She would let the three strangers eat their meal, then she would usher them out. They could find their own way in the world. They were not like Jonas. Not remotely like Jonas. But even as she thought this she knew she was wrong. They were exactly like Jonas.

Emily often heard voices in her head. She had heard them since she could first remember anything. They had always been there. Some people might have become anxious at this. Not so Emily. She took it all in her stride and used the words that came to her to write poems, stories, entire books even.

On one memorable occasion she had been about to buy new boots in a shoe shop, when words thrust themselves into her consciousness: 'And so what kind of dog is this that roams the city round?' Slightly unnerved she had looked to the ceiling as if she would somehow see the words suspended there. But, looking round, it was evident that no-one else had heard them. The words had materialised out of thin air. They had come to Emily alone.

Bemused, she had bought the boots and gone back to her car to search for paper. On the back of an old envelope she had started to write, beginning with the words she had heard in the shop: 'And so what kind of dog is this...'

She wrote until every part of the envelope was covered in tiny writing, then sat back and read the finished thing. It was as if another hand had written it – an entire poem that seemed to be about the Devil's Footprints. The footprints, reported to have appeared one night in Devon in 1855, were imprinted in light snow and travelled from Exmouth to Topsham. Scattered across the snowy roofs they ran, over walls, across fields. For miles and miles and miles they ran. The mystery was never explained though suggestions were many.

Emily was flabbergasted. Not for the first time did she ask herself: *where do the words come from?*

And today the voices were at it again. Scrambling to be heard. Echoing her thoughts from the previous evening, they would not leave her alone. *Find out more about these new friends of Jonas. Find out where they live. Find out everything. Do not rest until every stone has been turned. Your life depends on it.*

Emily was more than a little concerned about the last edict: *Your life depends on it*. How? In what way exactly? She knew she had nothing to fear from Jonas. Good, dependable Jonas. She was so proud of him. He had made every effort to fit in. Everything expected of him he bowed to and fulfilled accordingly. Even to the extent of helping out in the charity shop in town. *He's such a good boy*, she thought.

Never had anyone been so far from the truth. Emily, with her reluctance to see anything but good in Jonas, directed all her energies towards learning more about his friends, when all the time she should have been looking closer to home.

How blind we are when we avert our eyes from the obvious. Refuse to accept the inevitable. Ignore the truth, even when it is staring us in the face. Confer trust when trust is not earned or indeed warranted. Turn our back and face the wall. Refuse, on every level, to face the truth. A singular flaw in human nature.

Humans are hard-wired to survive by virtue of using all the skills available to them. Only when they fail to use their basic instincts will they be tripped up. Emotion can sway the mind. Present a false picture. Distort the truth. Lead to disaster.

Emily was not aware that the image portrayed by Jonas was a false one; that he was not what he seemed. Instead she turned her attention to three teenagers, in an effort to discover more about them. What were their names again? Yan? Tui? And? The third one had not offered even a vague semblance of a name. She would make one up for him. She would call him Bede.

18   Jack

Jack glanced out of the smithy window to see a figure lope past, heading towards the door. Then came the familiar knock. The knock of the strange boy. The strange boy that he had put in contact with his niece, Penny. What was he thinking of? The boy was obviously unbalanced – possibly even deranged. It had been niggling at him for days now. What on earth had possessed him to suggest a meeting between his beloved Penny and a boy who might as well have come from Mars, for all Jack knew about him which, he had to admit, was nothing.

Penny, however, had different ideas. She seemed quite taken by him, by all accounts. If her related tale of their meeting was anything to go by: 'the boy was interesting to talk to'.

Talk? Jack hadn't been able to get two words out of him. Good company. Really? And even more priceless, Jack thought when he heard it: She felt that she had known him all her life as there seemed to be a bond between them.

Jack reluctantly opened the door to be met by the boy who was the same, yet not the same. In subtle but extraordinary ways he had changed. Beyond all reasonable doubt he was different. Had he been the identical twin of the boy that Penny had referred to as Yan, Jack could perhaps have accepted the change in personality, in attitude, in the ability to engage in conversation. But, no, this was not the identical twin of Yan, this was Yan.

Jack was familiar with the expression *time can change a person*. He was sure someone could change, over a period of months, or years. But in the space of two weeks? Surely not. It was not possible.

'Is Penny in? She asked me to meet her here. We are going to look into the family history,' he announced to the nonplussed Jack.

'Her family history?' Jack enquired.

'Well, both of ours actually. It seems that we have a connection. Back in the mid-1800s. We are going to search the records to see what else we can find.'

The boy stated his case succinctly without faltering once. Jack was amazed at the heightened level of confidence displayed by Yan and his direct approach. No more furtive looking to the left and the right, like before. No meaningful glances into the house behind Jack, in an attempt to get an invitation to enter. Yan was not the same person.

Against his better judgement, but not wanting to appear rude to Penny's new friend, Jack decided to be civil.

'She'll be back soon. You can come in and wait if you like.'

'Thank you. I will,' and Yan entered the house and settled himself into an armchair. Jack frowned. It was one thing for Yan to be waiting for Penny, but quite another to be making himself at home, so utterly and completely, in Jack's house. Still, he must be polite to the boy, for Penny's sake. Jack went towards the kitchen and called back as he entered it.

'Yan?'

There was no response.

To try and attract the boy's attention he repeated himself with raised voice.

'Yan?'

Still nothing. *He's not responding to his name*, Jack thought. *Yan isn't his name. Whoever he is, he isn't called Yan. That's certain. That was never his birth name.*

As he mulled this over Penny arrived. Her soft footsteps crossed the threshold of the door and she greeted her uncle with a hug and Yan with a nod. *Well, at least they're not too close yet*, Jack thought thankfully. But the bond had already been forged. From now on Penny and Yan would be inseparable.

Anwen was on a train again heading north. Once more on the trail of her ancestors, she reached Manchester Piccadilly train station, disembarked and caught the connection that would take her to the northern parts of Lancashire. A chance discovery of a workshop, posted on Facebook, had led her to enrol on a weekend event.

THE NAMELESS CHILDREN

Do you have ancestors or family in the West Pennines? The words leapt off the laptop screen and in the space of minutes she had filled in an online form, submitted it and enrolled.

Armed with all the records she had accumulated, she was desperate to discover more about her origins. To see if the weekend could shed more light on what happened to 'little James'. What became of the burgeoning romance of Will and Emma? Where did the changeling come from?

As the train sped through the moorland of the West Pennines a thought struck Anwen. A dark thought that went straight to her heart and pierced it like an arrow. She had been dozing lightly, still aware of sounds around her, when she had become almost trance-like in mood – and it is then that moments of clarity occur, when startling truths are revealed to you. Concepts that would never be established in a month of Sundays, in a word – never – when in normal thinking mode.

Only when your thoughts are adrift, your mind wandering and your reasoning slightly askew, do such events occur. The piercing revelation that came to Anwen as she gazed out of the railway carriage window, eyelids half closed, made her sit bolt upright. Jolted her awake. The truth was inescapable. She was indeed descended from 'little James' – but little James was not who he appeared to be. He was a changeling. An imposter.

Anwen had trawled the records and knew many of the facts, absorbed all that she had discovered, all the evidence presented online. But for some reason it had only just dawned on her. If she had not descended from 'little James', then she had descended from the imposter.

Like many royal families throughout the world, at some point the blood line had been seriously disturbed. Distorted. Severed. And in this instance the blood line on the male side of the Elver family had died out with the death of the original little James. From that point in history everyone had descended from the changeling who, according to the note Anwen had found in the wall, had been born to a farm labourer in the locality.

The sudden awareness that her 'family' was not what it had originally seemed to be did not faze her in the least. It did, however, throw a different light on how she approached things. Her main goal now would be to focus on where the changeling came from. What had happened to his brothers and sisters? To his parents? Who were the people who had descended from them?

She hoped fervently that the workshop would show her a way forward, indicate how to cast her net further. And close on her trail would be the nameless children. Four dispossessed entities working together to avenge past miscarriages of justice.

Headed by Yan they would work tirelessly to avenge Bede, the original little James cast aside so easily by his father in the hours after his birth. They would not rest until justice had been seen to be done. Unbeknown to Anwen, she was not alone in her quest to establish what had happened – to get to the truth.

The three had invited Jonas to their living quarters. He was aghast and silently considered the abject misery that they must be experiencing day in, day out. So cold. So uninviting. Not a home. Not by any stretch of the imagination.

Tui looked at Jonas with soulful eyes, not by way of attempting to engender sympathy but by virtue of expressing her inner feelings. To Jonas it seemed as if she was baring her very soul. He looked at her kindly and thought of his home with Emily. Such a cosy, warm house with food on the table. The direct opposite of what he was witnessing here. Perhaps he could encourage Emily to let them stay. 'Just for a short while,' he would suggest over a meal one evening.

'I'll see what I can do,' Jonas comforted Tui, patting her arm lightly. He had no wish to raise her hopes so he kept his own counsel. Jonas, though, was like all the other nameless children, something he was well aware of. Once he had made up his mind to do something he would let nothing stand in his way. Come hell or high water he would make sure he achieved his goal. He would make it happen. He was determined. The other three children, with their recently conferred, given, names, would come to live with him at Emily's house.

Jonas bided his time, let the meal come to a close and watched as Emily's head began to droop as she sat in the armchair near the fire. He had carried out his usual chore of stoking up the fire and bringing in enough coal to last the evening.

'You know those friends of mine?' he enquired of Emily.

Emily did not reply. She did not stir.

Jonas could be forgiven for thinking that she had not heard him. But Emily had heard every word. Her eyes narrowed a fraction as she gazed into the glowing embers before her. Jonas persisted.

'Emily, are you awake? I wanted to ask you something to do with my friends. I wanted to ask a favour.'

But before he had even begun to detail what he expected from her, she knew what it would be. Emily was not stupid. Nothing escaped her finely tuned senses.

'Yes?' she replied.

'Well,' Jonas continued, 'I have seen where they are living at the moment and it's not good. Not good at all. I wondered if they could come and live with us for a short time. Just until they find somewhere of their own?'

'And how are they earning their living at the moment? Aren't they busking?'

'Yes,' admitted Jonas.

'So it could be quite some time before they earn enough money to be able to afford a deposit to rent somewhere?' She let her sentence trail away, the meaning implicit.

'Yes.' Jonas was temporarily defeated, but though he might have lost the battle he was adamant that he would not lose the war.

19   Dom

Dom was at his wit's end. Penny had not been returning his phone calls. He felt shunned. True she had sent him a text to say that she would be in touch soon but was 'busy right now'. *Busy doing what?* Dom wanted to know. He was keen to discover more about the child who had been born to his ancestors. *Who had fathered her? When was it exactly?*

He suddenly felt an awful feeling of foreboding creep over him. Way back in the 1800s a member of his distant family had committed murder. Well, maybe not actually been the perpetrator, but had certainly instigated it. In his blood line there was someone who had got away with murder. Had escaped imprisonment. Escaped hanging. Escaped death. An innocent child had been murdered before having the slightest chance to enjoy life. To become an adult. To see her own family thrive and grow. No chance at all.

Someone back in time, someone in the family Andover, had put paid to that. Made absolutely sure that she would not survive. Insisted on complete silence from the one charged with the drowning.

Who was the servant who had carried out this dreadful act? Had taken a tiny baby to the water's edge and lowered it into the freezing water, stifling its cries to avoid detection. It didn't bear thinking about but, try as he might, Dom found that he couldn't think about anything else.

If the child had been allowed to survive and had been accepted by the squire and his wife, and the son who had fathered her, things would have been so different. Inescapably altered. Dom might even have had a different blood line. He might have been born to those that had descended from the drowned child. The child whose life was denied her. He needed to talk to Penny – to discuss it with her. They needed to examine the links between No. 1 and No. 2 children, should there be any.

And always, in the background, simmering on a low burner, lay the hidden agenda: Dom's unrequited love for Penny. The feelings that he had initially thought might be reciprocated by her. But now any stirrings of romance, on Penny's part, seemed to have floundered and vanished following her recent acquaintance with the strange boy.

What was his name? Yan?

Dom's phone lit up. Penny was trying to reach him.

'Penny! Great. Thanks for getting back to me. Have you got time to meet later?'

Arrangements were made. He settled down to check his emails. Sitting in the front room at Grange Manor he was totally unaware that he was being watched. Yan had found him. It hadn't been hard.

As Dom sat relaxed, with his laptop on his knee, he glanced towards the window. It seemed as if a small bird (a wren?) had flashed past, casting a shadow and briefly, very briefly, partially obscured light from the room. In reality it was Yan, eager to avoid detection, who had flashed past and was now hidden beneath the window, out of sight. Dom shrugged and clicked 'send', propelling another message off into the ether. A request for information, any information, concerning the bloodline of the family Andover. He wanted to get to the bottom of things.

In a futile attempt to absolve himself, and his ancestors before him, of any responsibility or involvement in the death of the baby girl, he would go to any lengths. Penny, he hoped, would stand by him and support him in his efforts. He would soon learn that this would not be possible. Dom and Yan had conflicting goals and Penny stood between them, in the middle, unknowing. When it came to the crunch there was no contest as to who she might choose.

20   In Search of Saul

'I have looked for him everywhere.' Tui sounded plaintive.

'Who? Who have you been looking for?' asked Bede absentmindedly.

'The boy who saw my reflection in the water that day on the edge of the forest. I liked him. He was kind.'

Yan heard this and looked quizzically at her. Why should it matter to her whether the boy had been kind to her or otherwise? She was one of them. Those who were devoid of emotion, or so he liked to think. But could it be that they were, in fact, not immune to the behaviour of those around them? They absorbed their language so why not also their emotions? He tried to put aside this troubling thought but it refused to be dismissed and stuck rigidly in his mind, like a cobweb idly brushed away refuses to leave the fingers; persistent to the end.

'Why are you so keen to find him?' Yan was curious.

'I liked him. He had a nice face,' was all that Tui could offer. Not much, granted, but for her it was enough. Like the first word you learn in a foreign land, Saul had made a distinct impression on her. He was the first person she had made contact with after leaving the deep pit in the graveyard. The meeting between them would be forever etched on her mind. When she closed her eyes she could see him standing there.

She did not know that Saul had seen them leaving the graveyard and had been looking for them. Tracking their movements unreservedly until he had vanished from the world above. Vanished entirely without trace. He had left home one evening and not returned.

'He'll be back soon, mark my words,' the police had told his worried parents when they had phoned in a desperate state.

'He's only sixteen,' they had replied. But their words fell on deaf ears.

'It's normal for lads of his age to stay out overnight,' was the response. But however 'normal' it might be in the experience of the police it was not normal for Saul. Not normal at all. Unheard of in fact. His parents waited through the night and by 5 am, as light scattered through the curtains, the truth lay starkly before them. Saul was not coming home.

For some inexplicable reason he had not been caught on any CCTV cameras in the town. A couple of women thought that they might have spotted him down an alleyway, but they weren't 'very sure'.

Eye witness accounts of events are notoriously unreliable. The police knew this and didn't take the sighting seriously. They would need more information than that to be able to establish the whereabouts of Saul. Nevertheless they launched a full enquiry and search, and missing person posters appeared in all the usual places: on buses, telegraph poles, in shop windows. This merely added to the misery of Saul's parents who found their eyes being drawn to their son's face every time they left the house. It was as if they were surrounded by a sea that swam with the image of him. Bobbing on the waves, almost, but not quite, in view. Almost, but not quite, out of sight.

The inevitable Facebook page was set up.

Help us find Saul! it pleaded. But, after the initial flurry of useful suggestions and interest, the wind seemed to go out of the sails of those who had 'liked' the page and, in so doing, had appeared to promise so much. It was as if, by pledging their support, it was a guarantee that he would be found, that he would come back to them. That Saul was still alive.

While all the time he lay in the local graveyard, sealed in a deep pit, a vertical grave. A grave that had collapsed when four of those interned had upped and left. A grave that had taken Saul to itself. Where he had gone trustingly, drawn in by the voices. He had gone out of curiosity, out of a deep desire to know the truth, to discover more about the strange people he had seen, to find Tui and to see her again. And this had been his undoing.

Never go emotionally unarmed into unhallowed ground in a graveyard, as dusk falls. Saul now lay at peace deep within the grave. He did not speak, did not breathe. Showed no signs of life. But Saul was not dead and, more than that, he still had his soul. His soul that had life within it, invisible tendrils that could reach out and touch others, that could make contact with conscious beings – that could reach out to Tui.

In her search for Saul, Tui found herself drawn to the graveyard, to the spot where she had emerged from the ground. As she reached the grave, with the stone that marked what was meant to have been her final resting place, she had a strange sensation. As if something was plucking at her skin, stroking her cheeks. As if a fine tendril from a branch had blown lightly across her face, driven by the wind.

She could see nothing, no branch in sight, but was deeply aware that something, or someone, was making contact with her. And beneath the ground the dream-like state of Saul's consciousness began to stir.

Tui gazed, mesmerized, at the now-flattened mound that covered the grave. Colours began to dance above it. Tiny lights hovered in a fixed position, then shot off at an angle. Some of the colours merged with each other to create new colours. It was as if the Will O' the Wisps of the marshes had somehow found their way to this small insignificant graveyard and were putting on a light show. A magical display of all the colours in the rainbow.

Tui was unfazed by the lights. Objects changing colour around her was nothing new. Like the other nameless children she was a synesthete. Parts of her brain were not discreet and overlap occurred between those areas responsible for seeing numbers, hearing music, sensing smells and seeing colour. Her favourite number was seven. It shone a bright amber when it was spoken.

For Tui did not just hear a number, she saw it too. Some would say 'in her mind's eye' but to her it was as if the number was suspended in the air, unattached. It was not in her head but was there for everyone to see. Except that they couldn't. Only the nameless children and a few other gifted people had been blessed with this ability.

It was the same with certain words, though words that spelled out a colour were most susceptible to being draped in colour, suspended in full view: A 3-D image of a word or number hanging in the ether for all to see. She particularly liked the word 'walnut' as it conjured up a dusky pink colour, the colour revealed when the husks of the walnut had been soaked to produce a dye for wool.

Like bubbles emerging from a soapy bath, the spheres of colour rose steadily skywards from the canopy of the grave but, unlike soap bubbles, they did not pop when they reached a certain height and instead continued unbroken until they vanished amongst the foliage at the tops of the trees.

She looked back down to see a vibrant, iridescent green bubble appear from the ground as if created by a magical force, alchemy no less. This green sphere began to grow and grow until it was almost a metre wide and hung in the air in front of her. Tui was hypnotised by the rainbow show of colours and particularly captivated by the green rolling ball that turned as if on its own axis.

Then, slowly but surely, what appeared to be black spiders began to show themselves within the sphere. She peered more closely and saw that letters were starting to take shape. Letters that developed into words. Words that spelled out:

'Help. I am in the ground.'

Tui fell to her knees and began scrabbling at the earth with her bare hands, breaking her nails in the process and covering herself and her clothes with damp, clingy soil. She was struggling to remove all but small handfuls of soil and looked around in desperation for some sort of tool to help her. Coming towards her through the mist of the evening was a light. A torch that glowed brightly, flashing up and down, illuminating the path before it.

'Are you alright?' a voice shattered the silence.

'No, my friend has fallen down an old grave and is trapped.' Tui thought quickly and provided the explanation that she thought would be most likely to generate interest and, above all, help. She was right. The owner of the torch took one look at Tui's attempts to open up the grave and realised that there was no alternative but to act now. No time to wait for approval from the council and go through the lengthy procedure of obtaining permission to access a grave. He must go immediately for tools and assistance.

'I'll be right back. Don't go away. I won't be long.' And he was gone, lost in the night, swallowed up by the darkness. All except for the tiny light that refused to be extinguished even after the holder of the torch had long since vanished from sight. True to his word the torch bearer was back within a few minutes, carrying a couple of spades and accompanied by another man.

'This is John. He's used to digging graves. It's his job.'

John gave Tui a look that was meant to inspire both confidence and hope:

'It was me that filled in this grave only a few weeks ago. I'm amazed that you say someone has fallen down it. The earth seemed packed solid after we'd finished. There must have been another collapse, lower down, that shook up the earth and led to another deep pit developing. We should have him out in no time. Is it a 'him'?' asked John.

Tui nodded sadly, biting her lip with anxiety. Secretly, John and the torch bearer held out no hope for the inadvertent grave dweller to be pulled out alive. No hope at all. He would have used up his oxygen supplies. He would be a 'gonner' as they said locally.

Survival was extremely unlikely but, as with all probabilities, the outcome was not engraved in stone and when, finally, they pulled out the bedraggled filthy figure that was Saul, hauled him into the open and laid him on the damp ground, it was evident that he was very much alive. Saul had survived the impossible: being buried for weeks without oxygen, food or water. Granted, the two rescuers thought that he had been down there a matter of minutes only and even then they were incredulous when Saul gasped and breathed in his first lungful of air.

'Unbelievable,' John muttered, an opinion that was echoed by his torch-bearing friend. And he meant it. It really was unbelievable. A miracle no less. While from Tui came not a word. Not a syllable left her lips as she gazed in wonderment at the small grey figure. Saul.

It was indeed Saul, although not the same Saul who had been dragged into the grave some weeks earlier. For Saul had survived death by drowning. Drowning in soil. Had survived being buried alive and for that there is no explanation. None whatsoever.

Saul screwed up his eyes against the light. Crouching on the grass he looked, for all the world, like a cornered animal in fear for its life. The two men took a step backwards. What on earth had they released from its underground fortress? Their initial feelings of fear and trepidation they dismissed as being borne of superstitious nonsense.

John, the less intimidated of the two, stepped forward and offered Saul his hand.

'Here, let me help you. You must be freezing. And hungry,' he added less convincingly, trying to avoid Saul's eyes as he gripped the boy's hand and raised up the cramped, hunched figure from its crouched position. Rather awkwardly Saul attempted to stand but immediately fell back down.

'Maybe too soon. You will need to get the strength back in your legs before you can stand,' and turning to Tui:

'He's lucky to be alive. Very lucky. He needs to be in hospital. I'll phone for an ambulance.' As John reached for his phone, Saul seemed to regain full consciousness and take stock of the situation.

'I'll be fine,' he muttered.

'I'm sure you will,' said John, used to dealing with people who were showing signs of shock as he assumed Saul was; when in fact Saul was thinking hard and working out the best way to rid himself of his rescuers. They had saved him from the hole from hell but he now wanted them out of his sight and the sooner the better.

He needed time and a quiet spot to think what best to do next. To mull over what had happened to him. Right now he could only compute the fact that he was alive, conscious and in the graveyard that had swallowed him up. When was it? Two weeks ago? Two months? He had no concept of the length of time that had passed. Maybe the young girl could tell him. She looked familiar. A reflection in still water near a forest clearing. An unusual, captivating face that had disappeared as suddenly as it had arrived.

But what had happened here in the graveyard? What had caused him to become trapped under the soil? Locked in a grave by all appearances, judging by the stone marking the opening in the ground. His memory was hazy when he tried to recollect the sequence of events leading to his incarceration. He cast his eyes over the stone. No marks. No inscription. No dates. Nothing. Whoever had been buried here was clearly of no import. The words of a song seeped into his mind:

Nothing to mark their passing, no name upon the stone.

While Saul had been assessing his situation, John, the grave-digger, had been watching him intently. The other man turned:

'They're on their way. Estimated time of arrival eight minutes. They know the area. No traffic hold ups. Nothing to delay them.'

He smiled encouragingly at Saul, anticipating that the boy would be happy about this. But these were not words that Saul wanted to hear. Not in the least. Not one little bit. Without a moment's hesitation he grabbed the hand of Tui, hurtled away through the bush and scrub, and disappeared into the heavy foliage.

'Hey, come back,' the maker of the emergency call shouted after their retreating backs, to no avail. The words fell, not exactly on deaf ears, but on ears that had closed down with no desire to listen.

Saul and Tui ran, hand-in-hand, until they felt they could run no more. They crashed through a curtain of weeping willow and fell to the ground. As they lay there, clutching their sides, Saul turned to his saviour:

'You found me,' he whispered.

Tui merely smiled in return. Then, as an afterthought, Saul continued:

'Who are you?' Like a rabbit caught in the head lights, Tui looked stunned and was rendered speechless. Then, recovering her senses, she made as if to run away. But Saul, sensing her impending flight, laid his hand on her arm:

'Please stay. We must stick together.'

Tui looked at her arm, now covered in mud from where Saul had placed his hand, and smiled. As if they were both complicit in a crime, they shared a secret look that spoke of companionship and friendship that would be a life time in the making. 'I know where we can go for safety. I will take you to my home.' She turned to leave and Saul duly followed.

21 Bella

The three nameless children had acquired a dog. It was a non-descript little thing with part of its tail missing, as if it had been caught in a trap carelessly left out by people intent on catching rats on allotments. Tui called her Bella. The others couldn't have cared less.

Regardless, or in spite, of the loss of half a tail, Bella held her head high. She was a mixture of breeds but essentially whippet at the core. Bede had found her wandering aimlessly in the back streets one night. He and the others had done their busking stint for the day and were on their way home. Black plastic bin bags were strewn along the pavement, some torn with their contents scattered hither and thither.

A shadow seemed to flit behind one of the bags but Bede could detect a pair of pricked up ears, just visible above the rubbish. He reached out a hand and grabbed the little dog by the scruff of her neck. He met no resistance. She put up no fight. She was far too weak. If anything her heart began to race, not out of fear but out of recognition that she had been touched by a human. She was amongst friendly people. She had not been hit or kicked or shouted at. She felt waves of compassion roll towards her as a warm loving touch upon her head made her close her eyes in bliss and breathe out in relief.

'A little dog. So beautiful.' Tui wrapped her arms round the dog's neck and drew her to her. 'She's starving. She is homeless. She is just like us.' There was no need to say more. Her eyes said it all.

'What do you think?' Bede asked Yan.

'Well, if Tui doesn't mind contributing her own money to buy its food,' he replied. Tui's lip quivered but then she realised that this would never happen as she caught the glint in Yan's eye.

Saul had arrived in the disused toilets. A rushed thought fought its way into his mind as he looked upon the dog: *I am amongst strangers, in an unknown place.*

In turn, all the others looked at the dog. They used Bella as a barometer to assess a person's basic nature. Good and trustworthy – or devious and malicious. For the nameless children there were no in-between areas. No shades of grey. The barometer swung only one of two ways.

Bella slowly rose to her feet and trotted lightly to where Saul stood. Caked in mud, thin, and smelling of damp earth, he looked for all the world like a disreputable vagabond. But Bella saw through the tattered clothes that hung in shreds from the wiry frame that was Saul. She sniffed his feet, then his hands, looked towards his grime-smeared face then turned and wandered back to her bed.

'She likes you,' whispered Tui. 'For sure she likes you.'

The others nodded in agreement. A decision had been made. Not by them but by the dog. Saul felt accepted, though he was dimly aware of the fleeting thought that it was rather unusual for people to allow a dog to decide whether a stranger was safe or not.

'The dog knows. She always knows,' Yan confirmed.

Saul was actually past caring by this stage. It vaguely occurred to him to ask what it was that the dog knew but the question left his mind before he was able to ask it. The last thing he remembered before he hit the cold, white, tiled floor of the disused toilet, was a voice that spoke above him.

'He can stay. He doesn't know our secret. Let's keep it that way.'

What secret? thought Saul, then lapsed into unconsciousness.

Tui was having one of her dreams. Dark dreams she called them. This time though, before the finale when she was pushed underneath water and took her last breath, a beautiful image appeared. A glowing person. A woman. A smiling face that looked at her with love. Her mother. The image was so vivid, so real, that Tui shot bolt upright, wide awake.

'My mother! I saw my mother!' She cried out to the darkness. As one they came to her. Torches lit,

THE NAMELESS CHILDREN

three caring people gathered round her bed, and Bella laid her head on the pillow.

'Tell us,' urged Saul. 'Tell us what you saw.'

Tears welled in her eyes as she spoke, softly now.

'I saw my mother looking down at me. She was smiling. She loved me.'

Yan's lips tightened. It was almost more than he could bear. Seeing his adopted sister so torn apart. He wished he could resolve matters. Put an end to the dreams. Would it be enough to wreak revenge on Dom's mother through Dom? It might make himself feel better about things, but would it really, actually, help Tui?

He knew the answer. *No*. How else then, to remove these night terrors from Tui's life? What about hypnosis? It might help, but then again it might make matters worse. Impossible to know the outcome in advance. So easy with hindsight, after the fact. Maybe if he could find out from Penny more about their family; find out what became of Tui's mother, Yan's eldest sister, after Tui had been parted from this life. Maybe that would help.

22   A Worrying Connection

Jonas was running. As if he had winged feet, he flew over the ground. He had heard strange news. Unnerving comments. A brief conversation between Emily and one of her friends, instigated by Emily herself. Emily, his benefactor, who provided a roof over his head, put food on the table, enabled him to survive with very little contribution on his part.

'You know the three buskers who sit opposite the book shop in town, playing music day after day?' Emily was talking on the phone.

Jonas had been coming down the stairs when the words wafted through the open door of the living room. He froze one step from the bottom and held his breath. He wanted to capture every word. He knew instinctively that what he was about to hear would have a big part to play in his life, make a deep impression with a lasting outcome, but not necessarily a good one.

Emily's friend, Vanessa, replied that she knew who Emily meant, but surely the three teenagers weren't causing any harm? Just earning a living on the streets. Didn't cause an obstruction. Tried to keep a low profile.

But Emily persisted.

'They've been here!'

'What?'

'Jonas brought them for tea last week. They're his new friends apparently. Then he asked if they could move in.'

'What did you say?'

'Not a chance. He said: 'Only 'til they find somewhere of their own'. But when would that be? Probably never.'

'I can see your point,' Vanessa offered, 'but is there not anything else you could do to help?'

'Such as?'

'Well, putting them in touch with Social Services or groups that help the homeless.'

'It's not just the housing aspect. I don't trust them. At all. There's something evil about them.' Emily spat out the words.

'That's a bit strong isn't it? Evil? No-one is inherently evil. Well at least they don't start out like that. Maybe circumstances shape and mould their lives to make them less likeable, less sympathetic to others.'

'I understand what you're saying but I'm going with my intuition and it says *no*. Not under any circumstances should I even give a second thought to having the three of them under my roof, or even engaging with them in any context whatsoever.'

'What did Jonas think about your decision?'

'He seemed to accept it. I'd like to see the back of the three of them though. Get them off the streets of our town. Drive them out of town in fact. Will you help me?'

'Alright,' said her friend. 'If you feel that strongly, and are really that worried, I'll have a few words with someone on the council and see what can be done to encourage them to move on.'

'Thanks. Anything you can do to shift them would be great. I'm worried about the influence they may have on Jonas. He means so much to me and he's so different to them.' But, as Emily spoke, once again came the voice from within: *He's no different. He's exactly like them. You are deceiving yourself.*

'I'll call Jonas and see if he wants a cup of tea. He's just upstairs in his room.'

But there was no response from upstairs. Jonas had fled and was hot footing it to the disused toilet on the edge of town. The home of the nameless children.

At Grange Manor, Dom's infatuation with Penny was growing unabated. They continued to meet once a week though, while Penny seemed friendly enough, she showed no sign of being interested in anything other than friendship. This, however, was not the main concern in Dom's life.

He had become increasingly alarmed by what he had come to think of as 'visions'. Fleeting shapes that seemed to appear in his peripheral vision then vanish the minute he turned to look at them. Had he been remotely superstitious he would have attributed these 'phantoms' to goblins, sprites and other such creatures that inhabit the faery kingdom. Configurations that existed and yet did not exist. They could rarely be seen clearly as it was almost impossible to focus on them, so rapidly did they move. Equally, so complete was their ability to remain still, so that they were unseen in plain sight. Invisible.

But Dom was not at all superstitious and so the flashes of shadows, just out of sight, continued to trouble him. Out of fear of being ridiculed he had mentioned the visions to no-one, and certainly not to Penny. He was having enough trouble trying to engineer regular meetings with her these days, without throwing a spanner in the works by raising an element of doubt between them.

He smiled wryly to himself as he thought how any suggestion of fleeting demons, or 'flights of fancy' as he had heard them referred to, would dash all hopes of any sort of liaison between himself and Penny.

He had used what he fondly imagined were subtle attempts to discover how well she knew Yan. But Penny had not been forthcoming, and shrugged off any questions with a dismissive toss of her hair. Dom loved how her hair fell in curtains round her face, leaving much to the imagination. He never knew what she was thinking and had to rely on occasional glimpses of her elfin face to judge her mood and intent. While Dom, on the other hand, was as transparent as the day is long. Easy to read.

'Just like an open book,' his mother was fond of saying.

And, while Dom deliberated long and hard, Yan moved ever closer to the family Andover, with the aim of causing as much grief and consternation as possible to the surviving family members. Family such as Dom's mother but, in particular, Dom himself. Dom was the focus of Yan's attention. It was through Dom that his mother could be reached and through Dom that the appalling treatment of Tui could be addressed, her drowning as a tiny child avenged.

Tui, as Emily had chosen to call her, had not a malicious bone in her body. She was, however, closely bound to Yan, the only member of her immediate family to exist with her in the twenty-first century. As such, she hung on his words, listened attentively and was compliant when he suggested certain courses of action.

'We must get our own back for what they did to you,' he announced forcibly one evening. Tui nodded, while secretly thinking that what had happened was all in the past and was probably best left there.

She had recently learned some new phrases that she rather liked. Proverbs such as 'let sleeping dogs lie', 'turn the other cheek', 'leave well alone'. Having had the meanings explained to her she felt no inclination to open up old wounds and avenge people who were living now, for crimes their ancestors committed over a hundred years ago. No inclination at all. She thought it was meaningless.

By all means stand up for what you think is right. It is totally correct to act when action is required. No good to be one of the silent majority. No good at all. But seeking revenge for a deed committed in the past – well that is another matter entirely.

If she saw someone mistreating Bella, she would step up and challenge them. Some half-remembered words of a song came back to her. A song that had floated across the square from another busker singing a song about Raoul Wallenberg, a saviour of thousands of Jews in the Second World War. *How did the chorus go?*

'It's always so easy to keep your voice low, never to speak out of turn, never to say what you feel to be right, to keep quiet and never be heard'.

This was a perfect philosophy to follow. It ensured that change happened. That the helpless were thrown a lifeline. That justice was seen to be done. That unwholesome acts perpetrated through the ages did not go unchallenged.

With this last thought Tui contemplated that maybe Yan could be right; that there was some logic, tenuous though it was, in taking to task the descendants of those who had murdered her.

For now though she would choose to put these thoughts out of her mind. The sun was shining and she looked across at Saul. Sitting at the table, looking clean and refreshed after a wash and a good night's sleep, he looked up and smiled at her. It was as if a cloud of roses had fallen from the skies. Tui's heart lit up and she returned the smile.

'Tell me your name,' he whispered and the words danced across the shaft of sunlight that illuminated the dust in the air. Words that spun in hues of purple and orange.

'Tell me your name,' she repeated the words to herself.

'My name is Tui,' she said after some deliberation.

She had accepted Emily's gifted name for her and would now throw her conferred, automatic, name to the winds. She would no longer answer to No. 2. From now on she would be Tui.

23   A Plan is Cast

Jonas flew through the open door into the disused toilets that served as home for Yan, Bede, Tui, a dog, and now Saul. Truth be told he felt more at home here than he did at Emily's house, with all its creature comforts and regular supply of food.

Not for the first time he asked himself why he stayed with her. But he knew the reason and there were many to choose from. It was warm, comfortable and, above all, it was safe. It provided a retreat from the often hostile world. A retreat where he could hide away and remain largely undetected. Above all, though, it allowed him to portray a semblance of normality to all who met him. Who would doubt the authenticity of a person associated with Emily? No – not associated with – lived with. Emily, who was a pillar of society. Emily who had never hurt a soul.

But Emily's weakness lay deep within. Her every waking moment was tinged with sadness. She would do anything and everything to drive thoughts of David's death from her mind. David, her precious son, who had *departed this life aged four years following a short illness.* So said the words on the headstone.

She had never recovered from the shock of losing him and this would prove to be her undoing. Fate and an immense amount of bad luck had allowed

Jonas into her life. The chink in her armour was wide open. Enough to allow Jonas to creep in. To allow adversity to triumph and Emily to cast caution to the wind, wisdom to the heavens. To allow common sense to be seen to be completely and entirely lacking.

From the inopportune moment that Jonas sloped down the back alleyway, at the same time that Emily chose to leave her house through her back gate, she was lost. Life would never be the same again. Right now, though, Emily was deliriously happy. She felt that she had acquired an older version of David.

'He's so like David,' she would tell her friends who, in turn, would look sceptically at the object of Emily's adulation, Jonas, and see only a non-descript teenager with nothing special to recommend him. Nothing at all.

In the disused toilet at the edge of the town, Jonas felt at one with the company. He had passed the dog test on an earlier occasion and welcomed the soft muzzle placed trustingly in his hand by lovely Bella.

As he rushed into the home of the nameless children Jonas was surprisingly exhausted for one used to travelling at speed. Out of breath and gasping.

'What's happened Jonas?' Yan was first to begin the questioning.

'Give him chance to recover,' Tui ordered. 'Can't you see he's out of breath.'

Jonas raised his head to see five pairs of eyes staring questioningly at him, including those of the dog.

'Emily wants you gone,' he blurted out and related what he'd overheard when coming down the stairs in her house. The others looked horrified. Even Bella, who had picked up on the atmosphere, now wore a worried, fearful look.

'But it's not going to happen,' Jonas continued by way of reassurance. 'I won't let it.'

'How can you stop it? How can you stop Emily from using every method at her disposal to get rid of us?' Bede asked.

'I have a plan. It has been brewing at the back of my mind for some time, but now the time has come for me to bring it to fruition.'

Tui looked sad.

'I thought Emily liked us. She was nice to me when we made a meal together. She gave me my new name.'

'Oh, that was her was it,' said Yan dismissively. 'Well, however nice she might have seemed that night we were all round there, she was obviously not showing her true colours.'

'Her colours looked fine to me,' murmured Tui, taking his comment in the literal sense. Her words floated on the air.

'What is your plan Jonas?' Bede looked straight at him as he asked the question.

'I can't say at the moment.' Jonas looked away from all the eyes. From those curious to know how he was going to avert disaster and make sure that they could all stay in the town.

Had Yan and Bede been in possession of an ounce of emotion, empathy, or feelings for their fellow human beings, they would have heard alarm bells ringing when they witnessed the stance that Jonas had adopted; the body language that sent out an unambiguous message. But then they were not remotely concerned about their fellow human beings for the simple reason that they stood apart from them.

For the nameless children, Jonas included, were not human. The only one amongst them who was definitely human was Saul. Saul, who had spent time incarcerated with other nameless children. Saul, who would never be the same again. Saul who had effectively died and come back to life.

In essence, the only real difference between Saul and the others was that he still had his soul. He was not, however, tuned into the planned actions of Jonas, and Tui, his new friend, was too taken in with Saul to pay much attention to the whole scenario. Her sole contribution was to express mild disbelief that Emily could be anything other than she seemed to be – a caring, honest person.

But the pact had been made. A silent pact, closed and agreed upon through eye contact alone. Yan and

THE NAMELESS CHILDREN

Bede were in agreement with Jonas. Whatever he chose to do to safeguard their future was okay with them and would go unnoticed. They would turn a blind eye to the proposed plan of Jonas. After all, he was one of them.

24   Dilston Hall

The workshop at the isolated village in the West Pennines was proving to be well worth the trip for Anwen. It had the added advantage of being held in the conference centre, Dilston Hall, the focus of all her endeavours. It really was a stroke of luck to have landed on the workshop in the first place. Discovering it was here, at the Hall, was another unbelievable coincidence.

But Anwen didn't believe in coincidences. To her this was synchronicity, pure and simple. This was meant to happen. She let the words of a well-known quote flow over her consciousness:

Once you make a decision everything in the universe will conspire to make it happen. As a firm believer in this philosophy she embraced every opportunity with open arms. In a word she created her own luck, if there is such a thing as luck and, as Anwen knew, the jury is still out on this one.

The morning had been intense with two, hour-long, lectures followed by group discussion and a light vegetarian lunch. *No meat eaters here*, noticed Anwen with satisfaction. All the participants of the workshop had been shown how to choose the correct key words to optimise the chances of their online searches taking them where they wanted to go. It was

THE NAMELESS CHILDREN

exciting and stimulating but Anwen was starting to feel claustrophobic and needed to be outside in the fresh air.

At the first opportunity she left the rest of the group and made for the wall where she had found the note from Emma to Will. The note that had been carefully written and secreted in a gap in the stone work.

Arriving at the spot where she had found the note, she reached into her pocket and drew it out to read once more. Nowhere, amongst the neatly laid out sentences, was there the slightest hint that all was not well, that the couple would not be able to meet at the normal place and time, that disaster would befall one or both of them. None whatsoever.

Apart from the dire description that Emma had given Will, regarding the death of the son born to the squire and his wife and his replacement with a changeling, all seemed in order. Then it struck her.

How could she have been so stupid?

Emma had described a deed shrouded in deceit, lies and intrigue. This was no ordinary note, but Will had not picked it up, otherwise it would not have remained in the wall for all that time. Considering the weather conditions on these exposed moorlands it was a miracle that the note had survived at all. If only it could speak to her. If only the note could tell her more than the words written down. Who had been the last person to hold the note before her? It must have been Emma. But what if...?

Another scenario leapt into Anwen's mind. What if Will had indeed come to this very spot to collect the note that he knew would be waiting for him? What if he had been in the process of reading it when he had heard footsteps? Footsteps that, by the very nature of the ring they gave out on the cobbles, had told him that this was not a fellow servant. No softly trodden scuffed sound was carrying a person round the side of the building. This was the ringing footstep of the squire, striding out with purpose and intent, possibly on his way to collect his saddled mount and ride off across the fields. What would Will have done if he had found himself in such a position?

What would I have done? Anwen thought.

Will couldn't afford to be found in possession of the note, not by any stretch of the imagination. It would mean discovery of his forbidden dalliance with Emma and instant dismissal, with no employment references for either of them. No, the only option open to Will would have been to thrust the note back where Emma had placed it and where Anwen had found it 150 years later.

She examined the folds in the note. Impossible to know if anyone other than Emma had held it. How long did fingerprints last? Would it be possible to get the note analysed to check for them?

Anwen allowed her mind to wander still further. Assuming that Will had been disturbed while reading the note – what then? Would he have met Emma as planned, with everything carrying on as normal? But if this had been the case why hadn't he come back later to retrieve the note? She brushed her fair hair away from her eyes and squinted into the sun. Looking down once more at the note, she saw something flash into view then, just as quickly, vanish.

Curse our limited peripheral vision, she thought to herself. *If I was a hare I could see so much further behind me, be much more aware of what is going on in my surroundings.*

But Anwen was not a hare and hence did not see Bede secreting himself into position, a matter of only a few yards away from her. Bede who was delighted that Anwen was back on the scene and providing him with clues. Clues that would lead him closer to the Elver family, to the people who had dismissed him out of hand. Rendered him cold and lifeless to a pauper's grave in unhallowed ground.

Nothing to mark their passing, no words upon the stone. The words seemed to echo with the wind and circle both Bede and Anwen, before vanishing across the dark moor.

Following the afternoon workshop Anwen strolled into the town centre, a good walk which helped to refresh her. She was staying at the Hall for the weekend but felt a need to escape and mull things over from a distance, be it only a couple of miles. Meandering along the high street she heard fragments of a song drifting from a shop doorway. 'To Let', the shop was an ideal place to busk. Perfect in fact. Out of the wind, it provided a little sanctuary where you were not constantly under the scrutiny of members of the public.

She had often thought that busking was a strange profession. The busker was desperate to earn money but equally intent on maintaining a low profile; in most cases, at any rate. Perhaps not the escape artists and fire eaters. It was more likely that these characters were not hell-bent on hiding their talents under a bush.

The buskers that Anwen could see were positioned as close to the shop door as possible, set back from the street, with a cap laid on the ground in front of them. The only instruments being a bodhran and a whistle, it made for a quick getaway should a shop owner complain about the 'noise' to the police who would be duty-bound to move them on. The police were mostly kind and understanding:

'Sorry, if it was left to us, you could play here all day. It's just that we have to act when someone complains.'

So far, that day, no-one had complained and at least they couldn't be accused of obscuring a shop window as this particular shop was empty, devoid of goods and devoid of people. A perfect spot.

Anwen was wondering whether she would ever have the courage to busk then realised that, for the greater majority of buskers, it was not an option. The decision was made for them. It was out of their hands. They were desperate. They needed money so they busked. It was as simple as that.

Peering into the gloom in the doorway she could make out three people and a small, graceful-looking dog that lay on a carefully-placed rug. She reflected on what she had read about dogs that accompany the homeless.

Contrary to what many members of the public might think about the welfare of street dogs, the dogs had been found to be considerably better off, and happier, than the average house dog. They were in the constant company of people and wanted for nothing. The street person they accompanied valued them very highly, for protection, company and warmth. The busker and their dog were mutually beneficial to each other.

Not so the house-bound dog. Often left in solitary confinement, throughout the working day, these dogs did not fare so well. The well-known edict: 'There is nothing in a dog's nature that prepares it for being on its own' came to mind.

She was about to move on when something made her look back. She couldn't pinpoint what it was exactly. *Did one of the trio turn to speak to any of the others?* She couldn't remember.

Then she caught his eye.

Bede looked directly at her then, just as suddenly, looked away again.

I've seen him before, she thought.

Anwen couldn't remember where she'd seen him before, couldn't put a name to the face, but one thing was certain: he knew her. The sudden avoidance of eye contact, after it was initially established, was weird. Symptomatic of someone who does not want to be noticed; has no wish to engage with others. Anwen sought out his gaze.

There it was again. Bede looked up to see her staring straight at him and he quickly looked away again.

'Do you know me?' Quite bold for her.

'No, I don't think so.' He looked furtively from side to side and Anwen was convinced. He definitely knew her. She persisted.

'Have we met before anywhere?'

'Look, I don't know you. Just leave it will you!'

The unexpected hostile response: a sure sign of guilt, of a lie, of deception in the making.

'Okay.' Anwen turned and began to walk away.

Bede suddenly came to his senses. Why pretend? Why not try to get to know her? So much easier than stalking her and trying to gain information by stealth and subterfuge. Footsteps running behind her. A hand on her shoulder.

'Please stop. I didn't mean to be rude. Maybe we have met, or at least been in the same place at the same time. Do you live locally?'

Anwen looked at him suspiciously then decided to give him the benefit of the doubt.

'No. I'm just in the area on a course at Dilston Hall.'

'What's the course about?' Bede decided to follow it through.

'What do you know about family history?' Anwen fired back. Always a good idea to answer a question with another question.

'Not a lot, but I'm looking into the background of the Elver Family who used to live at Dilston Hall,' replied Bede.

Anwen's mouth fell open and she closed it again immediately. Then, unable to contain her curiosity any longer:

'What have you found out about them? I've been looking into them too.'

'Not much really. Would you like to share what you've discovered? It might make it easier.'

'What's your particular interest?' Anwen pushed for more information.

'I think I might have links to the family going back to the mid-1800s,' he replied.

Anwen said nothing. She didn't know this boy and wasn't about to divulge her hard-earned secrets. She would pursue her own line of enquiry and get the note fingerprinted. Anything else she could learn from this strange boy would be a bonus. She smiled at him, but deep down lay a feeling of mistrust. Always go on your intuition her grandmother had told her and Anwen always did. Trust is hard earned and it would come at a price. It's just that she, Anwen, would not be paying.

Anwen had no need to fear Bede. No need at all. She was not descended from the Elver family. She was descended from the changeling. They had all been deceived. Drawn the short straw. Anwen for having been led to believe, albeit unintentionally, that she had descended from a bloodline that in fact was not hers; it was the bloodline of the changeling.

The changeling, in turn, had been deceived as he had not been brought up by his parents. Had his parents died this would have been understandable, but his parents had not died. They had sold him. Not merely passed him on so that they would have one less mouth to feed. They had sold him. Money had changed hands.

Emma could testify to that. Emma... Will too, had he ever caught sight of the letter hidden away in the wall. The note that had waited patiently. The inscribed words that were still there over a century later. A silent testament to a wrong doing.

THE NAMELESS CHILDREN

Then there was Bede who had died from cholera such a short time after his birth. Inadvertently poisoned by the nanny. The nanny who had been there to help his mother recover from the birth of her child; to ease the pressure on her. The nanny who had dripped water into the mouth of little James to 'top him up' in between feeds. All this before it had become established that cholera was transmitted through drinking water.

In time, the work of a very smart person, John Snow, would serve to shed light on the cause of cholera, when he identified contaminated water as the culprit. His discovery allowed the belated link to be made between cholera outbreaks and the water supply and only then did a turning point occur.

Only when it was acknowledged that cholera was not a disease of the poor, but affected rich and poor alike. Only then, when the common denominator had been deduced, was it possible to move forwards. The common denominator that had been staring them in the face. Hiding in plain sight – as always. The water pump at the end of the street. The pump that supplied water to all the houses in the district.

And that was how little James, the first born of the Squire of Dilston Hall, came to die. He was fed contaminated water. In all innocence, it was true, but the bottom line was written there for all to see. He had, effectively, been poisoned.

Even Bede, with the scattered knowledge he had gleaned about the circumstances surrounding his death, could see that it had been an accident. A horrendous mistake. An inadvertent slip. Had a doctor been called at the moment of the demise of little James he would have had no alternative but to write under 'Cause of Death': Cholera. At no point would he have questioned the level of care meted out to little James. Not at all.

The symptoms were there for all to see, except that no-one had seen them. The disease took its toll on the tiny tot in a matter of hours. During the night, while his mother lay sleeping, and the nanny was turned away from her charge, little James slipped away to eternity. It was his father that had discovered the limp, lifeless body. Faced with having to tell his wife the appalling news, he made an instant decision and called for a trusted servant. He called for Emma.

Emma was duly charged with taking the little body to be disposed of, and of bringing a changeling child to take its place. The squire's wife would never know and it was this unfeeling act of seeming inhumanity by the squire towards his small son that Bede could never forgive. The apparent total disregard for him once he had died. The lack of a burial. The taking back of his name:

Nothing to mark their passing, no name upon the stone
Condemned to eternity with no acknowledgement, no dignity, no proper burial and, above all, no name.

For the name that should have belonged to Bede was given to the changeling. Bede was out for blood. He would not rest until he had seen justice done.

Not just done but seen to be done, he added silently to himself.

25   Background of a Murderer

Dom was growing ever more frustrated with his lack of contact with Penny. True, they met at fairly regular intervals, but the conversation was generally centred on Grange Manor. The more they discovered about the history of the Andover family, the less favourable did Dom appear in Penny's eyes.

'So, do you think there are any other murderers in your family?' Penny asked Dom, with a look of mischief on her face.

Dom visibly blanched.

'I don't think so. At least I hope not,' he replied quietly, thinking frantically of a way to turn the conversation round and away from the subject of murder.

This was harder to do than one would imagine, not surprising considering the clandestine, barbaric edicts issued by one of Dom's ancestors. It reminded Dom, in one of his bleaker moments, of Herod instructing his soldiers to put to death every boy child under the age of two in the city of Bethlehem, except that this was not murder on an epic scale. It was the murder of one. A small child. And the serious nature of the matter was not in any way lessened by this fact, as Dom knew only too well. He was amazed how much emotion was stirred in him whenever he thought of the baby girl, his distant relative, being drowned in a cold river and left floating. Which heartless person would instigate such a thing? Who indeed?

But Dom knew the answer and the implications chilled his heart. The genes that shaped the ancestor who was capable of murder were shared with himself. A horrific thought but inescapable. Within his body, like it or not, were the genes of a murderer.

He tried not to dwell on this too much. He was aware of the nature/nurture debate – still ongoing – but he tended towards the belief that genes did not make the person, rather that environment shaped your personality: worked on the genes that you were born with and was mainly responsible for the person you became. He hoped, fervently, that this was true.

Saul had adjusted surprisingly well to living with three street people and a dog in a disused toilet. He actually found it rather exciting; much like troops, following mobilisation at the beginning of the First World War, lived on adrenalin, their spirits buoyed in anticipation of promised adventures and challenges to come. All this naïvety soon to be replaced by the stark reality of war; the realisation that 'this was it'. They were knee-deep in mud in the trenches and the war, contrary to all expectations, would not be 'over by Christmas'.

Saul had ventured out once or twice into the town but had not risked exposing his secret life by daring to engage in busking with the others. He was the same, yet not the same, as he had been prior to his excursion into the graveyard and subsequent incarceration.

Every so often he felt a pang of guilt that his parents would be missing him and probably presumed him dead. One evening he had positioned himself under the kitchen window of the house where he had grown up. The house where his parents still lived. The house that represented security and stability. He had heard the whispered tones drift through the open window.

'Do you think he is still alive?' his mother was asking.

'I really don't know,' his father replying in words that he hoped were comforting. 'We can only hope and try to keep our spirits up.'

Saul did not wait to hear any more. He felt little compassion for these people who had nurtured him and cared for him since he was born. He felt more allegiance to the nameless children. Several weeks in the grave had changed him.

But Saul was still in possession of his soul and was not a lost cause. Time would tell if he would ever feel sympathy once more towards his parents and regain a desire to see them again. Feel a pull to be a person once more, in the land of the living, rather than existing with soulless individuals, hell bent on revenge.

Penny and Yan were walking along the street idly chatting, Penny with her head down, subconsciously counting cracks in the paving. Coming towards them, weaving in and out of the crowd, Dom did not initially spot the pair, but Yan spotted him and did not waste a moment. Slipping his arm round Penny's shoulders he turned her to face him.

'Would you like to see a film together this evening?' Penny's face shone radiant.

'That would be great,' she replied. As she turned to continue walking there, facing her, was the thunder-struck face of Dom. He had never been able to disguise his emotions and today was no exception. Shocked to the core he could not deny what he had seen with his own eyes. Yan and Penny were an item. Even Penny's obvious pleasure at seeing him failed to raise his spirits.

'Let's meet up this evening Dom,' she suggested. 'I'm going to see a film first with Yan, but there'll be time afterwards.'

Dom smiled while keeping half an eye on Yan whose eyes seemed to have narrowed to almost slits, making him look both furtive and dangerous at the same time.

Don't underestimate this guy, the words passed through Dom's mind. *But then never underestimate me*, he threw out the silent challenge to his adversary and rival in love.

The ongoing battle between him and this strange usurper who had forced his way into Dom's life, by virtue of his connection with Penny, was not having a good impact on Dom. It was bringing out the worst in him, accentuating his ruthless qualities, increasing his tendency to confront rather than back down to avoid a scene, introducing a sudden reluctance to 'turn the other cheek'.

Dom was meeting Yan head on. He had decided not to accept defeat where Penny was concerned. If he was going down he would go down fighting. *No, forget that!* He was not going down at all.

He would adopt the mental stance he took where mistreatment of animals was concerned. In those circumstances he would not budge an inch from what he believed to be right. He was known online for his unstinting attitude to those who do not respect other living things and who openly desecrate the planet. This unique planet that suffers so completely at the hands of the power-grabbers, the sociopathic leaders, at the hands of humans who should know better – but don't.

Dom's stance was one of zero tolerance and it was this approach that he would now level at Yan. From now on he and Yan would become sworn enemies. It was not just the obvious competition between the two for Penny's affections – there was something deeper. Dom was not entirely sure what it was, but what had begun as a persistent gnawing feeling that gripped his insides was growing rapidly into a deep-seated hatred for the entity that was Yan.

Entity? Where had that word sprung from? Yan was human like the rest of them, surely?

But still the thought churned through Dom's mind. He began to wonder whether he was losing it, with more and more episodes where clarity of thought temporarily eluded him; where the ability to process information seemed to be leaving him. Was this how mental illness started?

Then there were the visions. They were still there. Just when he was feeling calm, and at peace with the world, he would catch sight of a fleeting shadow that eclipsed his field of vision and brought his spirits crashing down, threatened his sanity, undermined his ability to function. And for reasons that he could not explain, and had no basis whatsoever in fact or reality, he felt that Yan was behind it all, that Yan was at the root of it, that Yan was out to do mischief. Of this Dom was firmly convinced. In what had been only seconds, these thoughts had flashed through Dom's mind. He jolted his attention back to the scene before him: to Penny's smiling face.

'So is that okay then? See you later at The Black Swan on the High Street. 10.30? We'll have time to get a drink and discuss a few things before they throw us out.'

'Absolutely. See you later.' Dom walked away but not before noticing once more the grimace on Yan's face. Posing as a smile it did not fool Dom for an instant. In fact, he doubted that it would fool anyone. He was now absolutely sure about one thing though: Yan was desperate to be with Penny and, while she evidently had feelings for him, her mind appeared to be not entirely made up. Dom was still in with a chance.

The truth, had he known it, was more sinister than he could ever have imagined. This lovely girl, with the curtain of hair that fell intriguingly across her face, shared a not insubstantial amount of her genes with the staring, grimacing creature that only weeks ago had been interred in the earth. Buried in unhallowed ground with nine other nameless children.

Had Dom trusted his own intuition he would have clutched at the word that thrust itself into his mind: *entity*, for that is exactly what Yan was. Not human but an entity. A revived creature destined to lie dead, buried and wholly inactive, for all eternity but, for reasons that might never be revealed, had suddenly emerged as dusk fell over a graveyard in a West Pennine village.

Yan, like the others who had materialised, appeared to be human. However, there were many subtle, but crucial, differences, the main one being the lack of a soul.

Having no soul did not seem to be a handicap in any way though. If anything, being in possession of a personality where sympathy, empathy, consideration and displaying feelings played no part was a decided advantage. How much easier to act from an entirely selfish viewpoint when you had no feelings for your fellow human. Very easy indeed.

Yan watched the retreating back of Dom and under his breath muttered 'loser'.

'What was that?' asked Penny.

'Nothing. Just can't understand what you see in the guy.'

'He's very kind and easy to get on with. Together we've discovered a great deal about his family.'

But that night she would learn something new that would blow the whole thing out of the water. It was not only Dom that was related to the drowned child, Tui, but Penny also. They were all intertwined.

Dom and Penny might continue to investigate the history of the family, but the pervading feeling of a shared interest and mutual trust would gradually be eaten away with the ever-growing realisation that one of Dom's relatives had murdered one of Penny's, and not too long ago. Less than two hundred years in fact.

For now all was quiet. Yan was pleased that he had Penny's company for the greater part of the evening, while Dom was elated at knowing he would see Penny as soon as the film finished.

The calm before the storm predominated but the cracks would soon start to show. And the carefully maintained façade that enables us to portray an image of confidence, competence and credibility to the outside world would begin to erode, as surely as water washes away a river bank and as inevitable as cliffs will fall to the sea. For nothing is forever.

The meeting in the pub had started well enough. Penny and Dom had managed to grab their favourite seats near the window where they could gaze out on the street. They were in a booth, hidden from the rest of the throng who had gathered to listen to a band at the other end of the pub. The music was amplified but not to the extent that they couldn't hear themselves think.

Penny had bid goodnight to Yan and fondly imagined that he would have gone home, though where 'home' was she had no idea. She suspected that it would probably be somewhere that might not be too luxurious and had refrained from asking Yan any more than she needed to know. Stick to the main points she had told herself. They worked well as a team. It was as if they had known each other forever, giving grist to the viewpoint: 'the genes will always out.'

But Yan was not at home. He was, in fact, secreted in the next booth at the pub, hidden behind a newspaper, occasionally darting out a hand to retrieve a glass of beer. It looked, for all the world, like a disembodied hand hovering in the air, feeling this way and that for the half full glass of dark liquid. But Yan was not reading. He was listening.

'I've found out something more. Tracked the family back another two generations,' Dom told Penny.

'What? As far as the time when the child was drowned?'

Every time Dom heard these words his heart missed a beat. They struck him to the core. He felt responsible.

But who can blame the sons for the deeds of the fathers, thought Dom, then realised that in fact everyone did. Virtually to the letter. This had been the root cause of wars and strife through the centuries. Sons avenging what had been done to their fathers. And with this came no reconciliation. No meeting at the half-way point. No chance for peace. The whole process just went on and on. The desire for revenge seemed to be part of the human condition. It was certainly inherent in the personalities of the nameless children.

Dom collected his thoughts. He spoke slowly.

'I think so. I think I know who the mother is. I think she was part of your family. She was a child of the blacksmith who ran the smithy. After her child died she went straight back to the smithy. All the family suspected foul play.'

'And that's why the blacksmith inserted the symbol and the inscription into the gate for Grange Manor,' Penny interrupted.

'It would make sense,' Dom agreed.

Penny set down her glass thoughtfully.

'Does this mean that I am descended from the woman whose daughter was drowned by someone in your family?'

'Well, maybe not directly descended. Hard to establish really.'

'But one thing's for sure,' Penny continued, 'the poor woman whose child was drowned at birth was my ancestor, my relation, only a few generations ago.'

'Yes,' Dom admitted. He wished with all his heart that he had not been so honest, that he had not spoken the truth, had kept it all inside him. Penny would never have known. But surely, she would not blame him for what someone in his distant past had done? Surely not?

While Penny might not blame Dom directly, a seed of doubt was beginning to grow and the flame was being fanned by Yan. For Yan most certainly blamed Dom and his entire family, both living and dead, for what had happened to Tui.

It was all in the telling. Whichever way a story was told would determine its meaning. Those light of heart would convey a story of promise, an outcome of a positive nature. The same story, when told by one with a hard heart, with a negative outlook, perhaps one with no soul, would paint a dark picture with sinister overtones and a foreboding nature.

And so it was with the story of the Andover family. On the surface one could see an intricate network of intrigue that burrowed its way back through the ages. One that had its inevitable black sheep. In this case a murderer. All families have their dark secrets, truth be told. But the truth is rarely told and many dark dealings are left hidden from the world.

Had the sinister episodes that took place in the mid-1800s been left in the past, or treated to only a light scrutiny, all might have been well. But Yan was determined to milk the event that had precipitated Tui's premature removal from the world. To milk it for all it was worth. He would revel in the details and bring them out shining in all their unearthly glory, for Penny to see, time after time. He would not let an opportunity slip by, when he did not raise the spectre of the drowned child and link it irrevocably to Dom.

Dom who was wholly innocent of any wrongdoing. Yan would engage Penny in discussion, while letting her think all along that she had already imparted the information to him – the fact that she was related to Tui – while in fact he had learnt all of this from eavesdropping in the pub. However, Yan had omitted to consider one vital detail: Dom possessed genes that he shared with his murderous ancestor but, had Yan realised this, should he have any cause for concern? After all, he and the other nameless children were already dead.

26   The Unthinkable

The results of the fingerprinting tests were back. Stuart, a friend of Anwen who happened to be studying forensic science, had offered to take the note she had found. He planned to test it for fingerprints and submit it as part of his third year dissertation for his degree. He was as delighted as Anwen when the note was shown to have not one, but two sets of prints upon it. The new test available was even able to shed some light on the gender of those who had made the prints.

'One female, one male,' he reported.

This means that Will could have touched the note, Awen thought.

Stuart continued: 'Do you mind if I hang on to the note for now and do a little more work on it?'

Anwen did mind but felt she owed it to her friend to help with his project, especially in view of how he'd helped her.

'Tell me all you know about this note. The background to it,' Stuart urged. Anwen hesitated.

'Well, only if you want to.' Stuart looked a little hurt and rather miffed.

'It's not that I don't want to tell you, it's just that I don't know very much. The rest is speculation,' she replied.

'Well, just tell me what you know. Stick to the facts. That, at least, will give me something to work on.'

'Okay,' Anwen reluctantly complied. 'I went up to the West Pennines to look into my family history. I'd already discovered quite a lot online. Way back in the mid-1800s a child born to one of my ancestors, the Squire of Dilston Hall, died shortly after birth.'

'Nothing unusual there,' commented Stuart.

'No, I realise that, but there's more to it.'

'Go on,' he encouraged.

'It appears that the child, a boy, was a very wanted baby, a child that was a long time in arriving. The parents were overjoyed that he'd been born and made an announcement in the paper. I've seen the article. Found it online. Then disaster struck. The baby, who they'd named James, died suddenly – from cholera apparently. From what I can establish, using the information I have to hand, the squire didn't tell the mother. Instead he arranged for a servant to dispose of his dead son's body and put another child in his place.'

'Wow!' whistled Stuart. 'And where does the note fit in?'

Anwen recounted the tale and watched the expression on his face change from one of vague interest to heightened anticipation then, finally, to unbridled curiosity.

'That is some story, Anwen. We really have to get to the bottom of this.'

'So, it's 'we' now is it?' she retorted and Stuart smiled.

Jonas was biding his time. Moving furtively round the house, saying little.

'Is everything alright Jonas?' Emily asked, concerned.

'Yes, why?'

'You seem a little on edge that's all,' Emily replied.

'No, all fine with me,' Jonas was anxious to stop the conversation in its tracks but Emily persisted.

'Those three friends of yours. What are their names? Tui, Yan and Bede?'

'What about them?' Jonas was cagey and apprehensive.

'I just wondered if they'd found anywhere to live yet?'

'No, they're still living in the same dreadful place they were in before. No change.'

Jonas might have been forgiven for thinking that Emily was concerned about the three, but he knew beyond any doubt that this line of questioning was not borne out of a desire to determine the state of well-being of his friends, but rather out of a need to find out where they were. Basically, had they left town?

'That's a shame,' and Emily left the room.

Jonas could hear her on the phone to a friend, speaking in low tones that would have been unintelligible to a normal person. But Jonas was not normal and neither was his level of hearing. With a spectrum of hearing that encompassed more low and high frequency sounds than humans were capable of detecting, he was well placed to hear every syllable uttered by Emily's lips. The words came through crisp and clear.

'So you know where they are then? ... 'Have you alerted the council? ... Excellent. And they will definitely take steps to shift them will they? ... Good. When will that be? ... Some time at the end of the month you think – in about two weeks' time? That's very good news. Lovely to think that this time next month I will have no further need to worry about any influence that they might be having on Jonas ... Yes, I really appreciate everything you've done. It's a load off my mind. A great relief actually. See you soon then. Bye.'

Jonas heard the handset being returned to its position and he backed away into the shadows. His friends would soon come under attack and would need a place to hide. He must act and he must act soon. He would act now.

The end, when it came, was as unpredictable as it was quick, as shocking as it was silently conducted. The overwhelming kindness shown by this woman in her middle years to Jonas, No. 4 of the nameless children, was no protection from the dreadful crime that befell her. It was not that Jonas was devoid of feeling. Not at all. But he was wholly devoid of any sort of empathy towards his fellow human beings, if in fact they could be considered as such.

Emily had no inkling it was to happen. Like some notable children before him, Jonas had been carefully nurtured and shown every kindness possible. Like those infamous characters who had made their mark in history had seen their every indulgence satisfied and their every need met in childhood.

But still, the gem of evil that lay deep within them, and within Jonas, surfaced without the slightest indication that there was anything wrong. No sign that in the heart of this outwardly pure child, that had never revealed a glimpse of any ill-doing or deviation from the straight and narrow, there was a gaping hole, a drive to meet an end goal that would not permit anything to stand in its way. It was as if he had never been born with a soul in the first place.

Emily had served her purpose. She had provided Jonas with succour and safety and he had taken all that she had to give him. But Emily had become surplus to his needs. An irritation that he wanted rid of. A thorn in his side. The only saving grace, if there was one, was that she never saw it coming. Emily had gone to her death seemingly with her eyes open wide. She had spent her last few months happier than she had ever been in her life since she had lost her only child David, all those years ago.

Bent over the sink, washing the dishes and singing softly to herself, Emily was in a world of her own. A world where nothing could touch her. Until it did. The thin rope bit deep into her neck and immediately obstructed her breathing. Her fingers clutched at the hands that held the rope. With a look of disbelief and horror in her eyes she fell to the ground, knowing that the hand that feeds you is not always met with the gratitude that it deserves and, in her case, most certainly wasn't.

Shards of light pierced the darkness. The thin curtains were no defence against the strong thrusting rays of the sun. Dom pulled the bedclothes over his head. He had no wish to be up yet. No desire to join the land of the living. The day, and all it held, could wait. But again and again memories jarred his sleeping reverie, refused to let the dreaming images return, prevented him from drifting back into a peaceful oblivion.

Penny knew. She knew everything. At least everything that Dom knew. Why had he told her? How stupid could you get? He should have left her in a state of innocent ignorance. But it was too late. Too late for regret, for recrimination. What was done was done and he would just have to live with it. Should he send her a text to check she was okay, or would it seem too keen, too early in the day? He would leave it for now.

Like sending emails late at night, when your decision-making ability is not at its best, sending a text first thing in the day is equally debatable. Not a good idea, especially when so much was at stake. In the event, Dom need not have worried. As he lay there in a state of idle inertia, a text came through on his phone. Penny wanted to meet to discuss more about last night and what they had talked about. At least she was still communicating with him. For now.

No-one noticed the flies hovering round the refuse bin. Council collections of refuse were now down to once every two weeks, so increased pest presence was inevitable. People were more concerned about the recent rise in the number of rat sightings on their streets than a few flies hovering round what they assumed were the remnants of meals, of decomposing food. No-one thought to check the bins. Indeed no-one had even noticed that anything was amiss.

At number 56 Watkins Street all seemed to roll along as usual. Emily's curtains were drawn to at night and opened again in the morning. The timing was almost to the second, which is how it always had been, for Emily was nothing if not precise. She had a methodological approach to everything and a strict routine that she adhered to with a fierce diligence admired by some of her friends. Not so others who viewed her behaviour as slightly eccentric and bordering on obsessive compulsive disorder. While waiting to buy stamps at the Post Office counter she would unthinkingly straighten out all the little stacks of leaflets and cards so that the edges were perfectly lined up and all sets were parallel to each other.

Yes, Emily liked an orderly life, a fact which had not escaped the attention of Jonas. If he was to avoid suspicion, or the eruption of alarm amongst her neighbours, he must instill in everyone a sense that all was well, that there was no need for any concern. None at all.

'Emily has gone away to visit a sick friend in the south of England and is expected back at the end of the month' was the line he churned out whenever he met one of Emily's friends in the high street in town. His explanation was accepted without question. All except for one. One person did not take this story at face value.

'Are you sure she's gone away?' Emily's friend, Vanessa, fired at Jonas, piercing his inner calm with her gaze.

'Absolutely, you can come to the house to see for yourself if you like.'

The challenge, thrown out rather recklessly Jonas thought immediately after he'd said it, had the desired effect. The friend seemed placated and a little flustered, almost as if she felt, with hindsight, that she had overstepped the mark by challenging Jonas. After all Emily thought the world of him. What harm could have come to her? Still, it was extremely strange that her friend had not mentioned a word about going on a trip.

'It was very quickly arranged. She got a phone call a few days ago to say that a friend needed her help urgently and she left immediately,' Jonas added as if able to see what the woman was thinking.

'Yes, of course. That sounds just like Emily. Always thinking about others. Well, I'll be off now Jonas. Enjoy your day.'

And all the time Emily's body lay undetected.

Jonas had his timing all wrong. He had not planned things carefully. The refuse bins had been emptied the day before Emily's untimely demise. There were now twelve long days to wait until they were emptied again. Strange how time appears to pass more slowly when one is desperate for it to pass quickly. If Jonas had looked out of the window once at the bin standing by the gate, he must have looked a hundred times. Like someone obsessed, as indeed he was, he could not tear his eyes away from the offending object. One night he woke up at 3.00 am with an almost uncontrollable urge to go to the bin, remove Emily's body and dispose of it elsewhere.

But where exactly? The town was nowhere near the sea, positioned as it was close to the West Pennine range. Likewise, no deep crevasses presented themselves as likely places to access easily and tip a body. Plus which it would only be a matter of time before a walker would chance to come across the remains of what had once been his landlady. No – not landlady. Benefactor. Still not quite right. How would Jonas describe Emily to someone, if asked?

A kindly lady who had taken him in when he was most in need, made him welcome, offered him a home, given him food, treated him like a son. The son she had lost.

Had Jonas been capable of emotion he would have felt deep remorse for what he had done. But this was not likely to happen. Not now. Not ever. The only consideration he had for anyone other than himself he reserved for the other nameless children and their recent acquisitions, Saul and the dog Bella.

Time continued to be meted out slowly, minute by each halting minute being drawn over the coals. Jonas found the pressing urgency of each day force him into a state of almost complete inertia. For two entire days he sat, trance-like, in his room, cross-legged and facing the wall. Like someone who has experienced a tremendous shock, by opening a letter to read that their entire family has been wiped out, he had adopted the posture associated with catatonic freezing of the body. Either intentionally, or otherwise, Jonas had removed himself from any emotional impact and potential suffering. When he emerged from the trance after two days, he observed only that he was several pounds lighter in weight and craved water. Other than that, nothing. It did, however, strike him as somewhat contradictory that he should experience nothing, one way or the other, now that Emily was no longer there to take care of him, and yet, at the same time, he was extremely anxious that her dead body should remain undiscovered.

Jonas was not wholly devoid of emotion it would seem, but was only affected when an event might serve to impact him and the life he had been accustomed to living. As all the nameless children had an unbreakable bond, what affected them automatically affected him, and so he had chosen to act to improve their living conditions.

Finally the day for the refuse collection came and went. The large wagon rumbled down the street, tipped the contents of the bin inside, returned it to an upright position and moved on to the next row of bins lined up sentry-like. From behind the curtains Jonas watched the whole process from start to finish. Only when the vehicle had reached the end of the street, turned a corner and vanished from view, did his shoulders finally fall and his breath leave him in a sigh of relief. There was not a moment to lose. As fast as his legs would carry him he went to the disused toilet, to the dwelling of the others.

'Emily has gone,' he announced, breathless.

'What? On holiday?' asked Yan.

'No, permanently. Don't ask any more questions. Just accept it. She has gone. The house is mine. You can come and live with me.'

'How is the house yours?' Tui this time.

Jonas was quick to reply.

'She left me the house in her will. Put me down as her next of kin.'

'What if she comes back?' Tui again.

'She won't be coming back.' His reply was both definite and final. As he imparted the words Jonas shot a warning look at Yan and Bede. A look that said everything they needed to know. Emily was not coming back, as Jonas had made sure that she wouldn't, and this topic was no longer open for discussion. Yan took control of the situation.

'Gather up your things everyone. We're on the move. Get Bella's lead. Keep her close.'

As the sun rose in the sky that day, the house that had once held Emily and Jonas now held four nameless children, Saul and a dog. The ownership of the house would never be disputed. When the will came to be read, some way down the line, there it would be in black and white: next of kin Jonas Chase. Emily had not only given her house and her life to the undeserving creature that was Jonas, she had, with typical generosity of spirit, also conferred on him her surname. As the seagulls picked over her bones, on a landfill site in the south of England, the group settled down under her roof to begin life in their new home.

27   An Element of Doubt

'What did you want to discuss?' Dom was nervous and apprehensive.

'Just what we were talking about last night. The bottom line, basically, appears to be that one of your ancestors murdered one of mine,' Penny replied.

'Yes,' agreed Dom, 'but it was a long, long time ago. Surely you're not holding me responsible?' He turned to face Penny, spirits downcast as he felt any connection with her slipping away, any bond that might have developed being broken, the threads of communication being stretched to breaking point.

'Of course not. That would be ridiculous. It would make no sense at all. You can't blame the wrong doings of the fathers on the sons.'

'But every day, in every part of the world, that is exactly what people do,' proclaimed Dom.

'Yes, but I am not other people. I think for myself.'

Dom breathed a sigh of relief. Penny continued:

'But there is something I think you should know: that you are entitled to know. Yan, who you have met on a few occasions, has rather a different view of the situation. Like me he is also related to the drowned girl.'

'How?!' Dom shot back, surprised.

'I'm not exactly sure. He won't say. It's just that he seems to be obsessed with finding out exactly who it was that committed the murder.'

'Why? What does he plan to do about it, if and when he finds out?'

'No idea. I just thought I should warn you.'

'Warn me?' Dom was now more than surprised. He was alarmed. 'He's not coming after me is he?'

'I don't think so. We have grown quite close recently but he doesn't tell me everything.'

Dom's lips tightened and his hands clenched.

'Why are you spending time with someone who is threatening?' he asked.

'Well, he's very nice to me.'

I bet he is, thought Dom.

'But recently I've realised he might not be all he claims to be,' she continued.

'What's that? What does he claim to be?' Dom was curious.

'He says he's been travelling round the UK with his friends, looking into their family history.'

'What! There are more of them?'

'Three actually and recently I understand that another has joined them – and a dog.'

'A dog?' The situation was becoming stranger by the minute. 'Okay, let's leave it for now. Thanks for letting me know. We're still friends, yes?'

'Of course.' Penny squeezed his arm before pulling her bike towards her to set off.

All is not lost with her at any rate, thought Dom. But as for Yan, that is another matter entirely.

Rain bounced off the ground. With harsh purposefulness it hit the pavement and Penny. At first she failed to notice the driving force. Only when she felt a seeping wetness dampen her skin did she make any attempt to cover herself. Facts discovered over the past few days had occupied her mind and rendered her insensible to external events. She had almost forgotten to eat until reminded by her Uncle Jack during a recent visit to the smithy.

'You look like you're wasting away,' he had told her. 'You resemble a mere shadow of your former self. Here, get some toast inside you.'

Absent-mindedly Penny took the offered toast and proceeded to eat it without comment.

'Anything bothering you?' Jack asked.

'Yes and no,' Penny replied with a wry smile.

'Well, which is it? Yes or no?'

'Sorry. I was miles away. Just something that Dom told me the other evening. To do with our family. Something he found out.'

'Good or bad?'

'Mostly not good,' again came the non-committal, enigmatic response.

'Bad then?' Jack concluded.

'Pretty bad,' she concurred. 'Way back in the 1800s, the period in history that I've been investigating, there was a child born to a member of our family. Someone called Dora. She was only fourteen and worked as a maid in the Andover household.'

'Isn't Dom an 'Andover'?' her uncle asked.

'Yes, he is.'

'And he knows all about this?'

'He told me most of it. His mother found out quite a lot, then Dom discovered more on the back of that.'

'And the gate is somehow involved in all of this?'

'Yes, that's what got me interested in the first place, as you know. A desire to discover the meaning of the inscription and symbol on the gate.'

'But you've known that for some time. So what's new?'

'I think I was related to Dora, the one whose baby was drowned under orders from the Andover family.'

'Well, yes, I can see that there would be a link, but it's equally possible that you were descended from one of her brothers, or even her sisters, isn't it?' Jack was keen to force Penny out of her brooding, dark mood. It was moods like this that took her down. Down to a dark place where no-one could reach her. Where communication was futile, talking was to no avail, all modes of contact became severed.

Penny would return to rocking in a corner, sitting on the floor against the wall, with her hands clasped round her knees and her head down. This could go on for hours and all the time a low moaning would issue from the automaton that she had become. Jack had no wish for this to happen and would avert impending disaster at all costs, using every method at his disposal. Then, just as the conversation appeared to have ground to a halt, it began again.

'I think I am directly descended from her,' Penny whispered. 'Going back five or six generations.'

'How can you be sure?' gently now Jack searched for answers.

'I feel it,' came the answer, pleading for acknowledgement, for acceptance that what she was saying was the truth. 'It is in the bone. In my bones.'

'Don't you mean 'in the blood'?' Jack contradicted, anxious not to upset her but keen to understand what she was trying to explain.

'No!' Penny was adamant. 'In the bone. When something has occurred repeatedly for several generations, such that the next generation automatically follows suit, it is said to be 'in the bone'. The first time a member of a family goes to university this change in tradition is said to be 'in the blood'. When this is followed by members of the next two generations going to university, it becomes the norm. It is then expected that all future members of the family will go to university. It becomes the 'done thing'. The practice is now 'in the bone'.'

'I still don't see how going to university has anything to do with you thinking that you are directly

linked to the serving maid whose child was drowned.'
Jack was perplexed.

'Don't you see?' asked Penny. 'I know it's true. I've seen it in my dreams. I have a fear of water, of open expanses of water, of deep ponds, of lakes, of the sea.'

'Yes, but...'

Penny cut him short:

'I have inherited this fear of water from Dora. She would have hated water after her baby was taken from her and drowned. It's in my very genes. It's in the bone.' And with that Penny smiled sadly at her uncle, took another piece of toast from the table and left the smithy.

Jack could only gaze after her, feeling helpless and exasperated that he had not been able to do more to alleviate his niece's pain, to help her in her hour of need, to lessen her suffering. Maybe there was something he could do though. Try to establish the exact truth behind the death of the drowned child. Hopefully, he would learn that Penny was not directly descended from the child's mother, Dora. That would ease Penny's mind and lighten her load. Unless, of course, what he found out merely served to consolidate her findings, fix them in stone and fan the flames of the inner turmoil that Penny was now experiencing. What then?

28   A Growing Intrigue

The weekend came to an end. So much learned. So much still to learn. Anwen was being overwhelmed by a growing sense that she belonged here, in this small town in the West Pennines. A town where she knew no-one and no-one knew her. A place where she had no living connections.

None living maybe, but many dead, the thought flitted across her mind. She was torn two ways. Whether to go back home to the Welsh Valleys, to the town that she had grown up in, where she had been born, where everyone knew her – or whether to stay here and find out more about her past.

'Living history'. Isn't that what they call it? To live in the place that held her ancestors, their gravestones, their secrets. To discover more about the family Elver who had lived for generations at Dilston Hall and who had brought into their midst the changeling. The innocent child who was removed from his family and assumed the role of family member of the Elvers. The child who, by default, continued the family lie. But this was not 'in the bone' as Penny would say. Neither was it 'in the blood'. It was by way of subterfuge, deceit and a web of lies that the changeling had superseded little James. Had become him.

Who had done this? Anwen wanted to know. Who had dismissed his son so easily and had, with equal heartlessness and apparent indifference, inserted a stranger in the child's place? A replacement son for his wife to love and rear as her own.

All would have been well if the deed had been above board, transparency established; if the wife had known that her little son had died and that here was another little boy that needed love and succour. A child whose own parents could not afford to keep him. Yes, if it had all been done by the book, and the original James had received a fitting burial and resting place, all would indeed have been well. But all was not well. No. 3 of the nameless children, Bede, was consummate proof that a serious misdemeanour had been committed and someone would be held responsible. Taken to task for it.

Anwen, in turn, was resolute that she would find her true source of origin, the farm labourers who parted with their child, handed him over without a second glance. It was not only the family Elver who should take responsibility for the exchange of a child for money so many years ago. The family of the changeling also had much to answer for. She would stay here for the foreseeable future and see what secrets she could unearth. And following her every movement would be Bede, who was eager to discover all he could for a different reason. Anwen wanted an explanation while Bede wanted justice and he would stop at nothing to get it.

Penny was drawn to Yan, not through words alone. The passage of time had not dimmed the genetic memory or laid waste the threads of history that connected them. But the attraction, if that's what it could be called, ran deeper, far deeper. Embedded within her psyche, at the very core of her being, lay crystals of purpose, gems of intent. Channelled within the deep recesses of the mind that belonged to Yan were almost identical concepts, particles of wisdom, seeds of knowing.

It was through these shared facts that Yan held Penny in his thrall. When she was with him time seemed to stand still, the future ceased to exist. All that she felt was a growing hunger. A desire to discover the whole truth and make someone take responsibility for the death of Tui.

The dead were dead. Or were they? In her more lucid moments Penny's thoughts appeared to challenge themselves, to offer contradiction upon contradiction. Left her mind churning like soup on the boil. Set her adrift like a small boat bobbing on the high seas. Only when Dom appeared did her thoughts begin to calm and rush to cluster together, to belong once more to her. It was then that her heart would beat at regular intervals, no longer speeding up and slowing down as if torn between a flight or fight scenario. Dom presented no challenge to her senses, let her think her own thoughts, let her be herself.

But still she was drawn to Yan. His persona blanketed her and removed her will, her ability to behave with reason and act from wholesome beginnings and benevolent thought. Stamped on any desire to spread her wings and pursue her innermost longings. Showed her other paths and opportunities. Took her on the road less travelled. For creative people this road normally holds great promise, dictates that new adventures will be found, new goals achieved, fresh opportunities realised.

Not so with Yan. With Yan, the road Penny chose was not welcoming and did not offer hope for the future. It was the road followed by someone with a focused obsession, a grinding determination to achieve one sole purpose. And with this road there was no turning back. It could be argued that the unbending attitude, held so firmly aloft by Yan, allowed no distraction from the object of his desire, and is one way – no – the only way to achieve success. But it is a dismal path to take.

Penny, should she decide to work hand in hand with Yan, would undoubtedly discover the underlying basis for the force that was driving him, but his might not be the most logical route to follow when attempting to draw a line under the drowning of Tui. For Yan uncompromising revenge might be the solution to the problem, but then Yan had no soul.

He would not be concerned by the effect his actions might have on others, on the living. The actions which seemed to be gravitating more and more towards an inevitable conclusion. The removal of Dom. Once Penny's eyes began to open, and she started to think clearly, the disturbing facts would reveal themselves to her in stark detail.

Yan intended to perpetrate a crime that would result in the disappearance of Dom – to vanish him from the world. His mother would never know what had happened to her precious son. She would never know peace. To all intents her life would be over for:

'It is not death that forces us to linger,
 O'er the passing of a loved one or a friend,
 Nor the fact that they are gone forever,
 But the lack of knowing what befell them at the end'

These words kept coming back to Penny. She had no recollection where she had first heard them, or seen them written, only that they were carved into her memory like an inscription on stone. Why they kept surfacing in her mind was a cause for concern for her. Why these words out of the hundreds of sayings that she had come across in her short life? She let them slide over her tongue effortlessly. What did they mean? Apart from an obvious dwelling on death, and the loss of someone close to you, they appeared to offer no great revelation concerning the meaning of life. *But the lack of knowing what befell them at the end*. Presumably this was a reference to not knowing how someone had died, or whether indeed they had actually died at all but were merely unavailable to the living. Were out of communication.

Then it came to her. Like the sudden slamming of a door within earshot, or a bullet fired at close quarters from a gun. She knew where she had seen these words before. Watching the trio busking one day she had suddenly become aware of the things placed in their collecting bowl. Other than money, and the inevitable odd foreign coins, there appeared from time to time little printed cards. Some held contact details for people desperate to promote their business, though how they thought that penniless musicians might be in a position to take advantage of this information, and avail themselves of the opportunities inherent in the promised words, was open to question.

A few wooden beads lay at the bottom of the bowl, day in and day out, looking like the discarded contents of someone's pocket. Someone who had worn long strings of wooden beads back in the late 1960s when it was the thing to do – if you were young, without responsibility, carefree or simply a hippy.

Amongst all these pieces of social driftwood lay a card with no website, no QR code, no contact details whatsoever. It merely held the words that showed themselves to Penny at every available opportunity.

THE NAMELESS CHILDREN

Whenever she let her mind wander, or felt herself drifting off to sleep, then they would appear. Unsummoned, and often unwanted, they would present themselves in her field of vision to be read. Even when she opened her eyes they would still be there, as if painted in the air or strung up, puppet-like, from a suspended bar. Now, as she focused on them, they began to sharpen in her mind and she could read them clearly. As if on demand she could recreate the scene.

She was standing in front of the trio as they performed on the street. Gazing down into the bowl she could see the card quite clearly. This time something different swam into view. Something that had been there all along but she had never noticed it. The last line had been underlined with red ink. Not once, but twice. *Who had done this?*

Then, in an instant, she knew the answer. Yan had done this. It was he who returned the card to the bowl every day. The defaced card with its singular notation highlighting these few words. He was using it as a mantra, as an affirmation. It served as both a reminder and a promise, a declaration to himself that something needed to be done. That he would be the one to do it and that he would move heaven and earth to make sure it happened. But what did he intend to do? Penny's brow furrowed with concentration as she sought the answer... '*But the lack of knowing what befell them at the end.*'

What act befell someone and who did it befall? Meditate on it, she thought. *Let your mind go blank and your question will be answered. Your search will be over.*

She slipped into a trance like a diver slips under water, seamlessly and without a trace of a ripple. *Who is under threat?* She asked silently of the universe. The answer came back crystal clear. An unambiguous response:

'Dom. Dom is under threat.'

With this revelation the trance broke and Penny stared into space. *Who was threatening Dom?* But before the last word had impressed itself on her consciousness the answer came back. As she saw once more the underlined words in the collecting bowl she knew who constituted a threat to her friend. There was only one possible contender: Yan.

Penny felt overwhelmed by terror and an urgent need to contact Dom, to alert him to possible danger. She fumbled for her mobile phone and, in doing so, managed to let it fall from her fingers. She clutched wildly as it fell to the ground, the case splintering as it hit concrete. Down she went, bending to retrieve her precious – her only – method of communication.

The light was fading and Penny blindly swiped her hands along the ground in her frantic search for the elusive object. Her hands made contact, but all too quickly, knocking the phone further away and into a puddle. Desperation began to take hold as she grew ever more frantic. She clutched the phone and saw that the display on the screen appeared to have gone – no – it was still there, although somewhat muted. She tried to phone Dom. The phone began to ring out, *Dom* clearly visible on the screen, but quickly went to voicemail.

'Pick up Dom. Please pick up,' Penny pleaded with him, venting her frustration on the elements. The thin wind that whipped her hair into her eyes, the splashes of rain upon her skin, did nothing to allay the feeling of dread that pervaded her being and cloaked her senses with helplessness. She tried again. And again. And again. No reply.

Penny tried to console herself with the knowledge that Dom often switched off his phone, or set it to silent, when he was practising his guitar. He tried to set aside half an hour a day to devote to this and usually played with his eyes closed. No need to look at the notes on the page, he played by ear and 'I can concentrate better when my eyes are closed,' he had told her. But a voice at the back of her mind began to grow and would not be stilled.

What if Dom was not playing his guitar? What if he was being stopped from answering his phone by something, or someone?

Black thoughts permeated her brain. With no further ado she began to run as fast as she could to where her bike was stationed. Head down against the wind, with the lashing rain beating upon her back and legs, she made for Grange Manor.

Dom still lived at home. Cheaper to study when you had no rent to pay, especially when the course he wanted to study was on his doorstep. Penny pounded on the door and Sue, Dom's mother, answered, with alarm written across her face. Before Sue had chance to phrase a sentence Penny blurted out her reason for being there.

'Is Dom in?'

'No, he's out in town with friends I think.'

'Are you sure?'

'What's this about?' Dom's father pushed forwards to the door.

'I just wanted to see him,' Penny replied.

'And you've come out here in the pouring rain and at this time of night? It's nearly 11 pm. You must be desperate. Come inside.'

Penny allowed herself to be ushered into the warm, cosy living room of Grange Manor.

'It's nothing really,' she floundered, hesitant to voice her anxieties with the realisation that they would sound like the ravings of a mad woman.

'It must be something,' Dom's father persisted. 'Can't you tell us? We won't bite.'

'I'm just a bit worried that someone might be out to get him.'

'Who, exactly?'

'Just someone who might be a bit jealous of him.'

'Like a love rival you mean? Someone else who's interested in you?'

Penny nodded and hung her head.

'Have they made any actual threats, whoever it is?'

'Not as such,' Penny admitted. 'It's just a feeling I have.'

'I'm sure he's fine. Let's try to phone him again and leave a voicemail.' As he spoke he looked at his wife who seemed anything but convinced that everything was going to be fine. The mere suggestion that her beloved son might be in danger was enough to put the fear of God in her and she began to tremble and sway slightly.

'Here, sit down. I'll get you both a cup of sweet tea, but I'll phone Dom first and leave him a message.'

Two cups of tea and five voicemails later, the three looked as one towards the clock as it began to chime 3.00 am. Dom was always home by midnight. No-one dared to speak the words, the words of finality, of fear. The words that would be held up and examined as a portent of doom. The words that held no hope or promise of a good outcome. Dom was not coming home. Someone was holding him against his will. His free will that had been abruptly curtailed by another. At some point during the last few hours Dom had been removed from his life, from his family and from Penny. Removed to an unknown place. It was now up to his family to get him back.

29   Trapped

His first sensation was of feeling cold. A cold dampness permeated his body. Unfamiliar sounds railed against his senses. A sweet musty smell hung in the air. Barely conscious, he stretched. His fingers met a soft wetness and his eyes opened. Alien walls confronted him. He closed his eyes. This would be a dream. When he opened them again all would be restored to normality. His bedroom at Grange Manor, with all the comfort and security it offered, would be there to greet him this time. Not so.

Dom had heard of lucid dreams where you were dreaming but were aware that you were. This was not a lucid dream. This was the opposite. Here he felt very strongly that he was totally and absolutely awake and in full possession of his faculties, but he wished with all his heart that it was a dream. For you can wake from a dream, but you cannot wake from reality.

He opened his fingers and moved them across a wall. Was the wall behind him or to the side? Hard to tell at first then, as his eyes became dark-adapted, the full extent of his surroundings became evident. Like a building that rises through the mist as you approach it so the objects in his immediate vicinity made themselves known to him. An upturned bin (plastic?) lay on the floor directly ahead of him, a low table to his left and what appeared to be a wall directly to his right – the wall that he was leaning against.

He tried to stand, managed a half-way position, and then fell back down. Something was restraining him, gripping his ankles. Nervously his fingers reached down to investigate. Cold steel. Unrelenting, unforgiving steel. He was shackled, held in position, restrained by metal grips round both ankles. Secured to prevent him from standing up. Fastened tightly to prevent escape. A wave of cold fear passed over him and he leant forwards to be sick. *Not possible. None of this. Not real!*

He began to hyperventilate and rock backwards and forwards as panic took over. He shook his head from side to side as his thoughts became scrambled and he desperately sought answers. Impossible to determine anything, solve any puzzles, when your mind is scrambled.

Clear your head. Breathe slowly. Calm down. Like a mantra he processed these thoughts time and again until, slowly, the fog that obscured his mental vision began to clear. In order to formulate a solution to a problem, first know your problem. Define the parameters clearly. Set out a plan, one step at a time. List the objectives by all means, but first assess the problem. *What did he last remember? Think now.*

Walking home from the library last night – or was it still the same night? What time was it?

Always dependent on his mobile phone as a time piece, he searched frantically about him. No phone. Panic was beginning to set in.

Do not panic. Keep calm. The inner voice of survival. The voice that lies within all of us and, when the going gets tough, when your physical being or your sanity is threatened, comes to the fore in your hour of need.

And so it was with Dom. No phone. No idea what time of day it was and hence no idea how long he had been down there. *Was it down – or was it up?* He had no way of knowing.

Back to last night. Focus. Walking home from the library. Missed the last bus – early in these parts – 10.30 pm. An impossible bus service but at least it still operated in these far-flung parts of the UK, in these small towns in the West Pennines. *Just leaving town. Hearing footsteps. Were they behind him or to the side? Think now! The footsteps growing louder. Someone approaching.* He turned to look, slightly apprehensive in case he was about to be mugged for his phone or the small amount of change he had on him. Then a face that he knew came clearly into focus. Dom breathed a sigh of relief.

Yan. It was just Yan catching him up for a chat.

All the alarm bells stopped ringing, all defensive mechanisms were withdrawn. No longer on full alert, Dom relaxed into an easy, strolling walk.

'Do you fancy a drink at my place?' Yan offered.

Like a spider reels in the fly, with cunning deception and subterfuge, Yan drew Dom in and Dom went with him. Nothing about Yan, his conversation, body language or mood, conveyed anything other than friendship. Dom was quietly pleased that he had an unforeseen opportunity to get to know his rival a little better, to get the measure of him. Never had Dom read anyone's intentions so incorrectly, got anyone so absolutely and completely wrong.

He remembered reaching a building on the outskirts of town.

'Is this where you live?' he asked. 'It's a bit off the beaten track.'

'Yes, I like to be away from the crowds,' came the reply.

'I thought you lived with your friends, Tui and Bede?'

'Sometimes,' Yan replied absentmindedly.

Dom thought this to be a rather strange answer but felt disinclined to pursue the matter.

'Here we are.' Yan pushed open the door to the disused toilet that had once housed the trio, and later Saul and Bella too, until their recent move to Emily's house. The place still had a slightly lived-in look about it. Dom stifled his temptation to voice what he was thinking: that this wasn't remotely a place where anyone would choose to live.

And he was right, the nameless children had not chosen to live here. They had had no choice in the matter. Faced with the option of a clearing in the forest, or the disused toilet, the decision had been made for them. But then curiosity got the better of Dom.

'What is this place? It looks like a disused toilet from Victorian times.'

'Exactly right,' replied Yan. 'Let me show you round.'

Back to the present now and a vague memory crept into Dom's mind: Yan opening a door to reveal a flight of steps. After that nothing.

Had he fallen and become trapped there or had Yan pushed him? But if he had fallen surely Yan would have saved him, brought him back up?

Truth, when it finally impacts the mind can deliver a devastating blow. He was not there by accident. He had been enticed there, pushed into a cellar, rendered unconscious by the fall and then shackled to the floor – and Yan? Yan was nowhere to be seen. In the glimmering darkness, with waves of claustrophobia pressing upon him from all sides, Dom faced up to his situation. He was trapped below ground in an unknown part of town without his phone and no-one, but no-one, knew where he was.

30   Still Missing

Saul and Tui had grown close, something that had not gone unnoticed by the others. Yan had initially been unhappy by this development but felt reassured that Saul, while not being a nameless child as such, was very closely linked to them. It was impossible not to admit that Saul fitted in well with their group and had taken easily to the life. Indeed it fitted him like a glove. Although still apprehensive about appearing in public, while the others were busking, he had become more and more confident of late and would go into shops and buy food with their earnings. He no longer looked like the 'old' Saul.

It was nearly three months since he had been swallowed up by the ground, embraced by the soil, dragged below by outstretched hands that reached out to him from the vertical grave that lay at the edge of the burial ground. His was now a 'cold case'. His file lay categorised as such in one of the many drawers at the local police station.

'We haven't given up on him. Please be assured of that,' the police reiterated for the umpteenth time, when yet again Saul's parents came on the phone asking for news. When all the time there was no news. No sighting to give them a slender thread of optimism, something to focus on, a reason to hope.

Hard to believe that their son had just vanished from the face of the earth.

'Does he ever go potholing in local caves?' One policewoman tried to offer a grain of hope, something to clutch at.

But, no, Saul had never been down a pothole in his life. So another avenue of possible investigation was closed, slammed shut and bolted tight. The 'missing person' posters grew tired and tattered and the wind carried them away. The case might well be 'ongoing', but essentially it was closed. The town had moved on. People were beginning to forget. Life had got in the way of thinking about Saul, the missing teenager.

But Saul was no longer missing. He was living out his life in the same town as his parents. He was, however, not easily spotted, having adopted a disguise which rendered him unrecognisable to his family and friends who had known him so well. This was no accident. Tui had mentioned that really he ought to change his appearance so he would not have to return to his former life. Cheap hair dye, growing his hair long and wearing a pair of dark-rimmed glasses with clear lenses, had done the trick. So effective was the guise that, on several occasions, Saul's parents had passed within feet of their son without noticing him. He was invisible in plain sight. Incredible though it seemed, it dawned on Saul that people only see what they expect to see. Had his parents looked closely they would have detected, under the unkempt locks and glasses, their son. Very much alive.

In the meantime Saul, Tui and Bella trod the streets of the small town. Wove their way in and out of the tight cobbled lanes. Hung about in the shadows. Sought out the corners where the hidden people lived. Led what could be called an existence of sorts. They belonged to the community of people who live on the edge. Today they ventured out into the sunshine.

'Let's sit by the fountain in the square and read our books. Bella loves the sun.' Tui looked hopefully at Saul. He hesitated, but only for a moment. Carried along by her enthusiasm he let himself be cajoled into sitting in full view of the passing public. It was market day and the crowds spilled over onto the streets which were closed to traffic. Saul leaned back on the bench, eyes closed, enjoying the sun.

Approaching the fountain, on her way to the market, was his mother. But she was not alone. In tow was the springer spaniel, Muffin, a dog that had been in the family since Saul was six years old. Adopted from a dog rescue home, Muffin had been rehomed and renamed. Her history was typical of most dogs that found themselves in a dogs' home. Not beaten as such, but still cruelly treated. Left on her own for up to ten hours at a time by a couple who thought it would be nice to have a dog but had given no thought or consideration to what its needs might be. The continuous barking of the neglected dog had led to complaints from neighbours and the eventual delivery of the dog to the dogs' home.

'We can't cope with her. She won't stop barking,' was the excuse given when they presented the innocent victim of their careless, selfish ways.

'How long was she left on her own during the day?' asked the staff at the dogs' home.

'Oh, no more than ten hours,' came the reply.

'Right,' said the staff member through gritted teeth. 'She's going to be better off here then, with us. Hopefully we can find her a loving home with people who will care for her,' staring at the couple, who backed away looking shame-faced, and then made a dash for their car. Once outside, the look of obvious relief on their faces that they no longer had any responsibility for the dog belied the supposed regret they felt. Betrayed the mask they had presented. Showed their total lack of concern for their dog and the fact that they had failed her. Showed them up for what they really were – people who should never be allowed to keep animals. Ever.

Finding herself in a household where she was cared for and loved, catapulted into a new world where loneliness was a thing of the past, overwhelmed Muffin. She formed an immediate and unbreakable bond with each member of the family. Truth be told, she was the only family member that

Saul actually missed. Had he thought about it more carefully he would have realised that he might be able to fool his parents with his new disguise but never, in a month of Sundays, would he be able to fool his dog.

They were now so close that Muffin accidentally brushed against Saul's leg. Instantly she stopped walking, swivelled round and became very animated. Like a sniffer dog that has suddenly found an offending piece of fruit in a backpack at a New Zealand airport, she leapt into action and proceeded to dance about. She pounced onto Saul's knee in delight. Jolted awake from his reverie, his first reaction was to throw his arms around his darling Muffin until he caught sight of the warning look from Tui. On no account should he acknowledge Muffin.

'Come on Muffin, let's get going,' his mother muttered, apologising at the same time to her son, without giving the slightest indication that she recognised him. Saul refrained from replying, instead letting Tui do it for him.

'That's okay. No problem.' The pair watched as Saul's mother and his beloved dog wandered off in the direction of the market.

'That was hard,' Saul commented.

'Yes, but it would have been harder still if your mother had recognised you and wanted to take you home with her.'

Saul nodded but a creeping thought trickled through his mind that perhaps it might not be too bad to return to his old life, as long as he could take Tui and Bella with him. Behind the façade of indifference and selfishness that was incessantly cultivated by the nameless children, there was a crystal that had begun to vibrate. A tentative reaching out to the past with a desire to combine this with his present, to form a different future. To break away from the chaotic lifestyle led by the five of them in Emily's house.

Again a persistent thought returned to his mind: *Where was Emily?* Jonas had given an explanation that had served to satisfy the other three, but for Saul had something lacking. He was uneasy and day by passing day he became more and more convinced that something untoward had happened to Emily and that Jonas was at the root of it.

31 Fingerprints

Stuart had been busy. After discovering two sets of fingerprints, other than Anwen's, on the note she had found in the wall at Dilston Hall, he had been propelled into action. He'd managed to persuade his supervisor to let him change the title of his project and was now able to focus fully on gathering all the information he could from the piece of paper.

Carbon dating confirmed that the note had been around since the mid-1800s and the ink used to write the note also fitted in with the same time period. Gradually a picture began to emerge.

'Who were Emma and Will?' Anwen wanted to know. Stuart admitted that he had no idea and that forensic science, while being an exact science, was not capable of seeing into the past where this matter was concerned.

'It will only show me what I can discern using the tests currently available,' he told her. 'The rest is up to you. Can't you find out anything by looking at records for staff employed at Dilston Hall in the 1800s?'

'I've already looked online but nothing so far.'

'Have you checked the local church? Looked at the Parish Records? They are a mine of information.'

Anwen felt greatly encouraged at this suggestion. She wondered whether Bede had uncovered anything of import and realised she hadn't seen him for a couple of weeks. Tomorrow she would look out for him busking in town, aware that he would most likely only offer her information if she had something to share with him.

She tried to think what she could say that would tempt him to reveal what he knew about the changeling, about little James. Even though they had formed a close bond Anwen did not trust Bede completely, not on every level. So far she had only mentioned that she was descended from the changeling. She had deliberately omitted any reference to the note in the wall. This was a journey of discovery that she wished to make alone. Alone but with Stuart helping her.

Stuart was not related to the Elver family that had dismissed little James, and so constituted no threat to Anwen's mission: her desire to find her original beginnings, the family that handed over the changeling to serve as a substitute for James. The substitute that grew up with a life of luxury and a level of finery and comfort unheard of amongst the farming people that included his parents, his family. Well, not unheard of exactly, but certainly not experienced.

Hopefully, Emma and Will, and whatever happened to them, would shed light on the circumstances surrounding the whole episode. Yes, Stuart would be a good companion to help decipher patterns, to piece together parts of the jigsaw. For Stuart had no ulterior motive, unlike Bede who was out for revenge. As the ousted child Bede had good reason to seek revenge. But sometimes revenge is best left, injustice not acted upon, the status quo maintained.

With Bede, his inner turmoil drove him on. He could not rest until he had achieved his goal. While Stuart, the hard-working science student whose face was like an open book – now there was someone who was dependable, an emotionally stable person who Anwen could lean on.

But people are not always what they seem. Once certain information has been made available to them, see how quickly the wind changes, how dramatically their personality flips, how quickly the façade of stability and normality deserts them. Yes, it is often those who present us with an ostensibly friendly and open nature who are found to be hiding a web of lies and deceit, are capable of turning on a sixpence and of becoming self-serving in the extreme.

For now all was calm and amiable between Anwen and her scientist friend, as the discovery that would change their lives had not yet been made.

The books were heavy in the extreme. And dusty. Anwen blew off the cobwebs and carried the first tome to an oak table in the library. Having promised to be very careful and only to 'turn each page by the corner, slowly', she began to read. Much irrelevant detail lay upon the pages but occasionally a gem stopped the flow and caused her to reread the sentence or paragraph. So many years ago, so many interesting lives led by the characters personified on these pages. Records that held dates and places for all those who were born and had died in the parish.

With no surnames to help her, Anwen felt overwhelmed by the task ahead. How on earth could she track down Will or Emma amongst this great mass of information? A difficult task indeed. *But not impossible*, came the voice of optimism that surfaced whenever Anwen needed a helping hand, a few words of comfort, a shoulder to lean on.

Most achievements are born of perseverance, through a desire to seek out the truth, to focus on the main goal, to not be distracted by anything or anyone. So Anwen continued. Long into the evening she read, until there came soft padding footsteps followed by a light hand on her shoulder and the announcement:

'We will be closing soon. We will be open again in the morning should you choose to come back.'

Anwen was hooked to the job in hand and would indeed be coming back.

32   A Step Closer

'Something a little odd happened today.'

Saul's father looked up from his book, eyebrows raised questioningly at his wife.

'We were at the market, Muffin and I, when she seemed to recognise someone. She certainly acted like that at any rate. In fact, had I not known better I would have said that she was greeting Saul.'

Her husband turned with renewed interest.

'It was the way she tried to jump onto his knee.'

'Whose knee?' interrupted Saul's father.

'A guy that was sitting by the fountain in the square. You remember how Muffin used to jump onto Saul's knee when she first came to live with us? Well that was what she did, or rather tried to do, today. Strangely enough she did it with a complete stranger.'

Saul's father became very animated and let his book fall to the floor.

'Tell me about this guy? What did he look like? Is there any way it might have been Saul?' he pleaded, desperate for answers.

'Well, to be honest, I didn't get a close look at him. I was in a hurry to get to the fruit and vegetable stall on the market, so I just apologised for the dog's behaviour and pulled her away.' She stopped and thought for a moment. 'But someone was with him. Someone said something. A girl. She said it wasn't a problem, or something like that.'

'Close your eyes and think carefully. Try to get a picture in your mind of the girl and the guy with her. See if you can conjure up their faces.'

'She was wearing a parka jacket, army camouflage colour, with a fur hood. He was a bit taller than her, long dark hair, dark framed glasses. I couldn't see his eyes through his hair. They had a dog with them.' Her husband broke in.

'A dog! So in spite of them having a dog, Muffin still made a beeline for the boy. Doesn't that strike you as odd?'

'Well, yes, now you mention it. Muffin is always drawn to a dog first and foremost, before a person. Strange as she didn't indicate that she'd even seen the dog.'

'Do you think...' He paused and breathed in and out slowly and deeply. 'Do you think there is the remotest chance that it could have been Saul? What if he has had an accident and suffered memory loss? He might not know who he is or even know that he has a family.'

'But surely he would have ended up in Accident and Emergency at the hospital and the police would have notified us as soon as he was flagged up on the system as a missing person? Usually that would all happen within 24 hours of an accident taking place.'

'Yes, but only if he was taken to a hospital. What if he had been found and someone took him in? I'm going to do an online search to see if it brings up any unusual happenings in the area since Saul went missing. Something that might not have been in the local newspaper or the media generally, but could have surfaced on Facebook.'

'How are you going to do that then? You don't have a Facebook account.'

'True. I've never thought it was worth bothering with before. Never felt the need. But it'll only take a few minutes to set one up. I'll create a community page with no privacy settings. That way anyone and everyone can post whatever they like on it.'

The power of social media being what it is, Saul's parents did not have long to wait. His father had phrased his request using words that were carefully chosen so as not to suggest panic or desperation on the part of the sender. Just a few words asking if anyone had seen anything unusual in or around the town over the past few weeks. Anything that seemed to be a little out of the ordinary and that involved a teenage boy. An incident, quite possibly minor, which when mentally revisited suggested that something of note might have occurred.

The response was meagre. One comment only. But the words riveting. There, on the page a post read: 'Found a boy trapped underground in the local graveyard a few weeks ago. A girl was calling for help and we went to her aid. Seemed he'd been trapped there for some time and we fully expected the worst when we finally got him out. Anything else you'd like to know? You can continue this in a private message if you want.'

Saul's father was about to bang out a reply then saw that 'gravedigger', the avatar of the person who'd posted the comment, was available for chatting online. Ten minutes of continuous online messages later, the pieces were starting to fall into place and a picture was beginning to emerge.

Roughly two months ago, 'gravedigger' and a work colleague had been finishing work in the graveyard and were about to go home when they heard shouting. They rushed to the aid of a young girl aged about fifteen or sixteen. She said that her friend, a boy, had fallen into one of the old graves. That a hole had opened up and just swallowed him whole. She said she'd been trying for some time, with no luck, to get him out.

What 'gravedigger' and his friend had thought strange at the time was that the grave in question had collapsed prior to the incident, which can happen when coffins disintegrate, and that they had immediately filled it in and flattened the ground. They could only think that yet more coffins in the mass grave had collapsed, opening up the hole again.

'Where is this grave? Did they say?' Saul's mother asked.

'Well, yes actually. They said it's really easy to find. It's one of the few found at the edge of the graveyard in what's known as unhallowed ground.'

'Has it got any inscription on the headstone to help us find it?'

'Well, no, that's the odd thing. This grave is only discernable by virtue of a slightly raised mound, though I understand that this has largely been levelled out, and a stone with absolutely nothing written on it stands close by.'

'How strange,' his wife murmured. 'Shall we go and have a look?'

'Why not? Nothing to lose.'

As they reached the graveyard the light was fading. Once they had stepped under the trees that edged the plot they found it difficult to see anything clearly but gradually, as their eyes adapted, shapes began to materialise.

'Here! Is this it?'

They stood gazing at the roughened stone. A headstone with no inscription. The grave itself looked fairly smooth and flat, the soil raked neatly over to preserve the notion that this was a tidy place, a place where order was sacrosanct. Never mind that this was a graveyard, it had to look, to all intents, like a park with a few headstones littered here and there.

Saul's father idly scuffed the ground near the grave's surface, his foot trailing through the leaves.

'Stop! What's that?' his wife shouted.

There, sparkling like a piece of silver amongst the leaves, was a tiny item, magpie's treasure, a ring. She fell to her knees and grabbed at the object. Cupping her hand she carefully blew and brushed away the dust and dirt. Like a precious jewel emerging for the first time into the light of day, the ring shone.

'It's Saul's ring,' she breathed. 'See, it has your Grandfather's insignia on it. The only piece of jewellery Saul ever wore. And only because he loved your father so much, held him in such high esteem. He said the ring was something to remember him by.'

'I remember,' her husband passed a hand over his eyes and blinked back tears.

'He was here. Our son was here.' His wife held out the words as a beacon of hope, as a lifeline, as a way forward in the search for Saul. They would begin again to look for their son with renewed vigour, this time with the firm belief that he was alive.

It is said that someone who does not want to be found can never be found. With the wisdom and cunning of a fox they can cover their tracks, make themselves invisible. But first they must possess the absolute conviction that they do not wish to be found. And in the case of Saul this conviction was beginning to waver.

33 Obsession

Yan refused to look her in the eye. Turned his face whenever direct contact seemed inevitable. It was this simple action, this indisputable demonstration of suspicious body language, that placed the first nail in the coffin as far as Penny was concerned. Any doubts she had been having that Yan was not really avoiding her, but had been busy, were now firmly dispelled.

She caught him by the arm as he rushed past her one day muttering that he had to be at his busking spot very soon if he didn't want to lose it.

'What's wrong Yan? Why have you been avoiding me?'

'Haven't,' he replied like a sulky child with the face to match.

'Can we talk when you've got time?' Looking full into his face she searched for any clues as to his sudden change in behaviour. He shrugged but Penny was persistent.

'I'll come back in an hour. There is something I need to discuss with you.'

At this Yan looked up and she detected, in his large brown eyes, a hint of surprise, followed by fear coupled with suspicion.

'What about?' he asked. Penny didn't reply. Merely turned and walked away.

An hour later Yan saw Penny approach well before she had reached the busking spot on the corner of the square. His heightened hearing, coupled with an acute sense of smell, reduced the competition to zero. No chance whatsoever that Penny would spot Yan before he saw her. One moment Yan was apparently engrossed playing the whistle, the next minute he had gone. A light breeze, no more, gave the slightest hint that there had been anyone standing there only seconds earlier.

Yan did not wish to be confronted by Penny. Not yet. Not ever, if he could help it. He needed to get his story right first. A watertight telling that would allay all her fears and calm her spirit. Well, perhaps not calm her down exactly, but at least convince her that he, Yan, was not involved in the disappearance of Dom. He would also use all means at his disposal: thought manipulation, trickery, sleight of hand, anything at all. For under no circumstances should Penny suspect him of any wrongdoing.

But Yan, clever as he was, had underestimated Penny. She had seen through the façade of innocence and a life plainly lived. After all, she and Yan were related and, as always, the genes will out. Of all the people Yan could have hoped to deceive, Penny was the least likely to be taken in.

As the busking spot swung into view Penny frowned. No Yan. Tui and Bede were performing, with Bella at their feet and Saul keeping a low profile in the shadows behind them. But there was no sign of Yan. Adhering to the laws of busking and common courtesy, Penny waited until the song came to an end before blurting out:

'Where's Yan? He said he'd meet me here when you had a break.'

Tui and Bede looked confused, as well they might. They understood full well that Yan had vanished in a matter of seconds and how he had done it, but they had no idea why. They assumed it would be for a good reason though. Most likely as he had no wish to talk to Penny.

'He was here a minute ago,' ventured Tui, while Bede nodded in agreement. 'And now he's gone,' she continued, stating the obvious.

'Well please can you tell him I'll be back,' Penny informed them, irritated that she had wasted her time.

'What's it about?' Tui wanted to know.

'Haven't you heard? It's been in the papers and on the radio. My friend Dom's gone missing. Two nights ago. Vanished without trace.'

'Why do you want to talk to Yan about it?' Bede asked.

'Just in case he might know something,' Penny replied.

Tui and Bede, by silent mutual agreement, said nothing and merely waited for Penny to leave. Within a few minutes Yan was back performing with the others.

'That was close,' he whispered in between songs. Bede looked at him.

'Did you have anything to do with Dom's disappearance? You can tell us.'

But Yan felt that he could not tell them. Tui, for one, was becoming less and less convinced that revenge was the correct course to follow. She might be far from happy about this turn of events.

Discovering that Yan, her 'adopted brother', had committed such a horrendous crime, by kidnapping a wholly innocent person, might be the tipping point. Might be the thing that decided her once and for all. Made her think that a life of normality was preferable to one of semi-anonymity living on the streets. Despite their recent 'acquisition' of a home, it might not be enough to keep Tui with them. Later Yan would tell Bede what he had done. Like accomplices in a crime, they could discuss what to do next.

Stuart had become a man obsessed. Not content with leaving the perusal of Parish Records to Anwen, he was conducting his own searches. Searches that led to new discoveries. As a scientist he was aware that all great advances were achieved by what is known as 'pure research'.

Unhindered by the boundaries and limiting factors set in stone by some grant-funding bodies, he knew that the only way to discover anything groundbreaking was to follow any new line of research unconditionally. To let any discovery, or promising set of data, dictate the route of travel, rather than the previously determined theory. It was not a case of looking for data to support a theory but rather following the data to develop a new theory. This tack produced interesting results for Stuart.

Instead of focusing wholly on Will and Emma and the note, Stuart found himself being led down a completely different route. Back in history, shortly after little James had been born and ultimately died, the changeling had been brought into the picture. While looking for information about the changeling, Stuart idly keyed in his own family history. The little he knew spanned only three generations.

As the evening ground on, and lights flooded the library, the realisation of what he had found caused Stuart to sit, frozen, pen in hand. According to the records that he had before him he was related, not to the changeling but to the changeling's sister. A girl, Clara, who was born to Squire Elver and his wife, three years after the changeling had appeared on the scene, and who had survived. Born to the man who had substituted the changeling for baby James. This linked Stuart inextricably to the family Elver who had deposed James and taken the changeling away from his own family – the family that were the blood line of Anwen, his friend.

The revelation was as unexpected as it was unwanted. He scribbled a few notes on a piece of paper, shoved it in his pocket and left the library. He had no immediate plans to share this information with Anwen.

Bede, who had been tracking Stuart, was secreted in the next booth in the library and moved like lightning once Stuart had vacated his seat. He picked up the book that Stuart had been reading, found the page by sensing the heat imprint left by Stuart's fingers, and absorbed the information.

He smiled to himself. If he had been anxious before that he had no-one to exact revenge upon, he no longer had cause for concern. In one short evening the answer to his quandary had presented itself to him. Stuart was a descendent of the Elver family. Stuart would be his target.

Yan and Bede met in the dark, hidden depths of the disused toilet on the edge of town.

'How long have you had him down here?' Bede wanted to know.

'Just a few days. But he's okay. He's got food and water – and a sleeping bag. A few books to read. A radio.'

'Sounds quite good to me,' laughed Bede. 'More than any of us had when we first arrived here. What made you decide to kidnap Dom? Why not his mother, when she is more closely related to the

Squire of Grange Manor than he is? Wouldn't that have made more sense?' he asked Yan.

'On the face of it yes, sure. But think about it. What is more likely to cause her distress? Being captured herself or being deprived of her beloved son, Dom? Not knowing where he is, whether he will be returned to her alive.'

'And will he?'

'Will he what?'

'Be returned to her alive?'

'Who can say? Depends on what I decide to do and whether I just decide to walk away and leave him here indefinitely.'

'Leave him to die?'

'Why not?'

Bede had no answer to this stark, unfeeling admission by Yan. With the injustices perpetrated against the nameless children, and considering their almost total lack of feeling for the people they came into contact with, it did not seem an unreasonable thing to do. Besides, it had not escaped their attention that the sudden availability of a house for them all to live in, courtesy of Emily, Jonas's benefactor, was somewhat fortuitous.

Only their wholly selfish approach to life had kept any of them from voicing their opinions, had stopped them from asking what had happened to Emily. Had she really gone off to visit a relative or friend and not returned? How convenient that she had written Jonas into her will and given him guardianship of her house and total control of her bank account in her absence. Too good to be true. So good that in fact it probably wasn't true.

'I have found someone to blame. Someone to direct my energies towards, to help me avenge my past,' Bede confided in Yan.

'Really? Who?'

'A guy called Stuart. A friend of Anwen.'

'Right, so I assume you are planning to kidnap him?'

'Who mentioned anything about kidnap?' Bede was surprised.

'Well, it makes sense don't you think? Bringing him here. It's a great spot for hiding someone. No-one ever comes here.'

'They did once, recently,' Bede pointed out. 'To search for us after Emily's friend tipped off the council. They found no-one. The papers reported that homeless people had been living here which, actually, was true. We were the homeless people they were after, but we had flown the coop. Very lucky that we got away when we did. Arrived home and dry at Emily's house the night before the authorities came here intent on raiding the place and ousting us.'

'Very lucky indeed,' Yan agreed. 'But what are the chances of them coming here again in the near future? Ask yourself. None. But tell me, who are you planning to punish by kidnapping Stuart, if you decide to follow that route?'

Bede had obviously not thought this through.

'His family, I suppose. His parents who will be related to Squire Elver, like Dom's mother is related to Squire Andover.'

'Okay, fair enough. Sounds like a plan,' Yan concurred.

Bede stood to one side as Yan stooped low through the gap in the brickwork to reach Dom. A head raised itself to look at him. A look of hope sprang into the eyes. A thought assembled fleetingly that he was about to be released. Then, as suddenly as it had arisen it was dashed to the ground. Yan spoke not a word as he fumbled around Dom, replaced his food and water, brought blankets to lay beside the sleeping bag.

Then he left. Walking away from the plaintive figure Yan did not break his silence. He failed to heed the calls as Dom pleaded for his release. Calls that did nothing to lessen Yan's resolve or make him consider, even for a moment, that he might be wrong, persuaded him that he should turn back, retrace his steps and release his prisoner. From this scenario there was no going back. Yan would have to see it through to the bitter end.

Yan and Bede made for home, feeling safe and secure in the knowledge that at least they had a home. A place of comfort where no-one confronted them and where all matters of finance were met by Emily's bank account.

As they gathered round the table for tea that evening, they could not have known the events that were about to unfold in the south of England. In a landfill site, nearly 200 miles from Clitheroe, a mechanical digger was turning over the rubbish. Rubbish that had lain there for some weeks now and needed levelling out. The driver of the digger would never know what made him look back but he did and there, exposed to the skies in a state of partial decomposition, was Emily, her body revealed to the elements.

34   Into Thin Air

The removal of Stuart from the streets of Clitheroe was as rapid as it was unexpected.

Aided by Yan, Bede, and a sponge soaked in chloroform, the mission went like clockwork. Stuart was easily overpowered and manoeuvred into the shadows. He was then propelled through dark alleyways and along back streets. Places where anyone who saw what was happening, and was suspicious, would say nothing. Not a single word would pass their lips. These faceless people had trouble enough of their own. Trying to eke out an existence in these hidden areas, with no protection from the elements, was not easy or, indeed, always possible.

Many a street person had fallen asleep at night, under a pile of cardboard, never to rise again. Never to surface when the mists trickled through the passageway to where they lay, eyes closed, lips blue, face staring at the sky. These people were the dispossessed. Lacking in material things, an address, creature comforts and, above all, hope.

Hope had long since left them, and with it any confidence they might have possessed in their previous life. Their life before bad luck, circumstance and poor decisions had landed them on the streets.

No, these people who had so little would not raise their voices when confronted with mysterious and possible wrongdoing.

Yan and Bede were safe and they knew it. It took an hour or more to half carry, half drag, Stuart to the disused toilet that already held Dom. Halfway there Stuart began to regain consciousness and tried to struggle his way to freedom. Yan quickly restrained him by tying his arms behind his back. Stuart was then frogmarched to his prison, the dungeon below ground. There were no conveniently placed iron rings on the floor in this part of the basement. Undeterred Bede shackled his unwilling victim to some pipes that ran from the boiler to provide hot water to the sinks in the room above.

'What have I done? Why am I here?' Stuart's terror-stricken words followed the two criminals with their recently acquired names, and refused to leave them. Stuck to them like glue. Even when they arrived home, Yan and Bede could still hear the words, quieter now but relentlessly persistent:

'What have I done? Why am I here?'

Yan and Bede had not fully understood the impact their actions might have. Only when they saw the newspapers in two days' time would it dawn on them that, perhaps, they had overstepped the mark.

One missing person in a small town was not unheard of and could just about be dealt with on an emotional level. It equated fairly well with UK crime figures for towns of a similar size. The disappearance of a second boy of similar age, also a student, followed by yet another, within the space of a few weeks, was another matter entirely. It broke the mould. Suggested organised crime. Spoke of something wholly unsavoury taking place in the town.

Whispers of *serial killer* did nothing to help calm the increasing anxiety felt by the townspeople. The media knew how to handle this. With typical diplomacy and tact they announced:

'Third student goes missing!!' and:

'Is there a serial killer in our midst?'

While media interest, both national and international, in a single disappearance was limited, this rocketed exponentially once a second, then a third person was taken. Within 24 hours there was a full house-to-house search of the entire town, with extra police and detectives being drafted in, coupled with forensic scientists and the obligatory helicopter hovering above.

The media were having a field day. This frenzy of interest continued unabated for the best part of three weeks then, as suddenly as they had arrived, they left. Virtually en masse, as a circus leaves town, so did the media and police depart. And throughout it all no-one thought to check beneath the disused toilet buildings on the outskirts of the town. Had they searched with more diligence they would have discovered a door to the basement that served as a prison for the two captives. No-one knew that there was a basement and hence no-one thought to look.

Entering week four for Stuart and week five for Dom, the two captives lay disconsolate on their filthy mattresses, surrounded by uneaten food that was covered in flies. They were separated by two brick-built rooms and sound did not travel easily through the air. Through the air, no. Through metal pipes, yes.

Dom had never known boredom like it. He was now intimately acquainted with every inch of his domain. Strange word 'domain' especially as he had no sense of ownership over it and was merely a captive here. The roof was low. He had no memory of being brought to this place but, looking round him, thought it unlikely that he would be able to stand upright fully, should he ever be freed from his shackles. Measuring 6 feet 1 inch, in his stockinged feet, he was fairly confident that he must have been dragged into the room then chained to the floor.

Disintegrating brick work formed the walls, while the plastered ceiling hung low down in places, sometimes broken entirely to reveal a hole through to the room above. No view of the sky from where he was positioned. Reasonable to assume that he was below ground in some kind of basement. Assorted broken bricks and rubbish littered the floor. The only saving grace in his sparse, unstimulating world, was a single light bulb. Yan had rigged up an extension cable that trailed across the floor then disappeared through a jagged hole in the ceiling.

At no point during Dom's imprisonment had Yan engaged in conversation with him. Dom had not the slightest idea why he had been brought there, what the reason was behind Yan's actions, what he intended to do with him. All Dom's questions had been met with a stony silence, complete indifference, a refusal to acknowledge that Dom had even spoken, never mind pleaded.

'Have you no heart? No soul?' Dom had shouted at Yan one morning.

Yan had merely smiled, shrugged and left.

Now entering week five of his confinement, Dom had taken to charting his experience. He had only a half-filled note book at his disposal, found deep at the bottom of his college bag, but decided to commit his thoughts to paper using the tiniest writing he could produce, while still being able to decipher what he had written. Keeping his records to the point, he quickly learned the art of summarising, something he had never been particularly good at, comments on his submitted college work being testament to this.

He described his surroundings and used dots to document when he suspected a new day had begun. Roughly speaking then, if his calculations were correct, he had been in his underground chamber for about a month. Why had no-one come for him? Surely he would have been reported missing and the police informed within 24 hours of him not returning home? That was a given.

Something else had been troubling him. A vague memory that he was not the first person, the first young male, to go missing in recent months. What about that lad – Saul was he called? He had never turned up. Not so far at any rate.

Then another niggle thrust its way through. Not long after 'Saul' went missing, a young teen had turned up with the trio that included Yan. Dom had never met this boy but he remembered Penny commenting on his appearance. He just seemed to turn up out of nowhere and the group had adopted him.

Dom had not met the whole group, only Yan through his connection with Penny. *Could the boy who now lived with the others be the same one that went missing previously? If so, why hadn't he gone home to his parents? If nothing else to put an end to their misery.*

Ideas and solutions to the puzzle tossed round in his mind. Perhaps the missing 'Saul' was not the same as the one that now lived with Yan and the others, or maybe he was but had run away from his parents and had no desire to go back there.

His head was thumping. Prone to migraines Dom always carried tablets with him to alleviate the pain. *Take on immediate onset of the migraine as delay might result in failure to absorb the medication to a satisfactory level due to reduced efficiency of the digestive system caused by progression of the migraine.*

The words were so definite they might have been written in stone, but Dom's supply of tablets had dwindled away to zero. Now he must simply lie down and try to relax. No access to a cold wet flannel to press to his forehead. Ironically, through no conscious decision on his part, he was following the advice typically given to migraine sufferers to help alleviate the pain: *Lie still in a darkened room.* He smiled, or rather grimaced, to himself. Once the headache had subsided he would try to formulate a plan. A plan to help him escape.

It must have been in the early hours of the morning, hard to tell with no way of knowing the time and no access to the sky. A tapping sound with a ring to it. Like metal on metal. Had he been found? Was someone coming to get him? He raised himself onto his elbows. A harsh striking sound echoed throughout the underground space. It could have been Morse code. Dom had no way of knowing for sure as he had never learned Morse code. There it came again, a sequence of tapping that seemed to form a pattern. Not continuous tapping but with a definite sense of order to it.

He remembered that some prisoners of war learned to communicate with each other by developing their own tapping method. In their efforts to use sound as a substitute for flashes of light, to send messages, they produced their own code. Known as a tap code, this code managed to avoid the problems inherent in trying to distinguish a dot from a dash. It achieved this by using two groups of taps for each letter.

Prisoners would arrange the alphabet into an array of letters and tap a row and a column number for each letter. By tapping the metal bars, pipes or the walls inside the cells, they were able to use the tap code which, while not perfect, acted as a primitive method of communication, when previously there had been none.

What an amazing thing the memory is, thought Dom, *that it can recall such details of seeming trivia, read over two years ago. Maybe not so surprising*, he then thought: *when survival is at stake, the mind and the body will use everything at their disposal to prolong life.* Whatever the taps might mean, there was only one course of action: To tap back.

'One, two, three, stop.'

Through the silent, dark, cavernous space came the response.

'One, two, three, stop.'

Someone is there! Someone is trying to get in touch with me – with anyone. Someone else is captive down here in this dungeon.

THE NAMELESS CHILDREN

Dom then shouted with all his might. A scream essentially. He waited until the echoes died down. Nothing came back.

Okay, think clearly. Whoever is trying to make contact with you is out of hearing distance but is contained somewhere that has metal pipes. Pipes that connect with here. With my chamber.

He tapped again:

'One, stop.'

'One, stop,' came the response.

Hoping beyond hope that the other detainee, if that is what it was, had some knowledge of the tapping method and the tap code, he quickly drew up the Roman alphabet tap code. Slowly and with precision he methodically typed out:

'I am Dom.' It seemed to take forever to do this and he waited anxiously for a reply. When it came it was somewhat halting.

Dom wrote down the number of taps, noting as he did so where the pauses came. When he had finished deciphering the message, he realised that this was indeed another captive but that they had merely repeated what Dom had sent. Not very helpful, but a start. At least they were communicating. The relief poured over him. He was no longer alone.

Stuart, in the meantime, was frantically trying to assess the situation. He was not alone. Someone was responding to his taps. Now, how did the tap code work? He remembered that the Swedish Diplomat, Raoul Wallenberg, had been taken prisoner at the end of the Second World War and placed in Lubyanka prison in Russia.

Mostly held in solitary confinement for the rest of his life Raoul, and other prisoners, would communicate by tapping out messages to each other using the metal pipes that ran through the cells and across the entire prison. It was in fact the only method of communication and a life saver in terms of helping to preserve the sanity of these people who would never see their families or the light of day again. Ever.

Stuart struggled to remember how a tap code worked. He scrawled a table onto the hard dirt floor and tried to mentally work his way round it. Ten, fifteen minutes elapsed and Dom was beginning to doubt that he had ever heard the taps in the first place. Then it came. Strong and strident the sounds rang out into the empty stillness.

'I ... Stuart.'

Dom began to cry with relief. Tears rolled down his cheeks as Stuart began tapping again.

'Where?'

'Disused toilets.'

'Who brought you?'

'Yan.'

'Two,' was all Stuart could remember.

THE NAMELESS CHILDREN

The tapping went on until they fell asleep from exhaustion. The conclusion arrived at was clear. They were trapped underground in the disused toilets on the edge of the town. But they were not alone. There were two of them. Between them they could devise an escape plan. It had been done before by people in far graver circumstances than they found themselves in. It would now be done again and hope was on the horizon.

Anwen was searching for Stuart. She had not accepted the conclusion drawn by the investigating bodies that he had 'probably gone away to visit a friend and not told anyone.' Like Dom, this was not in Stuart's nature. Stuart was a dedicated scientist, wholly devoted to his course and his subject. Forensic science captivated him. It absorbed him. It was his life. He would not simply uproot himself and leave. It wouldn't happen.

Another thing. There had been no phone contact from Stuart since his abrupt disappearance. Neither was he posting on Facebook or Twitter. Identical features to those that figured in Dom's disappearance. Also, no activity had been detected at cash points.

What were they both surviving on? thought Anwen. *Thin air? No, it was rubbish. Stuart had not merely gone off for a few weeks without notifying anyone.*

She poured over the incidences of missing persons in the locality, searching for any pattern that might emerge. Looked for a common denominator for the cases that belonged to Dom and Stuart. She arranged to meet Bede, ostensibly to share and update any information they had discovered concerning their family histories, but really to check him out for any 'on the street' news. Arriving early at the busking spot she happened to see a young girl engaged in conversation with Yan.

'Who's that?' she asked Bede as the two of them moved off to find a café.

'Just a friend of Yan's. She's also a friend of Dom...' Bede let drop this piece of information without thinking, without stopping to think at all.

'What? Dom who is missing? Like Stuart?'

'Well, yes, but I don't think she's worth talking to.' Bede took Anwen's sleeve to persuade her to walk more quickly, away from any possible meeting, any confrontation that might point the finger of suspicion at himself and Yan.

But Anwen was having none of it. Arm outstretched she offered her hand to Penny, who took it in hers.

'Hi, I'm Anwen. I understand you're a friend of Dom and that you're searching for him?'

Penny nodded and looked close to tears.

'Do you want to talk? I'm looking for Stuart. He is my friend. Maybe we can help each other? Give each other support – swap ideas?' Anwen suggested. Penny shot Anwen a look of gratitude and Anwen's mind was made up. She turned to Bede:

'I really want to talk to Penny. Sorry Bede. Let's meet another time – okay?'

Conflicting feelings shattered Bede's previous composure. Pleased that he would no longer have to answer any of Penny's searching questions, he was scared witless that somehow her meeting with Anwen would not have a good outcome; not where he or Yan were concerned, at any rate.

He began to protest but his pleas fell on deaf ears. Penny and Anwen were already walking away, Anwen with her arm round Penny in a display of comfort and support that was unambiguous.

They sat with their hands cupped round a mug of steaming coffee heavily laden with froth and Anwen waited patiently. Penny was only now starting to calm down.

'Sorry. It's all been so upsetting. Dom disappearing and not knowing where he is.'

'Do you have any suspicions? Any idea who might have taken him?'

'Well, yes actually I do, but I have no evidence and don't want to voice my opinions in case it drives away the person I suspect or, worse still, makes them do something even worse than kidnap.'

'Such as what?' Anwen asked.

'Such as killing him!' Penny blurted out.

'So you think he's still alive then?' Anwen had to ask the question.

'Well I hope he is. Once I find out why he was taken in the first place I will be a step closer to finding out what might have happened to him. What about you? Do you suspect anyone?'

'I'm not sure. I have nothing whatsoever to base my theories on. Nothing concrete that would help the cops put a case together, build up a body of evidence. I'm going it alone at the moment, trying to find Stuart myself. That is, until I met you. Do you want to pool our resources? Work as a team?'

Penny beamed her response and the pact was sealed.

35   A Process of Identification

Emily's friend, Vanessa Bright was at the police station, registering her concern that Emily Chase had not been placed on the missing person list. The rest of the town might be easily lulled into a state of denial, into accepting that Emily had gone away to visit a sick friend and would be back soon, but not her.

She had done as Emily had asked her and the disused toilets had been duly raided by people acting under instructions from the council. The report came back that, while there were signs that people had been living there fairly recently, no-one was there now.

Someone warned them, she thought when she heard the news. *They knew they were about to be raided and they scarpered. Where to?*

Each time she had gone to Emily's house, to see if Jonas had any news, she was given scant welcome. Jonas held the door open, by inches only, and never invited her in. *It's as if he's treating me like a vampire*, she had thought at the time, *while really he is the one who most fits the picture of a creature of the night.*

Once, when she had knocked on the door, she could have sworn that the curtain moved in an upstairs room and that the pale face of a young girl looked out from the window. But when she looked again the face had gone.

Jonas portrayed no emotion, no change of expression came over his face while being mildly interrogated by Emily's friend. He would not be moved and would never back down. In the face of intimidation he was a master at remaining calm. Easy to do when emotions wash over you, you have skin as thick as an ox, and you can flick away disparaging, contemptuous comments like a gazelle bats at annoying flies with its tail. All of these Jonas was able to accomplish with ease.

On each occasion Vanessa left the house empty handed and very concerned, but at no time did she ever consider giving up. The phrase did not exist in her vocabulary. She was a fighter and had achieved much in her life, largely as a consequence of her refusal to give up and her determination to see things through to the bitter end.

It was due to her never-ceasing persistence that she found herself at the police station that very morning, arms resting on the counter in an unsuccessful attempt to make herself appear taller. She had scarcely uttered the words:

'Is there any news...' when a shrill ring broke her sentence in two.

By way of an apology the desk sergeant nodded at her, then at the phone. Then followed a pause punctuated by monosyllabic responses.

'What? Just now? Where?' He scribbled furiously then spoke into the mouthpiece a final time by way of signing off. 'Thanks for letting me know. I'll update everyone here, cancel all leave and arrange a press conference.'

Vanessa froze. *What had happened that was so bad that all police holiday leave would be cancelled and a press conference organised?*

The sequence of events was eerily familiar. It had happened three times recently. Each time when someone had gone missing. Three male teens – vanished. Within a few weeks of each other. Disappeared without a trace. *Surely another hadn't gone missing? What was wrong with this town?* She looked at the officer's face that appeared to have aged five years in the same number of minutes. It was lined and ashen. He turned towards her.

'Sorry. I have things I have to act on. Would you mind filling in another form please, giving a full description of your friend: height, age, hair colour, type of clothes she normally wore, any significant marks such as birth marks – and anything else you can think of,' he added.

'I've already filled in a form before,' Vanessa protested.

'Yes, but if you wouldn't mind completing another. There might be something else you remember. Something that would help us to identify her, should we find a body.'

'What! You've found a body?' she cried out.

'I only said *if*,' replied the officer.

But it was too late. An idle comment had been jumped on by the woman and devoured hungrily. One look at him confirmed that her assumption was correct. They had indeed found a body and now they wanted another full report preparing on Emily, no doubt to see whether the descriptions matched: that of Emily as she remembered her, and that of the body they had found. Suddenly Vanessa knew the truth. Emily's body had been found and she had been murdered.

Saul's mother held the ring to the light, passing it backwards and forwards through her fingers, like a devout catholic saying the rosary. She had become obsessed with the shiny object, never letting it out of her sight. Her husband rested his hand lightly on her shoulder. An action that conveyed so much. The soft touch that said 'I am here and all will be well'. She fervently hoped that it would be.

'What do you think we should do next?' she asked. 'Where can we turn for help?'

'I think we should let the police know we have found Saul's ring and tell them what the gravedigger told us.'

'Do you really?' She was surprised.

'Why what do you think we should do?'

'Well, I wouldn't go to the authorities. All that will do is raise the profile of Saul as a missing person. Put him back on people's radar.'

'Isn't that what we want?'

'Well, possibly not,' his wife disagreed. 'Think about it. Say Saul has had an accident of some sort and lost his memory. If he is out there somewhere he might not respond to requests for information, but anyone holding him might be alerted.'

'You think he is being held against his will?'

'I don't know, but it's a possibility and one that we might ignore at our peril. I think I'll go alone to the market and look round the square. Take Muffin of course. Hopefully, I will spot them. If I do I can phone you so you can wander past and see what you think.'

'Sounds like a good plan.'

They looked towards the window where rain splashed onto the glass, blurring the view to the garden.

'About time it rained.' They spoke at the same time and laughed at the synchronicity and predictability of their words. As vegetable growers, whatever the seasons threw at them was mostly accepted with good grace and a degree of inevitability. Anything short of gale force winds or torrential rain was generally looked on as being 'good for the crops'.

Dom held his breath and concentrated as he deciphered the message being tapped out.

'You hear rain?'

'Yes,' he tapped back to Stuart.

'Any escape ideas?'

'Not yet.'

Then it came to Dom in a flash. If only he could persuade Yan to release him from his shackles, just long enough to stretch his legs. If only he could orchestrate this. Yan, of course, would be watching him intently but only while there was no distraction. All that was needed was for Dom to tap on the pipe. That would be a signal for Stuart to start tapping as if his life depended on it, striking the pipes in his own prison with relentless intent.

Yan would be bound to look away and that was all he, Dom, would need to be able to leap at Yan and overpower him. To strike him and pin him to the ground. To shackle Yan to the floor in his place. See how he liked being imprisoned, unable to move, for weeks on end.

But Dom knew, even as this scenario ran through his mind, that he would never subject another human being, or any living creature for that matter, to such appalling torment. Through his online scrutiny of wildlife cruelty he was only too aware of the Moon Bears of China, imprisoned for up to 30 years in crush cages, unable to turn or even breathe properly; all for the excruciatingly painful extraction of bile from the gall bladder, ostensibly for use in Chinese Traditional Medicine, in which it was wholly ineffective.

No, he would not subject Yan to the same treatment that Yan had meted out to him. He would turn Yan over to the authorities. The plan was communicated through the pipes and Dom waited anxiously for Stuart's feedback. Then it came, a resounding 'Yes!'

Game on, thought Dom as he experienced, for the first time since being kidnapped, a ray of hope on the horizon.

Emily's friend, Vanessa, had been correct. Her worst fears were confirmed when she heard the six o'clock news that evening.

The body of a woman has been found on a landfill site in the south of England. It is thought that she might be Emily Chase, missing for several weeks from Clitheroe in the north of England, although a firm identification has yet to be made. In the absence of close family it is hoped that someone who knew her might be able to assist in this matter.

Vanessa knew it would fall to her to make the identification and she knew beyond all doubt that the body would be that of Emily. Heart beating nineteen to the dozen she picked up her phone.

'Hello, I would like to offer my help in identifying the person' – she could not bring herself to use the word 'body' – 'who was found on a land-fill site in the south of England, earlier today.'

How could Emily have ended up like this?

'I have reason to believe it might be my friend, Emily Chase... Yes, I'll wait to hear from you... Thank you.' Vanessa's mind then went into overdrive.

How many enemies did Emily have? Precisely none. How likely was it that she had been mugged? Highly unlikely as Emily never carried much money on her person.

But even before she began to process the list of possibilities, Vanessa knew that there was only one person who would benefit outright from Emily's demise – Jonas.

36 Thwarted

Had he had the slightest insight into what made Yan tick, Dom would have realised that the plan, so carefully thought out by himself and Stuart, would not be brought to fruition. Had he had any contact with Jack, Penny's uncle, Dom would have known that Yan was not all that he seemed. That this rather disreputable individual could move at the speed of lightning and possessed hearing that could rival that of a dog. Had Dom known any of this he would have known that his plan was a lost cause, a recipe for disaster, destined to fail. But Dom did not know any of this. When Yan's footsteps could be clearly heard echoing through the discarded Victorian toilets, his spirits lifted. *Today is the day*, he thought. *Escape is certain.* But, as with all things in life, nothing is certain.

'Can you at least untie the shackles? Just for a few minutes? Please!' he implored Yan. 'I'm in constant pain from pressure sores. Look, I'll show you.'

Yan had no desire to look, but neither had he any wish for his victim to perish from infected pressure sores. Sores which, if left untreated, would only worsen and could eventually result in the premature death of Dom. And Yan had not yet decided whether or not to let Dom live. For the moment he was enjoying too much the feeling of power and control he had over the situation. Reading the comments on the Facebook page set up to 'Help find Dominic Andover'. Seeing how desperately people would clutch at straws only to have them snapped in two and for the rug to be dragged from under them.

Someone thought they'd spotted Dom a week ago coming out of an Indian Takeaway shop, but CCTV footage quickly revealed the supposed 'look-a-like' not to resemble Dom remotely. No-one thought to question why Dom might be walking about in the middle of town early in the evening buying Indian food as if nothing had happened. 'Perhaps he's lost his memory' was a common theme and, in the absence of any other more realistic theories, was the scenario that most people chose to believe. Plausibility and common sense flew, hand in hand, out of the window in these circumstances.

Everyone was in denial. No-one would face up to the probable truth. That he had been murdered and his body disposed of – most likely in the nearest river. Although that had been searched it was common knowledge that the river only gave up its dead when, and if, it was willing to. Often only after a bout of heavy rain that swelled the river more than usual and led to bursting of the banks. Only then was there the remotest chance that a body might float to the surface. Even after local flooding it was not inevitable that a body would show itself. More likely when the water level fell would a person suddenly be struck from the 'missing' list, their remains starkly revealed on the river bank, trapped by a mass of weeds.

At some time or other, in the minds of all those who cared for and loved Dom, such thoughts had drifted past and been hurriedly discarded. Without exception, the people who knew and loved Dominic Andover were in denial.

Against his better judgement, but in the knowledge that he was totally in control of the situation, Yan bent down and unfastened the shackles that held Dom to the floor. Immediately Dom tapped out the signal and instantly Stuart replied, firing out a series of taps in quick succession. Yan spun round to see where the sound was coming from and Dom pounced. But, like a magic trick when a black curtain is thrown over a person, then removed to reveal an empty space, the figure that Dom leapt at seemed to trickle through his hands like sand. The phrase 'shape-shifter' sprang into Dom's mind.

'You thought you could outwit me did you?' Yan laughed in his face as once more the shackles were locked in position and Dom fastened securely to the tiled floor. 'You have somewhat underestimated me, I think.' And with that parting comment Yan left the basement, turning once to throw a bag down on the ground. 'Some food and drink there. If you can reach it that is.' Dom was crushed. *Was there no way out of this place?*

37   On the Scent

Anwen and Penny had decided to back off from meetings with their respective collaborators, Bede and Yan. Instead they chose to spy on them from a distance. Track them even.

'I have a better idea,' Penny suggested. 'Why don't we use my dog Norman, a Border Terrier? Rather than trying to follow in the footsteps of either Yan or Bede, when we stand a good chance of being caught, why don't we see if we can find them – before they're about to leave a pub for instance – and Norman will follow their scent? That way we can find out where they live!'

'Good idea, but first we need something belonging to both of them for Norman to get the smell of them in the first place.'

Ultimately, this proved easier to do than either of them had anticipated and belongings were acquired from both Yan and Bede. In both cases the stolen items were missed but assumed to be lost.

'I seem to have lost one of my gloves,' Bede complained one evening as he joined the others for tea in Emily's house. 'Very annoying, especially when it's so cold outside!'

'You're not the only one. I lost a pen. Don't even remember when I last used it. All I know is that it's gone.'

The two items were indeed lost, but only to them. They were in fact well hidden, wrapped in tissue paper and placed inside separate, sealed plastic bags to preserve the scent.

'We must choose our time carefully. We can't afford to trip up. One mistake and all will be lost,' Penny entreated.

'I quite agree. We must tread carefully.' Anwen was happy with the arrangement.

The curtains in the morgue were tightly closed and an acrid smell of antiseptic pervaded Vanessa's nostrils.

'Are you ready?' the attendant asked Vanessa who nodded, although she had never been less ready for anything in her entire life.

A button was pressed and the inner sanctum of the morgue revealed a pale-faced woman lying on a slab, her body covered by a sheet. The tears began to fall and Vanessa was unable to reply to the question posed by the police officer overseeing the procedure.

'Do you recognise her?'

As she clutched at the barrier, and began to fall to the floor, it was evident that Vanessa did indeed recognise the person on the slab. Emily Chase was no longer in the land of the living. She had become one of the deceased and was now the centre of a murder investigation.

A dark, foreboding sky lay over the town and threatened rain. Saul's mother frowned and clenched her knuckles as she looked out of the window.

'I really must go to the market today but why does it have to rain? Today of all days!'

'You could always leave it 'til next week,' her husband suggested, knowing even before the words had left his mouth that they would not be heeded. Market day was only once a week. This was not an opportunity to be missed.

'Maybe the two people you saw would be there any day of the week?' he persevered.

'Possibly, but I don't think so. I think they had been hanging around hoping for leftover fruit and vegetables, judging from what they were holding.'

'In that case what are we waiting for? Let's go.'

As the first lashes of rain beat down upon their faces they made their way towards the market.

'I don't think Muffin much likes this weather.'

'Neither do I!' exclaimed her husband.

'Don't forget to drop behind as we near the market. We don't want to appear too conspicuous,' she reminded him.

'I'll stay hidden amongst the crowd and watch Muffin. See how she behaves towards the boy who might or might not be Saul.'

By the time they reached the market square the rain had eased off. She hardly dared to look at first but, yes, there they were, sitting on a bench, backs to the fountain, dog in attendance. She noticed, with affection, that the dog had been given a blanket to lie on and a few biscuits to keep her occupied.

Whoever they are at least they're caring, she thought.

The rain began to grow heavier and more insistent. The girl reached down and placed a waterproof cover over the dog. Saul's mother warmed to her more and more and edged closer, trying to appear ambivalent and not look directly at the two. She would leave that to Saul's father.

In the event, any attempt to appear indifferent was overridden by the dog. Well before she and Muffin had reached where the couple were sitting, Muffin went into overdrive and tugged hard on the lead, dragging Saul's mother with her.

Then Muffin was upon him. Leaping onto Saul's knee she licked his face, covering it all over with a wet slavering tongue. The response was instant. Saul did not have time to prepare his defences. Suddenly confronted with his beloved dog he reacted.

'Muffin. Stop it right now! Get down! Do you hear me? Stop it!'

But all the time his arms were round the dog, pulling her to him in a contradictory act typical of dog owners; chastising them and rewarding them at the same time. His mother wasted no time.

'Saul? Is that you?' the voice, almost shyly questioning, appeared plaintive to Saul's ears. But he was unable to deal with the situation. Looking up he could see his father moving towards him through the market day crowds. He did what any cornered animal would do. He looked for an escape route and he ran.

'It was him,' Saul's mother gasped as her husband caught up with her. They watched helplessly as the retreating heels of Saul vanished into the crowd.

But Tui had not gone with him. She had remained sitting on the bench, holding Bella tightly to her. Part of her wanted to run after Saul but another part was curious. She wanted to know about these people who had parented Saul, raised him since birth. Obviously loved him. She wanted to know why Saul had run away from them. What was he afraid of? Timidly she held out her hand to Saul's mother.

'Hello. I am Tui, and this,' she pointed to the dog at her side, 'is Bella.'

Saul's parents were in a state of shock and bemusement. They had just discovered that their missing son was alive and still living in the town. Had been living alongside them all the time most probably. The joy that came with this knowledge was tempered by the massive disappointment they felt when he had run away. Run from them – his parents.

THE NAMELESS CHILDREN

Saul's mother was the first to get a grip, to take control of the situation. She breathed in deeply, let her shoulders drop to help her relax, and took Tui's hand in hers.

'I am Saul's mother and this is Muffin, his dog.' They smiled at each other and the charged atmosphere of alarm and fear dissipated.

'Can we talk?'

'Yes, I would like that,' Tui accepted the invitation. Saul's mother nodded to her husband that she would go alone, that she needed to talk on a one-to-one basis. Her husband understood immediately. Words were not necessary. They knew each other well enough that facial expressions could speak volumes when the need arose.

Side by side, each with a dog in tow, Saul's mother and Tui moved away from the fountain and found a small café where the noise level was a mere hub-bub. Enough to provide an atmosphere without grating on the senses and obscuring most words spoken. An ideal situation to engage in light conversation. But trying to keep it light today proved far from easy for Saul's mother. So much was at stake. She was terrified that if she put a foot out of line, or alarmed her companion in any way, that Tui would be off, much like Saul half an hour earlier. Against all expectations Tui began:

'You are Saul's mother.' More of a statement than a question.

'Yes. And you are his friend?'

'Yes. He was trapped under the ground and I found him.'

'It was you that raised the alarm in the graveyard. Thank you,' his mother breathed.

'Yes, I was looking for him. I hadn't seen him for a while and was on his trail.'

'You knew him before he vanished? He never mentioned you.'

'We only met briefly and had not become friends really. That happened after he was rescued.' Then, the question that Saul's mother was desperate to ask:

'Why didn't he come home after he was rescued?'

'He changed. He was in the ground for a few weeks. He was not the same Saul that fell into the grave.'

Saul's mother paled and tried frantically to understand the story that Tui was telling her. Tried to put together the pieces of the jigsaw.

'How did he change?'

'He became one of us. Not completely. Just a little.' Then she stopped, aware that she had probably said too much already.

'Where do you live? Can you tell me?' knowing as she asked the question that an answer was unlikely to be forthcoming, for Tui had pursed her lips together and started to fasten her coat as if ready to leave. 'Will you tell Saul that we love him and we are always here for him? He can come home whenever he likes, even if only for a visit. He is free to come and go as he pleases – and of course he can bring you with him and Bella.'

Tui nodded and smiled.

'I must go now. I will tell him.' With that the girl of the streets left the café, holding the rope lead of Bella. No fancy leather here, merely a functional attachment that kept Bella close.

As Tui walked away Saul's mother looked after her and saw her stop. Halfway across the square Tui turned and looked back and gave a small wave. Saul's mother returned the wave and, with tears in her eyes, left to join her husband, safe in the knowledge that she would indeed see her son again. Tui would make sure of it.

Saul's father was pacing the floor.

'So close. So close,' he kept repeating.

'Calm down,' his wife spoke, more out of a desire to save the carpet from being worn to a thread than anything else.

'I am calm,' he protested. Then: 'what do you think we should do next?' he pleaded, turning towards her with eyes that held fear and desperation.

'I think we tread carefully. I know you are keen to get out there and bring him home, but think about it. Saul must have a very good reason for not coming home. At least we know now that he remembers the dog.'

'And us,' added her husband sadly. 'The thing that made him turn and run – the final straw – was when he looked up and saw me coming towards him across the square.' As he sat, with his head bowed, he could not remember ever feeling so low and helpless in his entire life.

'I think we go back to the square. Well at least I go back with Muffin. See if I can talk to them again, or with the girl if Saul isn't there,' his wife suggested.

'What was her name again?'

'Tui.'

'Strange name. Isn't it a type of New Zealand bird?'

'Yes, I think so,' his wife murmured but her mind was elsewhere, already imagining her next visit to the square.

His mother was right. Saul did indeed have his reasons for not going home. He was not himself. Ever since he had been incarcerated below the ground, trapped on every side by damp, crumbling soil, he had been unable to shake off the overwhelming sensation that part of him was missing. Had been taken away. Had been destroyed. That the soil had taken the essence of him to itself.

He could still recall the dank earth smell and felt it would never leave him. He had been enticed by subterfuge, by evil voices that called out from the grave and urged him to help them, that pleaded with him. Voices that tugged at his heart strings and pulled at his soul. And in a matter of minutes he had been dragged into the pit. The pit that had held him fast until he was rescued.

Tui. He would be in her debt forever. His friend who had tracked him down, sought him out, trailed him to the spot where he had lain, unseen and unfound for weeks.

The second he had breathed fresh air once again, set foot on firm ground, seen the light of day, held the hand of another, Saul knew one thing for certain. He was not the same Saul who was cajoled and enticed into the pit in the ground. True, he had the same features, but that was where the resemblance stopped. Dead. His soul was intact but that was not enough. Being in close proximity to the six nameless children interred with him in the vertical grave had left its mark. As if a hand had reached inside his head, messed about with his thought processes, altered the hard-wiring a little, confused his main aims in life, moved the goal posts.

Yes, Saul knew beyond all doubt that he was different. The knowledge rendered him wholly unwilling to return to his parents. Amongst other things he could not bear the look on his mother's face when she realised that her darling son had changed, was lost to her. Had essentially fallen by the wayside. It would be worse, almost, than if he had become a heroin addict, for at least there was the slight grain of a possibility that he could overcome a drug addiction.

But no hope could he see that he would ever be able to sidestep the turmoil that existed inside his head, the voices that surfaced with alarming regularity:

'Come back to us, Saul. We are waiting for you.'

But Saul had no intention of going anywhere near the graveyard and now had a deep mistrust of strangers. Indeed anyone who asked for help alarmed him. Seeing an outstretched hand on the street or a tremulous voice from the shadows – either of these could trigger a memory so dark that he had no desire to revisit it.

He even found it difficult to watch the others busking, as this could be loosely construed as begging, despite the fact that they were offering something in return for money: music and entertainment. But so badly had Saul been affected by his experience that even the simple act of busking appeared in a different light to him, and he had no wish to attract the attention, inadvertently or otherwise, of strangers.

38   Following Leads

The police, fired up by the recent discovery of Emily's body, had opened a murder investigation and were asking for 'any information that might help with their enquiries'. The leading detective, Geoff Blunt, was attempting to draw together all the threads. Anything that might be linked to the killing of Emily Chase. On the interactive board at headquarters he had placed details linked to all the people who had been reported missing during the past year.

'Why not longer than a year?' he had been asked.

'Maybe we will later. For now let's just stick to the recent past. See what it brings up.'

The stark reality of the grave situation they found themselves in was brought home to the entire team as they came into the office ready to begin a new day.

'Three missing boys?' Geoff spoke the words as if he couldn't believe what he was seeing on the board, as indeed he couldn't. 'I didn't realise that we'd lost three. How could I not have known this?'

'You're not alone Geoff,' a female colleague, Jean, comforted him. 'But each time another student was reported missing the normal procedures were rolled out. All the requirements set in place. Nothing was omitted. All done by the book.'

'I didn't think anything else. I'm just amazed that it had failed to really impact on me.'

'Well, we carried out all the usual investigations and were none the wiser at the end of it. All we could do then was leave the cases open and hope that we received some new information. Which we didn't. Until now,' another colleague added.

'Who's saying that the death of Emily Chase is related to the disappearance of the three boys?' Jean again.

'There might be no connection but we'll look nevertheless. These things can be more interconnected than they might at first appear.' Geoff based his comments on years of experience.

'By 'things' I presume you mean murder?' Jean asked.

'Well, yes, I suppose so,' he agreed.

Three young faces stared out from the board. Three teenagers who had been torn from their families and friends and taken who knew where?

'Let's start at the beginning.' The meeting had convened and Geoff was leading it.
'I know it means going over old ground,' he added quickly, seeing the disheartened, disgruntled looks on the sea of faces that surrounded him. 'But it's important. We might have missed something. What has happened during the past year? Has anyone new moved into the area? Did we search thoroughly every

possible site where someone might be held against their will?'

Jean was first to answer:

'In terms of newcomers, there are three young buskers who play near the square. They just seemed to appear out of nowhere one day about six months ago. In fact we received a complaint from a woman who was concerned that they were squatting in the disused toilet block on the edge of town.'

'What was this woman's name – the one who made the complaint?'

'Vanessa Bright I think it was,' Jean offered. 'She was a friend of Emily Chase. It was her who turned up at the police station recently, asking if there had been any new leads relating to Emily's disappearance. The desk sergeant was about to explain that we had nothing new to report when the call came through that a body had been found that answered the description of Emily.' She stopped as Geoff threw his pen down on the table.

'So straight away we have a link. Emily Chase, or at least her friend, wanted rid of these three newcomers, and shortly after a complaint was lodged by this friend Emily goes missing. Did anyone check the old toilets for any trace of Dominic Andover? Stuart Hopkins?'

'Well, yes we did at the time, when responding to the complaint.'

'Any sign of habitation at the toilets?'

'It looked like someone had been living there fairly recently but had scarpered.'

'And did anyone think to check again, when the second and third boys went missing?'

On both sides of the table heads hung, as eyes refused to meet his own.

'Right then, first thing in the morning we need two teams. One to go over the old toilets with a fine tooth comb, and another to go over the house belonging to Emily Chase. Let's see what we find. Regroup tomorrow evening at 16:00.'

The room cleared as each member of the police force returned to their individual roles and work stations. Tomorrow it would be all systems go when the operation stepped up a gear. Always the case when the heart of an investigation was focused on murder.

39 On Track

Anwen and Penny chose their moment well, took their time, made no attempt to rush the job in hand. Patience was crucial to achieving their goal, to discovering, by fair means or foul, where Yan and Bede had hidden Dom and Stuart. Convinced that their quarry would slip up at some point, commit a serious error of judgement, they had bided their time.

Today their patience was rewarded. Until now they had failed to set Penny's dog, Norman, on the trail of either Yan or Bede. With stealth and purposefulness the two culprits had always managed to avoid the eyes of their stalkers, despite the persistent vigilance of their erstwhile companions.

In the meantime, Penny and Anwen had managed to keep up a semblance of appearance that all was well. They had even arranged a foursome one evening in the pub, in an attempt to perpetuate the illusion that the friendships were as close as ever and that the pacts formed to investigate the roots of the Andover and Elver families were still intact. That it was still 'game on'.

It was indeed still 'game on', but not as Yan and Bede imagined. Not remotely. At the end of the evening the four of them were persuaded out into the street by the pub landlord, as the pub closed and they said their goodbyes.

The two girls understood the foolishness of attempting to follow their chosen prey. Having learned a little of their superhuman abilities from Jack, Penny's uncle, they knew it would be futile. Instead they persuaded the two boys to linger longer than usual outside the pub. The more they scuffed their boots on the pavement, the more scent did the stone slabs acquire. It was a dry night. They waited.

An hour later, when they felt that Yan and Bede would be long gone from the vicinity, they set Norman on the trail of their ex friends, now suspects in a possible kidnapping. Border Terriers are not hounds bred for trailing quarry but are known for their 'ratting' talents, their ability to unearth and dispatch rats with the minimum effort. Despite this shortcoming as a tracker dog Norman behaved splendidly. Nose to the ground he ran, without breaking his stride, until he reached the edge of town. There he stopped abruptly.

'Oh no, he's lost the scent,' Anwen muttered.

'Give him a minute. Be patient. Let him get his bearings,' Penny replied.

As if he had heard her words Norman leapt once more into action. The two stopped, breathless, as the dog finally sat back on his haunches as if to say: 'job done!'

'Where are we?' Anwen asked.

'I know this place,' Penny said. 'Yan brought me here once, a long time ago, just after we first met. It's the Victorian toilets that have been sitting here unused for some time now. I think they must be scheduled for dismantling by the council at some point.'

'I don't like it here. I don't like it at all,' Anwen whispered. 'I want to go back. What if Yan and Bede really have captured Dom and Stuart as we suspect? What if we find them down there with them? I really think we should turn round.'

'I think you're right. But I do think that now is the time to tip off the authorities, ask them if they have searched this place since the disappearance of Dom and Stuart.'

Anwen breathed a sigh of relief. 'Let's go now.'

With a hollow feeling that accompanies the sense of dissatisfaction that comes from a job only half done, they retraced their steps as fast as they could. Allowing the dog to lead the way, they fled back to the protection of their small town and the comforting presence of other people.

40 Assembling the Truth

Sleep did not come easily to Vanessa. Ever since she had seen her friend's face, borne witness to her untimely death, served her role as identifying person for the pathologist, life had become filled with dread. She was fearful on several counts.

No-one knew why Emily had met her death. The cause had been relatively simple to establish, despite the time that had elapsed between her murder and ultimate discovery on the landfill site. The pathologist had no difficulty in reading the signs. The tell-tale ligature marks were the first thing that the eyes focused on when viewing the body. Emily's eyes were no longer present but her body was otherwise reasonably intact. Important evidence could be found underneath the fingernails. Such a useful place to obtain incriminating tissue samples from the perpetrator of the crime, especially in cases of strangulation, such as this one.

A person being strangled does not go down without a fight, unless of course they have been rendered unconscious before the attack is staged. And Emily was most certainly conscious when Jonas crept up behind her and put his plan into action.

Even allowing for the few seconds lost when she was shocked into a dazed stupor at the initial attack, the minutes that elapsed while she was slowly suffocating at the hands of Jonas were well used. She had clutched at the thin rope that cut into the skin of her neck and, finding there to be no gap, no space to gain a fingerhold, to be unable to get a purchase on the rope however temporary, had automatically turned her attention to the hands of her protégé. To Jonas who she had taken into her home when he most needed help. Jonas who she had treated as her own son, who had become a surrogate son, a replacement for little David.

Even when faced with such horrendous certainty that Jonas was trying to kill her, would most likely succeed, a tiny seed in Emily's mind still managed to bring forth the thought that Jonas was a good boy, that he was acting under the influence of others – those strange friends of his.

But the final images that floated past as she lapsed into a world where pain and despair no longer existed, were not of Jonas. They were of little David, her beloved child. And as the mist began to cloud her vision she held out her hands to David and he took them.

Vanessa could only imagine the events that led up to her friend's death and that finally overcame her. Try as she might she could not shift the image from her mind. Emily on a cold slab. Emily murdered.

There was another reason for Vanessa's concern. The murderer had not been found. He or she was still out there, though Vanessa erred on the side of 'he' for reasons that she was not entirely able to explain. She had resisted all urges to go once more to Emily's house and insist on being allowed in. It all seemed rather pointless now. She knew where Emily was. She was in the morgue. No amount of house searching would bring her back.

A niggling thought came to her. When the authorities searched the disused toilets they had found no sign of the three teenagers that had so aroused the suspicions of Emily, caused in her such a great sense of concern. Where had they gone? Could they be in Emily's house?

The forensic people had been 'all over the body' as they described it in the trade. They had obtained samples of skin from underneath Emily's nails. The DNA results had been released.

The next stage of the investigation was for the entire male population of the town to be interviewed and a cheek swab taken. This would enable, 'beyond all reasonable doubt', a match to be made between the tissue samples taken from Emily and the person who had strangled her. The detective sergeant sounded very confident when he informed the assembled team of these facts, then rather punctured the balloon of hope by adding: 'assuming, of course, that he hasn't already left town.'

Jonas had not left town but was extremely aware of the measures being taken to identify and capture the murderer of the defenceless little woman who was the bedrock of the community, who had never harmed a fly and whose loss had been felt deeply by everyone. Whether these were true sentiments, or otherwise, the fact remained that they were out to get someone. And that someone was him. He travelled with furtive intent, keeping to the walls and the shadows. The harsh truth came to him. He could not stay here. He must leave – and soon. But where?

That evening, when all were safely installed at Emily's house, he would confess the truth to Yan and Bede and await their decision about what must be done. The relating of the murder he had committed would have a dramatic effect on the others but it would not be the one he had anticipated; for once confessions start to roll off the tongue, more tend to follow. One loose tongue leads to another. By the end of the evening Jonas would learn that he was not the only one who had secrets to hide – and a reason to run.

41   Discovered

They came under cover of darkness. With a plan formulated by precision thinking. Hidden in the shadows they crouched patiently. Waited for the command in their ear pieces. The words that signalled that action should be taken. That a gradual advance on the target should begin.

The target that was the old toilets on the edge of the town. So unassuming as a crime scene, so inconspicuous to the discerning eye, so wholly innocent-looking to the bystander.

The lead investigator had been succinct in the extreme. There was no ounce of ambiguity in his words, no degree of uncertainty held within his speech. The message was clear. They were to remain hidden in the trees that surrounded the toilets. No movement was to be made, no sound uttered, until the signal came. Acting on information received they had reason to suspect that one or more of the missing boys might be on the premises.

They sat and listened and waited. An unexpected sound rang out into the night air. The sound of metal striking metal. A sequence of sounds. A tap code. Someone in the vicinity was sending out a message, a communication of sorts.

The commanding officer lost no time in issuing the signal which was simultaneously received in all headphones. The team sprang into action. All doors and windows – all possible points of exit – were covered in less than a minute. This was followed by armed officers who descended the steps that led to the basement. The basement that held, in two separate rooms, the captives Dom and Stuart.

Strong beams lit up the faces of the despondent teenagers. A look of despair that rapidly changed to one of disbelief, followed by sheer delight. Tears flowed down their cheeks as the shackles that bound them were forced open. Amidst reassurances that they were now in safe hands, and had no further cause to worry, came the simple rhetorical question:

'I take it you are Dominic Andover and Stuart Hopkins?'

Out into the moonlight hobbled the two young men, warmed by the blankets round their shoulders, emotional almost to the point of collapse. They stumbled to the cars waiting for them and began their journey home and away from their place of imprisonment. Questioning would have to wait until the morning. For now, peace of mind and sustenance were the main consideration for the two rescued captives.

News of the raid on the toilets hit the internet before it appeared in the tabloids. The power of social media cannot be underestimated. The story took off on Twitter and was quick to surface on Facebook and news bulletins on radio and TV stations.

'Missing boys found shackled to floor in disused toilet block. What monster did this?'

But the police already knew the answer. Directly the two teenagers had recovered sufficiently to be questioned, the whole story was revealed. They knew who had captured them, or at least Dom knew for certain that Yan had kidnapped him. As for Stuart, it was a matter for conjecture, but it was probably not too much of a long shot to speculate that Yan had also had a hand in his capture, with quite possibly co-operation from Bede. It would not be difficult to put together the other pieces of the jigsaw.

42   Nowhere to Run

Word was out on the street. The police knew who had captured Dominic Andover and Stuart Hopkins but they weren't telling. In the absence of hard evidence the rumours flew thick and fast.

'They're looking at newcomers to the town. Anyone who's moved in over the past few months.'

The rumours reached Yan and Bede, not by word of mouth but through the wind. Through the dew on the grass in the early morning. The cry of the curlew on the wing. Impacted their consciousness and threw them into a state of full alert.

As if a butterfly had flapped its wings at one end of the town the news filtered through to them, travelling with the utmost speed. Heightened senses were pivotal in this, in the bringing of the knowledge of this threat to their hearts and minds. To allow them a chance to react. To give them a chance of escape. But where to?

Tui was the first to respond. Not to the rumours that drifted into her mind, and rested lightly on her consciousness, but to a general feeling of unease for which she could find only one possible cause. They were in danger. Each and every one of them were at risk.

'We need to go,' she announced, waking the others in the dead of night. Barely had their head touched the pillow, and sleep overtaken them, than they were rudely wrested to full consciousness.

In a flash Yan, Bede and Jonas were on their feet and dressed. Bella needed no such prompting. She stood trembling in anticipation. A dog always knows what is afoot and she was no exception. They were about to be on the move. About to flee.

'No time to take our belongings,' Yan instructed. 'They are on their way. I can hear them.'
As he spoke a fully briefed party of police officers, some armed, some with dogs, were travelling towards Emily's house. Speeding along in cars that might have been borne on the wind so silently did they move. Perfect for a dawn raid, for descending on their unsuspecting target. But however quietly they travelled it did not escape the astute hearing of the nameless children. Crouched low, with never a look back, they evacuated Emily's house.

An unspoken agreement to disperse, as soon as they left the house, was followed to the letter. They scattered like a flock of gazelles who suddenly find a lion in their midst. Safety in numbers does not always hold true. Indeed this was a profound example of when it would undoubtedly not prove to be the best option.

Instinct dictated the path each of them took. Without conferring, Yan, Bede and Jonas ran for the graveyard. They catapulted headlong through the trees, down the alleyways and back streets of the town, along the lesser known tracks seldom frequented by the townspeople.

They flashed past the down-and-outs, the street people, who kept their heads down and saw nothing, a practice that guaranteed that the escapees would not – could not – be identified to the police. Easier, and safer, to report: 'I saw nothing', when indeed you had not, than to fabricate a lie. No danger when telling the truth. Not so when a lie unravels.

They were nearly there. The only option open to them. The only harbour in a storm. The only place of safety left. The grave that they had emerged from so many months ago. Their search almost, but not quite complete. The search for the families that had deserted them. The families that had left them to be buried without ceremony in unhallowed ground; had dismissed them without a second thought.

The nameless children had sought retribution and vengeance and nearly achieved it. Nearly, but not quite. Now was not the time for deliberation. Not the moment for hesitation. Now was the time for immediate decision making, and the decision had been made for them. Their only chance of survival was to go below ground, enter the pit in the graveyard and to stay there.

All did not go immediately to plan. The hollow space, that they had anticipated, was no longer there.

It had been filled in with compacted soil and the ground levelled. Patted flat with a heavy spade. Only the unmarked stone bore witness to the presence of a grave in this part of the churchyard.

Nothing to mark their passing, no words upon the stone, whispered the breeze.

They began to dig furiously. Two dug while the third removed the earth and distributed it over freshly dug graves. It was important to leave no trace, no sign that the ground had been disturbed – not in the slightest. Then they slipped soundlessly beneath the soil and vanished.

The words of a song were held suspended in the air above them:
Across the graveyard fast came he, heart beating like a drum, running creeping o'er the ground, looking back where he had come.
Another night had turned to dust and with it all hope gone, his dreams had crashed around him, dashed his spirits to the ground.

They were back beneath the ground where they belonged.

But not all the nameless children had returned to the grave. At a house not far from the market place the door was opened to let in the cold night air – and with it two bedraggled figures. Saul had returned to the fold. And by his side stood Tui and Bella the dog.

THE DEAD SPACE

1   The Return

In the chill darkness they stood, framed by the doorway, silhouetted against the sky. Two waifs and strays returned. The calm after the storm. Saul's mother reached out to them both and tentatively two hands reached out and took hers. One belonging to her son Saul, one to Tui. Gently drawing them to her she knelt on the ground, tears falling out of relief and happiness.

'You've come home,' she whispered. 'You've come home.' Her husband appeared behind her, wondering what was keeping his wife at the door. Seeing the scene he took a step back. No wish to upset things, to set Saul on the run again. The three moved into the house and warm drinks were produced. No questions asked.

'We need sanctuary,' was all Saul would say. 'We were lost in the wilderness.'

And now you are found, thought his mother.

THE NAMELESS CHILDREN,
Part 1 of THE SOIL CHRONICLES,
continues with Part 2: THE DEAD SPACE

ACKNOWLEDGEMENTS

Many thanks to Carol Arnall for her invaluable help, reading the manuscript and for providing constructive comments. Also to my husband Paul for his continuous support and contributions during editing. Finally, to my fellow authors of Castle Writers, Pickering, for providing useful feedback.